Terroir

for Maggie

Terroir

Graham Mort

Seren is the book imprint of
Poetry Wales Press Ltd
57 Nolton Street, Bridgend, Wales, CF31 3AE
www.serenbooks.com
Facebook: facebook.com/SerenBooks
Twitter: @SerenBooks

© Graham Mort 2015

ISBNs
978−1−78172−230−5 Pback
978−1−78172−231−2 Kindle
978−1−78172−232−9 Ebook

Typesetting by Elaine Sharples
Printed by Bell&Bain Ltd, Glasgow

The publisher works with the financial assistance of
The Welsh Books Council

'We are our own dark horses'
Laurens van der Post, *Venture to the Interior*

'Terroir can be very loosely translated as "a sense of place",
which is embodied in certain characteristic qualities, the
sum of the effects that the local environment has had on
the production of the product.'

Wikipedia, 2014

'In spite of the arguments, I remained firmly convinced
that consciousness was not reducible to science, namely
that there would always be something – the terroir of the
individual – that defied science to explain.'
Sophieb, *Brooklynguy's Wine and Food Blog*

'Laissez le vin de se faire.'
(Let the wine make itself.)
Old French saying

CONTENTS

TERROIR

André turned from the road, dropping the bike into a lower gear, twisting the throttle, taking the sloping track gently. Through the wrought-iron gates, past the closely planted vines to the white house with green shutters and pantile roof. His breath misted the visor as the bike slowed, gravel popping from its tyres. Something felt right about this: the way the vines fell away from the house, the spire of the church beyond, gun-smoke clouds, the metal roof of the winery glinting. He'd arrived: André Arnault. *Enologist.* That sounded good. Fresh leaves shone on the vines. They were young, grafted onto American root stock. The yellow flowers of hawkbit and the white trumpets of convolvulus showed where the weeds were moving in. It would all need work, and quickly.

A black Mercedes saloon was parked on the forecourt, beside it a battered bicycle and a dusty Peugeot van with a dented wing. André switched off the engine, resting the bike on its side stand. It was a BMW twin: sixteen valves, air-cooled and fast as a snake. He could feel the heat coming off the cylinders against his legs. He hung his helmet from one handlebar and draped his leather jacket over the saddle. Since his last visit someone had put up curtains in the plain two-storey house and there were new padlocks on the winery doors. An old man in overalls was

1

brushing out the garage, pulling his head back from the dust. He paused to watch André dismount.

Lower down the valley he'd passed a scarecrow dressed as Osama bin Laden. The locals must have a sense of humour. The old man put a finger to his nose and blew out a stream of snot before wiping his fingers on his trousers. Maybe not. André gave him a curt nod as he passed.

– *Monsieur.*

Raising a hand from his brush, the old man nodded back and muttered something towards the bike. He reminded André of his grandfather, knotted to the land like thorn roots, a real *paysan*.

The door opened before André could ring the bell. Gaspard dressed like an American: Nikes, a blue polo shirt pulled tight over his gut and low-slung Levis. He was a head shorter than André with flat ginger curls and moist blue eyes. He held out a damp hand, small in André's grip. His arms were hairless, his eyelashes pale. He wore a gold watch with a chunky metal bracelet.

– André! You're on time. Cool! Come in. *Ça va?*

– *Ça va,* Gaspard. Good to see you.

He'd insisted on first names. Now he walked ahead of André, slightly bow-legged; a walk that made up for his lack of height with its swagger. *Like a dog with two cocks,* his father would say. The house had been tastefully furnished with plain modern cabinets and armchairs. The only gesture to tradition were the lace hangings in the windows. The house was new by local standards and stood in just over thirty hectares of vines, west of the village with its square-set church and tidy houses with gabled

2

windows. All built from clean honey-coloured stone. Typical Bordeaux country.

A slim black-haired woman appeared behind Gaspard carrying a folded newspaper. Maybe ten years younger, thirty-ish, dressed in a dark pencil skirt and cream blouse.

– Ah, Ghislaine. Meet André, my – our – *œnologist*.

Gaspard smiled as he said the word, rolling it around his mouth as if tasting wine before spitting. He said it the way André thought of it, with relish. As if he'd been taught a certain pronunciation. As if he'd learned to savour things he had no right to. His wife had a firm nose, small ears set close to her head, strong dark eyebrows that gave her face a slightly severe look. Green eyes, like slate under water. She didn't smile. Her hand was cool. André noticed a single silver bangle on her wrist above a square silver watch. Matching. Tastefully understated. Expensive, of course.

– *Enchanté!*

He thought he noticed a glimmer of amusement at the formal greeting. Maybe she thought him old-fashioned. Maybe he was trying too hard. Her husband was scratching his chest under the polo shirt. He had white scars on the underside of both arms as if he'd defended himself against a blade. It was weird how someone as meaty as Gaspard Hubert could have such a delicate wife. Gaspard turned to her now.

– Coffee, darling. Do you mind? We have to talk.

She smiled then, a formal grimace. No make-up.

– Of course.

Her calves flexed as she walked away. Her voice was smoother than Gaspard's with no trace of a regional

3

accent. As soon as Gaspard had called him – after that first contact from Gaultier – André had him as a Breton. Cider country. What he knew about wine was questionable. What he knew about making money? Well, that was something else.

Place de L'autel was a typical small vineyard on Bordeaux's Right Bank. After generations of the land being split into small parcels, younger wine growers were trying to build up their hectares again. Place de L'autel had been sold to pay inheritance tax. The old wine grower was the last of his line and his kids couldn't wait to part with it. It was tiny by the standards of Bordeaux or Languedoc where André's father managed a cooperative that drew in over a dozen growers. In Burgundy, where they grew wine on a handkerchief, they'd understand. The only way to get land there was to marry it.

Place de L'autel had been bought up by a *garagiste*. One of the new breed with new ideas. The idea had been to rip out the old vines, re-plant, reduce output, increase quality, sell the wine on the stock market before bottling, then sell the land at an inflated price. Only in Bordeaux was that possible, where wine was sold as a future – like tin, or copper or coffee. So far, so good, but the new owner had been in a hurry. More interested in growing money than wine. Without the quality – and without a good wine agent to get him into foreign markets – the enterprise had gone under after two poor harvests. And it wasn't just the harvest that could do for you. The old wine-growing families still controlled a lot of Bordeaux. Aristocrats or *nouveaux riches* who'd blended in after a few generations. *War profiteers and grocers,* his father called them. They could freeze out newcomers if they thought they were rocking the boat – and it had been rocking for a good few years now.

Truth was, most of the *garagistes* had made their money doing something else. They could afford to take a long-term view, wait for their investment to mature. It was wine, after all, something that was harvested, that lived and breathed, that was aged to perfection. Or close to it. After all, nothing was perfect. Gaspard was a typical entrepreneur. He was getting rid of a chain of small supermarkets in Tours and Limoges. He didn't believe in standing still. Better to shift your money around. Some here, some there, some hidden. He was worth millions. Part of the money was going into a new chain of internet cafés, part of it into wine. The rest into property and … well, who knew what? Somehow, André didn't want to know.

They moved into the living room. When the coffee came, there were brown sugar cubes in a bowl and a homemade almond biscuit on each saucer. André murmured his thanks and again he thought he saw a glimmer in Ghislaine's eyes.

Gaspard was talking about Gaultier, the wine agent who'd tipped him off about Place de L'autel, suggesting that André – only in his third year as an enologist, but one of his best students for years – should be brought in to inspect the property and the vines. Gaultier had been a visiting lecturer when André was studying for his degree. He'd survived Dien Bien Phu as a teenager, walked with a stick and had a lazy eye where a bullet fragment had hit the nerve. Wine had made him successful, charismatic, and he had connections all over the wine-growing world, from Chile to California, Bordeaux to the Barossa Valley. So

André owed him one. And the *terroir* was promising – well-drained, gravelly soil with plenty of limestone on south-facing slopes. The last owner had got most things right, planting Merlot vines on the lower slopes, Cabernet Sauvignon and Cabernet Franc a little higher on lighter soil. The winery was well equipped with a new hydraulic press, stainless-steel fermenters that were temperature controlled and inspection tables that could be steam cleaned. There was a white-tiled laboratory that doubled as an office with refractometers and a computer. The cellars were in a long hangar-like building, also temperature controlled. The house and the annexe were eighties build. There was nothing of the chateau here. Everything was modern, built from breeze blocks and cement, but, above all, hygienic.

They sipped the coffee. Gaspard crossed his stubby legs and looked expectant. André's plan was simple: to reduce production, discarding excess fruit; to de-leaf, discouraging mould; to harvest and sort as late as possible. All by hand. Then to carry out the second fermentation in new oak barrels. The result, if the harvest was good, would be a new-style Bordeaux – rich in berry and cherry flavours, high in alcohol and with a long chocolaty finish. None of that leather and incense taste that the old wines had. The rest would be up to the agent. Gaultier was on first name terms with Robert Parker and a decent score in *The Wine Advocate* would ensure that the whole batch could be sold before bottling. If not in the first year, then maybe in the second or third. But none of that was André's concern. He was here to make wine, that was all, to have the free hand that Gaspard had promised him back in April, slapping him on the knee as they sat in the garden with a beer and looked down at the vines.

– I'm in your hands. I know about marketing and finance…

Gaspard took a pull at the bottle, wiping his lips.

– I love wine like I love women – but it's just as mysterious.

He grinned, showing teeth that were too white, too even. They looked unnatural. Veneered. Expensive.

– But I learn quickly. And what I learn…

He tapped his forehead with the bottle neck.

– …I don't forget.'

André was watching a white van speed along the road towards the village. He knew already what his father would think of Hubert. An *arriviste*. A bullshitter. Get rich quick and then fuck off out of it. He was still talking. Talking about André's future somewhere beyond the veil of heat that made the treeline shimmer.

– Gaultier tells me you're one of the best. Up and coming. I'll add twenty-five per cent to your current salary and five per cent of our annual profits over fifty thousand after we've settled overheads. I won't interfere with what you do, if you stick to the job. But I want to retain Gaultier as a consultant. That'll give us both back-up.

That was sensible. More than sensible; it was a no-brainer. Stay where he was making a mediocre Pomerol with a vineyard that was owned by a multi-national through several subsidiaries. Or be his own man, start something new. His father always said that you couldn't grow wine in a test tube. You had to put your hands into the soil. That's where *terroir* began, that was how to

7

understand it. With the hands. Soil was like sex Gaultier had said in one lecture – it was everything you needed to know and never could.

– Ok, it's a deal. But I'll need to start work soon.

– Move into the annexe as soon as you're ready. Ghislaine will be here in the week to help out. We can hire labour in the village when we need it. Old Raymond'll help out. He worked for the last owner and knows the ropes. I'll be busy in Tours for a few months yet, but back some weekends. We'll harvest in October?

– October, or even early November if we can wait that long. It depends.

André looked up at the sky.

– Timing is everything with wine.

A platitude, but one Gaspard would grasp.

– Cool. Can't wait. Look after the grapes and I'll look after you.

And they had clinked bottles to clinch it. André knew that Gaspard liked him because he was a peasant at heart, just like himself. Despite the bullshit and fancy car and the bling, he'd always be more at home with his own sort.

Early July and the grapes were already hanging on the vines. André borrowed the old Peugeot and moved his things into the annexe. Like the house, it was plainly furnished but had its own shower and kitchen area. Apart from tending the vines and cleaning and testing the equipment in the winery, his main job was to watch over the construction of the new oak barrels. The staves had to be toasted to perfection – a light shade of chestnut that would add smoke and complexity to the brambly wine he

8

imagined. That meant hurtling backwards and forwards on the bike to the cooper, leaving the two lads he'd engaged from the village with Raymond, who'd grumble at them when necessary. Eric and Paul. Brothers. Both with bleached hair and gold earrings and wide brown eyes. They'd proved to be decent lads, hard working if you watched them, and willing to learn.

Each day they'd work their way down the vines, weeding, removing leaves to allow air to circulate. Later they'd take out excess fruit. To make a new-style wine it was necessary to return to some – not all – of the old methods. That was the irony. At the cooperative he'd watched his father fume as tractors drew up, unable to unload the fruit that was already badly bruised, watching it stew in the sun. Picking was by machine and machines detached the fruit from the stems, but a lot of that went into the must. Quality control was scant when production was on such a vast scale. They produced five wines from a *vin de pays* to an *appellation contrôlée*, but they had no pride in it any more. And the label meant nothing.

The only real way to harvest was by tasting the fruit, then picking, then sorting by hand. It was painstaking and time consuming. To make wine, Gaultier had taught him, it was necessary to become intimate with the fruit. That's where hygiene started, by rooting out the spoiled grapes and treating the rest as precious. You had to love the vines. You had to immerse yourself in the soil and its history, every stone, every drop of sweat and blood it had soaked up. That was to understand *terroir*, what it had meant to families before mechanisation. It wasn't just land and weather and minerals, but everything that had happened

on the land and to it. It was history and future together.
When you drank wine, Gaultier had said, you're sipping
time and weather, the rising and setting sun, even tasting
your own mortality. That had taken a long time to
understand. That's what the cult of Dionysus had been
about. Gaultier had taught them about that too, how a
libation of blood had blessed the new wine.

Each day André rose at six-thirty, showered, then went
into the main house for breakfast. He'd sit down at the
kitchen table where Ghislaine had made coffee and laid
out bread, croissants and jam. On the first day she'd been
wearing jeans and a pale green tee shirt. He couldn't help
noticing that her breasts were small and pointed. Neat, like
everything about her. He'd stood awkwardly in the
doorway.

– *Bonjour, Madame.*

She'd smiled then.

– *Bonjour André!* But *Madame*? Ghislaine, please.

– OK. Sorry … I…

– No need to be sorry, but no need to be formal, either.
Now: *à table…*

She ate with deft and refined movements. Breaking the
croissants in slender fingers, buttering slices of bread
delicately. He eyes caught the light, intensely green under
dark hair that was shoulder length. Glossy with health or
wealth, or both.

– What?

She'd caught him watching her. He smiled.

– If it's to be informal, may I?

He broke off a hunk of bread and dunked it into the
bowl of coffee.

10

– That's how we had breakfast on my father's vineyard when I was a kid. Me, my mother and brother.

– *Touché*!

She tried the same trick, but dribbled coffee down her tee shirt. When she laughed her eyebrows tilted and her mouth showed rounded teeth that crossed over slightly at the front. Her face lost all severity and her tongue moistened her lips quickly, like a cat's.

All day he was busy with the vineyard. He ate with Ghislaine each evening, then went into the village for a drink, or took the bike for a spin, or called his father, or chilled out in his room listening to rock music on his iPod. Otherwise, there was a TV and a satellite dish, but he used it only for the news. Days at Place de L'autel passed comfortably enough: little by little the grapes swelled and the vineyard came back under control.

Each day brought another flawless sky. A fortnight passed. A month. One evening Ghislaine appeared with her hair cut short. The next morning she was wearing shorts and a man's check shirt tied at the waist. Her belly button was decorated with a silver ring piercing. André must have looked surprised.

– I'm going mad around the house, I want to help.

He poured a bowl of coffee and went stupid. Like his father used to say: *act numb*.

– With?

– With the vineyard. I'll do anything. I need a change from playing mum.

– You sure? It can be tough if you're not used to it.

There was a flash of thunder across the eyebrows.

– You think I don't know what work is?

11

– I didn't say that.

–You thought it.

– Maybe. You're the boss's wife. What would Gaspard think?

– Nothing, probably. Like he does.

André took that one in silence. She dunked her croissant and gave him a grin, quick and impish. It was decided.

He put her to cleaning out the winery, first with a yard brush, then scrubbing the sorting tables. It was heart-breaking stuff, but she didn't complain, humming as she worked in a pair of yellow rubber gloves. By dinnertime she had showered and changed back into a long skirt and tie-dye top and had omelettes ready on the table. As they ate, he sensed her watching him.

– How was your day?

He'd been back to the coopers, checking the barrels. They'd looked – and smelled – gorgeous. He'd run his fingers over the new oak, savouring the smoked vanilla they'd impart to the wine.

– Good. The barrels are nearly ready. They're the best I've seen.

– That's good.

– And your day?

He gave a wry grin, sorry he'd tried to punish her.

– Good, actually. Did you check?

– Of course.

– And?

– Spotless. You can come to work again.

They clinked glasses and he watched a tiny green lizard flicker away from the open kitchen door where the rays of evening sun were lingering to tempt it.

The next day, they all worked together, tending the vines. Spoiling them, *like fucking orphans,* as Raymond put it. André had fitted a new battery to the tractor and he cranked the engine to life. It caught in a puff of black smoke, a sweet rumble. Now he and Raymond were clearing out a ditch, hoiking out dead leaves and tangles of convolvulus and piling them into the trailer. Raymond paused to lean on his hoe, watching Ghislaine carry a basket of weeds on her hip.

– Well, she can work, I'll say that. Who'd have thought it?

There was sweat in the cleft of her breasts as she brushed past. He pale skin was taking on the sun. In a few days she'd be burnt brown like the rest of them. Raymond spat in the dust.

– When will we see that fucker of a husband?

André was surprised at the venom. He let it pass. He didn't fancy playing the boss's man with Raymond. That wouldn't wash.

– Gaspard? Oh, he's busy in Tours. Lots of business meetings right now, I guess.

Raymond laughed, then sucked in his cheeks and hooded his eyes.

– You mean the five 'til seven kind?

It had never occurred to André that Gaspard would have a mistress. But it didn't surprise him either. Gaspard wasn't handsome. He was even grotesque – fleshy, corporeal. You could imagine him taking a shit or fucking a woman, but not making love. But he had the energy that made money. Success. And, of course, he *had* money, the oldest hard-on of them all.

13

Ghislaine leaned back to scratch the back of her leg. André watched the white mark fade. She brushed past again and he watched the subtle movement of her hips, her slender legs and neat feet. Even in hiking boots she went down the slope with a kind of elegance. Understated, like her bracelet, the sparsely furnished house. Raymond was smiling, showing the gaps where his eyeteeth should have been.

– You think she's nice, so that'd stop him going for other women? Just because he's an ugly little bastard? He can buy them like that!

Raymond snapped his fingers theatrically.

– Then he's a fool.

Raymond grimaced.

– He's a fool all right, of a kind. But then he's no one's fool. Never cross him, son, he's not the kind to mess with.

– Why would I?

– Why wouldn't you? Reasons are like fish in the sea.

The hoe sliced away a dandelion so that the yellow head fell to the soil. He looked up again as if through afterthought.

– We had a sergeant like him in Algiers. Thebeau. Short-arse. Dead eyes. One day we caught an Arab kid in the *souk* with three rifle rounds in his turban. Thebeau drove him back to the barracks.

Raymond leaned on the hoe and stared across the valley. The veins on his hand were silted rivers.

– He was a beautiful kid. And he was frightened. It took courage to do what they did. They found him the next day by the roadside. We were hardened to it by then. But what that bastard had done to him made us all sick. Hubert's out of the same mould, believe me.

14

– What happened to him afterwards? Was he punished?

Raymond gave his cracked laugh.

– Thebeau? He was always too clever for that. He got an alibi all worked out in advance. Not that anyone gave a shit about a rag-head kid.

– So? What then? Nothing?

Raymond smiled and spat beneath the vines.

– My unit was there for two years. He had an unfortunate accident. Never made it home.

André dropped his shoulders into the silence, letting his eye drift to a hawk above the church, ascending in slow spirals, an angel of light. He started the tractor and they moved on.

After that, André watched Gaspard carefully. He came home every other weekend, always relaxed, always affable. When things went wrong he stayed cool and sorted them out. On those weekends, André dined in the bar or cooked for himself in the small kitchen. Ghislaine seemed to adapt easily to his coming and going and Gaspard had no objection to her working in the vineyard.

One day, when they were checking equipment in the winery, Gaspard put the pen behind his ear so that his sleeve fell back. André wanted to ask him how he got the scars on his arms, but he has the sense to let it lie. It was now late August and he had the feeling that things were finally under control. Gaspard trusted him to do things properly. The small team they had recruited was working well and most of the crap from the past had been cleared away. He was looking forward to the harvest. In the mornings there was dew on the vines and the air was sharp, drawing mist across the valley. Martins flickered from the eaves of the house to feed, their white rumps semaphoring the long flight ahead.

André had been into town for some spare pressure bolts for the wine press, returning late afternoon, just as Raymond was wheeling his bicycle down the path, limping slightly as he always did when he was tired. Then the boys careered past, waving from their old Cleo with its cracked sunroof. When he pulled up outside the house, Ghislaine was watching from the kitchen window. André cut the engine and unstrapped his helmet. He felt a sudden flush of sweat under his jacket. The day's heat was pulsing back from the walls of the house, from the glare of the gravel path. She walked out to greet him. Neat steps like a deer. There were freckles across her nose and her skin was tanned. Her top was low-cut showing the parting of her breasts. He could see her legs through the thin skirt as she moved.

– Do you have a spare?

André looked at the bike, stooping to switch off the petrol.

– You mean tyre?

She laughed and jabbed him in the midriff with her finger.

– I mean helmet.

There was a hollow sensation in his stomach.

– You like bikes?

– I don't know. I've only been on a moped, when I was a teenager.

– It's a hundred horsepower. Sixteen valves. It's not a moped.

16

Ghislaine rolled her eyes in mock amazement.

– Well, it's a big one, I'm sure.

He was thinking about Gaspard. First his wife was working the land like a labourer, now this. Her green eyes glinted. He could smell her scent, feel the subtle emanation from her skin as she stood close, radiating the day's sun.

– Not here. I've got an old one at home.

– If I buy one will you take me out? Tomorrow?

His mouth went dry. He already knew the answer, which was the wrong answer.

– OK. Get something decent in town. Full face. Go to Lafarge's.

She laughed, showing her teeth.

– Don't worry, I won't leave it lying around.

They had a secret. He felt a squirt of acid in his gut. That evening, they ate quietly, lost in separate thoughts. He asked about her children to break the silence. Françoise and Joelle, seven and nine. They were at a private boarding school. She shrugged, as if she didn't know why. André told her about his parents, about his younger brother, Antoine, studying to be a vet in Poitiers. He noticed her deft gestures as she ate salad, examined the dimple above her collarbone and wanted to drink from it. He watched her piling dishes, each movement making the dress cling to her thighs. His mouth was parched. He gulped water, clinking his glass against the jug. When she turned and smiled, meeting his eyes, dropping the tea towel on the table, he rose, avoiding her gaze. He needed a drink.

André set off to walk into the village, noticing how raw and unfinished the house seemed. There was the scent of soil as it cooled, a sappy odour from the vines. He picked up a caterpillar and watched it crawl over his hand. Its hairs were spikes of glass. He paused to examine the grapes, bloomed with dusky yeast, then crushed one against his tongue. It was tannic and bitter. There were slugs coupling on the path, slugs eating slugs. It was hard to tell which.

The football was showing on the big screen – Manchester United against Real Madrid. He knocked back a few beers with the crowd in the bar. They were getting to know him now. The girls looked curiously at him, but they all had boyfriends and he knew better than to try anything here. When he returned to the house it was after eleven. He tried to step quietly on the gravel so as not to wake her, but Ghislaine had the lights on and he could hear faint voices from the television. He had no idea what she did in the evenings. Sometimes he heard her talking to Gaspard or the children on the phone. She had a different voice for each. A dry tone for Gaspard, a little weary, without surprise, but a bright, questioning tone for the kids, the two little girls who were away at school.

André let himself into the annexe, cleaned his teeth and dropped straight into bed. The little room was hot and it was hard to sleep. He dreamed of motorbikes. Not the smart BMW he had now, but the old Kawasaki 125 he'd learned on. In his dreams it never fired, the starter motor howling in smoking oil. He had to push it home, past fields of maize and tightly braided vines.

He woke at 2.00am, the numbers on the alarm clock glowing green. It was weird how dreams always seemed to take you back home. His head was thick. He needed to piss. Floor tiles were cool underfoot as he padded to the bathroom. He drank a glass of water and thought of the grapes swelling out there in the night, of pressure building in their dark skins. André lay awake for an hour then dozed lightly. When he woke it was to an erection and the beeping of the alarm. The room was smitten by a glowing bar of sun where he'd forgotten to draw the curtains.

At breakfast Ghislaine wasn't dressed for work. She was wearing cream trousers, a damson silk halter-top. A grey jacket was hanging from the back of a chair. There was a vase of freesia on the table and the room was full of their scent. He must have looked surprised, though he tried not to. She looked beautiful. André avoided her eyes, pouring black coffee, pushing away the jug of hot milk she made for him. The coffee tasted oily and bitter.

– I have to go into town to the bank.

She said it casually, as if it was nothing to do with anything. He drank his coffee slowly, breaking a croissant and dunking it. There was a gold cross on a fine chain between the rise of her breasts. He had a slight hangover. Not bad, but too much to put up with in the sun.

– OK

– No problem. We'll manage.

She pulled a little face as if he was mocking her.

– I'm sure.

– Do you have any Aspirin or Paracetamol?

– Yes, here.

She rummaged in her handbag, pulling out her mobile phone and checking it quickly for messages.

– Thanks, I didn't sleep much.

She placed her hand on his forehead, a cool touch, then brushed back her hair with mock seriousness. Her armpits were shaved, but dark with stubble. He wanted to put his tongue there. To lick against the bristles. He could never understand why women shaved there. Or elsewhere, for that matter. He preferred the scent of skin to the smell of perfume.

– You seem OK.

– I'll live.

André swallowed the tablets then tipped the milk onto the last of the coffee and gulped it. He walked out, lacing up his boots against the low garden wall, aware of her watching behind the kitchen blind. Or maybe that was his imagination. A thrush hopped ahead of him and the grass was thick with bluish dew. He loved this time of year, when there was just a hint of autumn, when the vines were maturing, the grapes swelling. Swallows gathered on the power lines, yearning to make the journey they'd inherited through their genes. Like desire. Or land. Like *terroir*. The air yielded wood smoke, burning leaves, the scent of change. The season was turning on shortening days.

That evening Ghislaine served a guinea fowl casserole with sautéed potatoes and haricot beans. There on a side table was a square box in a Lafarge carrier bag. André had deliberately worked late until the sky was streaked with sunset. It was dusk outside as they finished eating.

– Is it still ok?

André nodded, pushing his plate away.

– Thank you, that was great. You're starting to cook like my mother!

He must have said it on purpose. She didn't look too pleased. She gave a little shrug.

– I didn't mean *that*. Don't tease!

She glanced towards the carrier bag, as if he ought to be pleased. He was.

– Is it still okay?

–Yes, it's still OK.

– I'll get changed.

He nodded, feeling his throat close up again. He went outside to check the bike until Ghislaine appeared in jeans and a tee shirt, carrying a white Bell helmet. She looked at it, frowning.

– Is this alright?

–Yes it's great. Good make. British. Take this.

He handed her his leather jacket and helped her do up the zip. She turned the cuffs back, laughing.

– It's huge.

– It's safer.

He helped her fasten the helmet buckle, then put on his own helmet and gauntlets, showing her how to climb up onto the pillion seat and put her feet on the pegs. His voice was muffled.

– Hold tight to me. Don't lean over on the bends. Just relax.

She gave him the thumbs up. He felt her arms go around his waist and belly, their helmets bumping together. He started the bike and her hands tightened in a little surge of panic. They nosed down the path to the road. The bike felt cumbersome with her weight on it, tricky on the gravel. André took a left, away from the village, twisting the throttle in a show of power. The road was straight and he eased up the gears until they were cruising at sixty, a steady blast of air pushing against his

21

chest. They hit a series of bends and he swung the bike through them, dropping the gears, feeling her hands tighten and relax, watching the hair on his arms ripple into goose pimples.

They came to a crossroads and he paused, then swung the bike left again, away from the river, climbing through pine woods. A few cars passed, their headlights dim in the half-light. He thought he saw an owl rising from the road then entering the trees. They passed a boy freewheeling down the hill, no lights, no hands, his face split by a delighted grin. André pulled out of a bend, feeling the brutal power of the bike as it took on the hill in third. Then fourth, then smoothly into fifth, hurling straight as a slingshot. He thought of pistons hurtling, the camshaft turning, the driveshaft, blurred spokes, tyres scorching the road. They approached another bend and he touched the brake, feeling pads grip disks, the bike slow. It was a miracle it all kept working so perfectly.

They rode for twenty kilometers without stopping, sinking into the clotted dusk of the next valley, through hamlets and villages, past lit bars where smokers stood outside, heads turning after them. They caught the scent of tobacco, bread from a bakery, sour dung from a farmyard. Then they were following the silver loops of the river, a thin moon to the east, the swollen sun still falling. The headlight bobbed against walls and trees. They rode in a bubble of golden light. Finally, in the closing dusk, not far from home, he pulled into a layby, patting her thigh. She dismounted awkwardly, catching her knee in the small of his back. She was fiddling with the helmet strap, her eyes dark with excitement or fear. He couldn't tell.

– Well?

She flashed him a little smile, intent on the jacket zip.

– Amazing! I love it!

He laid his gauntlets on the saddle and rubbed his arms. The engine ticked as it cooled.

– You're cold?

– Frozen!

She came up behind him, rubbing his arms gently, electrifying them. He tried not to turn around. He could smell her skin, her hair. His heart fluttered at his ribs like a bird at a window. She smiled, dangling the helmet from one hand like a veteran. They watched the sun dropping into the wooded hillside opposite, then climbed back on the bike.

He woke with the memory of Ghislaine's knees against his thighs, her arms around his waist. They'd parted in silence the night before, almost as if they'd quarrelled, dismounting and removing their helmets, lingering towards the house. They said goodnight casually and she'd thanked him for the ride, then he'd lain awake for hours, imaging her footfall in the corridor outside, bathed in expectation. The slightest sound put him on high alert. Then he'd fallen asleep in the early hours to fitful dreams of the wine harvest. Everything had gone wrong: late workers, the press seizing, rain, and a grey fungus spreading over the grapes. Then vats of grapes fermenting and splitting open in a stink of sulphur.

At breakfast, Ghislaine greeted him with a wry expression, deliberately distant, putting the coffee jug down with a bump. There were dark smudges under her eyes.

– You look tired.

She didn't answer, but sat down, pulling a plate towards her.

– I'm OK. I hope I didn't keep you up late.

Did she mean that? Did she know he'd lain there, expectant, counting hours pass in the chimes of the church clock? Her face was impassive as he ate, dunking her bread expertly in the coffee.

– No it's OK. I didn't sleep very well. Bad dreams about the harvest. Weird.

– You're getting anxious. It's natural.

– Maybe.

He spread a thin glaze of apricot conserve over the bread, dipping the corner into his coffee.

– Do you need me today?

– Only if you want to work. We can manage. And Gaspard will be back this weekend. He usually does enough for two.

That was true. He wasn't just thinking of things to say. The Breton knew how to graft.

– Not this weekend. He has to be in Dieppe for some reason.

– OK. Well, we'll still manage.

André had been to Dieppe with a school trip when he was a teenager. There was a little horseshoe beach where three hundred Canadian boys had died in the war, gasping out salt and blood. There were long wooden groins rotting in the sea and green weed on the pebbles. Then cliffs that overlooked the beach where the German machine guns had been waiting. A diversionary raid, so they'd all been sacrificed.

24

He wondered what kind of business Gaspard had there. He liked to spread his assets, keep on the move. He'd made it back three or four weekends so far. They'd worked together on Saturdays, catching up on progress, even doing some maintenance jobs together. André had kept out of the way beyond that, making his own breakfast and eating at the local bar or *créperie* most nights. It had become a routine. He'd even started to like the guy. He had charm, made himself interested in things. Like he said himself, he was a quick learner and André had enjoyed teaching him about the vines, showing him the new barrels and explaining how they'd been scorched for the wine. He was good with his hands, confident with any machine.

It was Friday and it had been a long week. André decided to work the morning, then take the afternoon off to do some personal stuff. He needed some new clothes and a haircut. He'd ride into town and take a little down time. What Antoine called *me time*. But just before lunch Ghislaine appeared, dressed in cut-down jeans, a tee shirt and work boots.

– Changed your mind?

He was cleaning the leaves from a blocked drain at the winery as she came up behind him.

– I got everything done.

– I'm going in to town. Would you like me to cook tonight? I could get some things?

Ghislaine gave out a little spurt of laughter, leaning against the winery wall. Down among the vines Raymond had stopped working and was pretending to clean something from the blade of his hoe. He lit a cigarette and spat.

– So you're not just a mean biker. You're a mean cook?

– I can do most things.

– OK. Surprise me!

It was carelessly said. Thrown back over her shoulder as she turned away and approached Raymond with a bright greeting. He noticed she had a tiny dark birthmark on the back of her right leg, how brown her skin had become where the sun had touched it. He remembered that first formal meeting when she'd worn a dark skirt and cream blouse. She was like another woman, then. Now she seemed to glow, lit by the summer.

At two o'clock he sent Eric and Paul home early. They were touchingly grateful. When he spoke to Raymond he noticed how unmoved his eyes were, chipped from river pebbles.

– I'm going into town for a haircut and a few things. Knock off early. We've done a lot this week and it's too hot.

He pointed down the rows of vines where the weeds they'd pulled were withering in the sun. Raymond was taking a bunch of grapes off a laden vine, the curved knife glittering. He tossed them in the basket beside him, his boot crushing one like a cockroach as it rolled towards him.

– We're wasting a lot of fruit.

– No we're not. It'll make a better wine. Trust me.

– It's not me who has to trust you, it's Hubert.

– Don't worry, we've got back-up, we've got Arnault.

Raymond laughed. He took the stub from his mouth to gob a ball of phlegm after the grapes.

– That ponce? Do you think Gaspard'll beat up on that monied bastard if things go wrong?

26

He chuckled coldly, far-off water in a well.

– That's not how it works. Believe me. Watch your back, son, that's all.

The old man patted him on the shoulder, passing in the smell of garlic and sour sweat, grunting as he lugged the half-full basket.

André gave a wave to Ghislaine as he turned to go. Her tee shirt had fallen away from her shoulder as she stooped at the vines. Her skin gleamed where she'd put on sun cream. She wore a baseball cap to shade her eyes and worked like a country girl now. You'd think she'd been born to the land and not to … but André realised that he had no idea what she'd been born to. Who she was or where she came from. He knew less about her than he knew about Gaspard. Apart from her touch. He knew that. She'd touched him, lit another mystery. Gaspard had said that hadn't he? About women being mysterious. Like wine. He fetched his gear and fired up the bike. The jacket smelled faintly of perfume.

André got back at five-thirty with short hair, a couple of new tee shirts and some groceries. There had been grey strands in with the brown that fell onto the barber's sheet. He'd wandered the town square wondering about flowers, but that had seemed ostentatious, risky. When he got to the kitchen it was deserted, but there was a bunch of blue campanula in a simple glass vase on the table. The Peugeot was parked outside, but the house seemed deserted. He'd bought fillet steak and shallots, broad beans and baby carrots, cous cous and two good bottles of Bergerac, a white and a red. Then some cheese: a blue Fourme d'Ambert, some Epoisses and some fresh Chevre. With

wine, cheese was half the story. For starters he'd toss a
green salad with olive oil and anchovies. He made the
salad first, pouring in the oil from the anchovies as a
dressing, prepping the vegetables and dicing carrots to mix
with the *cous cous*. He popped out the broad beans into a
pan and got the skillet ready. Then he put the white wine
in the fridge and went for a shower, washing away the dust
and pomade, putting on a clean shirt and jeans.

When André got to the kitchen, he expected Ghislaine
to be dressed for dinner, but she was wearing combat
trousers and a cotton sweatshirt and carrying the helmet.

– Can we ride first?

It wasn't really a question. Still, he hesitated.

– Please? I need to cool down.

– OK.

He put the salad and steak back in the fridge. There was
already a big moon rising over the village when he fired
up the bike and she climbed behind, clunking helmets. A
flock of jackdaws puffed out from the church steeple like
smoke from a censer. Swallows darted over the vines. A
dark ribbon of cloud rose at the horizon. André
remembered that he'd missed the weather forecast that
evening. They rode towards the cloud, feeling the air cool,
following the ridge of the valley as it rose from the river.
Ghislaine's hands were light around him, tensing as they
cornered, relaxing as they pulled clear.

This time he stopped near a forest trail. The bike
smelled of hot metal and oil and cow shit that had caked
onto the exhaust. He leaned it on the side stand and they
laid their helmets down. She unzipped the jacket, smiling,
her lips glossy. He wanted to put his mouth to hers, to feel

her hands on his neck. She was wearing a perfume he hadn't noticed before. Faint honeysuckle. It reminded him of something. Someone. She shook her hair out, fluffing it with her fingers. They walked the woodland path, past stands of primroses and cowslips where shadows deepened between the trees. They didn't speak. Silence arced between them like stifled lightning. They paused to watch the sunset and his breath was tight in his chest. He saw her swallow awkwardly and tried to meet her eyes, but she was already heading back, walking casually with that neat turn of the hips. They reached the bike, tilted and cooling on its stand as a furtive breeze was whipping at the larch boughs. By the time they were halfway home, drizzle was darkening the road.

André rode carefully. Light rain was always the worst, the most treacherous. It raised a patina of grease on the road without washing it away. He was a fool not to have checked the forecast. It was probably just a summer shower, but the last thing he wanted was rain when the vines needed a few more days of sun. Luckily, the shower was localised and hadn't reached Place de l'autel. When they turned the driveway and approached the house Ghislaine's hands tightened around him. The downstairs windows were brightly lit against the dusk and Gaspard's Mercedes was parked in the driveway. He was sitting on the low garden wall with his legs crossed smoking a cigarette, watching the clouds gather.

André parked the bike with exaggerated care. Ghislaine took off her helmet and handed André the jacket. Then she ran towards Gaspard and kissed him lightly on the cheek, her short hair falling over his face. André's heart was hammering at his throat. He stroked away the goose pimples on his arms. *Shit, shit shit! What a fucking mess!* By the time André had got his helmet off and walked over to where they were sitting, Gaspard was smiling.

– What have you done to Ghislaine? She's put on weight.

André smiled and took his hand. It was sweaty at the palm and the scars on his arms seemed suddenly livid where they'd been stitched.

– Oh, she's been working with the rest of us. Tending the vines.

– Well, it suits her.

Ghislaine laughed, putting her hand on his shoulder and touching her head to his.

– You always wanted a woman who was some use didn't you?

Gaspard said something in reply, but André was only half listening. Gaspard would have seen the food in the kitchen, the wine in the fridge. Not that anything had happened. Had it? Something and nothing, maybe. They'd ridden up with his wife's arms around him. He realised he was being spoken to.

– André's cooking tonight. Will there be enough for three?

– Sure. I'll just clean up and make a start.

She made it sound normal. Easy. It was weird Gaspard hadn't mentioned them riding the bike together. Unless he'd said something to Ghislaine in those first few seconds. André was going to have to tread very carefully from now on.

At the house, he rinsed his hands and face quickly. Ghislaine and Gaspard were still in the garden, seated on the wall, her head resting on his shoulder. André washed the steaks, patting them dry, then fried them with thinly sliced shallots. He'd de-glaze the pan with a little wine to make a sauce, then steam the *cous cous*, mixing in butter and steamed baby carrots. He called them to table and they started with salad and bread, following it down with white wine as André updated Gaspard on the harvest. As the evening went on, André gradually started to relax, avoiding Ghislaine's eyes, trying not to see her hand touching against her husband's as they ate and passed things to each other. Like man and wife.

It was a bright morning with a fresh airstream, but no rain. André caught the early forecast on the television. They were in for a few days of high pressure. Gaspard was helping André strip down the tractor engine, changing the oil and filters. He was surprisingly deft. He noticed André watching him.

– I started out as a mechanic. Trained at a Citröen dealership in Lille.

– I'm impressed.

– Don't worry. I like to get my hands dirty.

They knocked off at lunchtime and André took the bike for a long slow ride, following the river towards the coast, studying the other vineyards, the harvest that was ripening everywhere. He imagined Ghislaine on the back, clinging to him, her legs apart, her body warm under his leather jacket. He shook the thought off, focusing on the harvest that could make or break him. So far it was looking good. But he couldn't figure out Gaspard. He couldn't really understand why Raymond had taken such a dislike to him. Instinct?

Prejudice or envy, more like. It was no use telling himself they'd done nothing wrong, he and Ghislaine. They'd come so close that the air was thick with it. The road swept away under the bike and that feeling nagged at him. A feeling that wouldn't go away: desire and fear mixed together.

Gaspard left on Sunday afternoon and on Monday he and Ghislaine had breakfast as if nothing had happened. Mealtimes became more formal, as if she was holding something in check. She still came to work in the vineyard, but she spent more time with Raymond or the brothers. There was a subtle avoidance of André's company. It was a relief. It felt as if every day he could put between himself and that last bike ride would wipe away what had nearly happened. Sometimes he thought he saw Raymond watching them with a kind of cynical amusement. Fuck him. It was time to get his head down, to work on the harvest, to pull clear of all that stuff.

By late August the new barrels were delivered and stood ready. By early September the wine press had been serviced and cleaned. They'd sterilise it again before pressing. Gaspard had hired a local man to supervise crushing the grapes, whilst André would keep an eye on the whole operation, moving from the fields to the winery. They had casual labour lined up to pick and load. Raymond would drive the tractor, Gaspard would be on hand as a gofer and Gaultier would drop by once the first fermentation was under way.

By mid October the final growth hung heavy on the vines, carrying its bloom of wild yeast. Mornings began with a pall of mist that burned away under the autumn sun. There'd been a run of clear weather, then three days of showers and distant thunder had made everyone in the valley nervous. Every day André sampled grapes from different points in the vineyard. The sugar content was running at an average of 22 parts. That would yield an alcohol content of about 13%. But sugar wasn't everything. Every day he tasted the grapes too, testing the thickness of the skins against his palate, looking for the appearance of noble rot. On October 28 a run of hot weather was forecast, followed by a weather front from the west. The grapes had begun to take on a slightly wrinkled appearance, like raisins. Now sugar was peaking at 24 parts. Raymond watched André crush grapes in his mouth and spit out the skins.

– Well?

– We harvest the day after tomorrow. Thursday. I'll call Gaspard now.

André left Raymond to supervise the last cleaning of the press and sorting tables and went to the phone. No need to check with Gaultier. This was his call. In three days the new wine would be fermenting in the vats; in three weeks, a secondary fermentation would be taking place in the new barrels, smoothing out acidity, drawing out the flavours of tannin and oak.

That night it was chilly in the annexe. André was planning to spend the winter at home. A few weeks away, at least. He was too agitated to sleep, thinking of ripe fruit being picked. He saw it being lifted from the vines to baskets, then to the trailer and the winery to be sorted. He saw the hydraulic press bursting their skins, the sugar-

saturated juice running towards the vats. Then a faint
scratching sound outside his door, the handle turning softly.
When Ghislaine got in beside him she was naked. Her hair
was long again and he could feel her bracelet scratching his
spine. Then her mouth was hot against his, tasting of honey
and coffee. Without speaking he ran his fingers over her
hips, the curve of her back, the unbearably soft skin of her
thighs. *Chérie!* She was whispering, her breath warming his
ear. *Chérie!* André put his leg between hers, pinning her
hands, and she was laughing softly. Then Raymond was
there, looking on, leaning on his hoe and smiling, his eyes
luminous as a wolf's. When André touched himself against
her it was over. He came in slow, hot spurts. When he woke,
it was to cold sheets damp from his sweat. At the window,
mist was evaporating from the vines. Then, as he turned to
check his clock, the crunch of Gaspard's tyres on gravel.
André piled the sheets into the laundry basket and went for
a shower, his head splitting.

The harvest was completed in three days of steady graft,
dawn to dusk. There was a curious sense of closeness, even
Gaspard taking on a fatherly presence, cajoling the younger
workers, joshing with the women, getting things done. In
the end, less than an eighth of the fruit was discarded after
sorting. The grapes that went into the crusher were as good
as any André had seen. His father had harvested two weeks
ago and it had been the usual mess. *A real fuck-up, but it's
done. What do you expect?* Gaultier made a flying visit,
clapping André on the shoulder, nodding approvingly at
Gaspard before shooting off to another vineyard.

The yard was cleaned up, the casual workers paid off,
the whole operation dropping down to tick-over as

fermentation began. From now on, control was the issue. The temperature in the vats and in the winery itself was governed by thermostats linked to a computer. André had estimated ten days for the first fermentation before running the must into barrels for the malolactic process. In the end, it ran to twelve days before all the barrels were filled. He'd worked for over two weeks without a break. Gaspard had promised to be around for a week or so and André showed him how to look after the wine and check the temperature, which was automatically adjusted. It wasn't difficult. He showed him the thermostats.

– Here, Gaspard, I'd check them twice a day. Just in case. You can also use manual control, if need be.

– No problem, boss. Now, pack your stuff and take a break.

Gaspard had insisted that he took a few days off, went home to see his family. The next day he got the bike ready, checking the gearbox and fork oil, putting a change of clothes into the panniers. Before he left, Gaspard called him into the office.

– First, take this.

He stuffed an envelope into André's leather jacket.

– What's that?

– A bonus. Cash. You've worked well beyond the call of duty.

He took André by the arm and led him to the desk.

– And I'd like you to sign this.

– Which is?

– A new contract for next year. Plus three per cent on your salary. Same commission.

– But what if the wine…?

– What if the wine's shit, eh?

Gaspard chuckled.

– Gaultier's sampled it. He told me it's very promising. You did everything right. I don't want you to slip away from us just yet.

André signed. He remembered Ghislaine's face in the woods, the scent of her skin. He remembered where he'd smelt that perfume. On the Paris subway once, standing next to a beautiful middle-aged Parisienne who was watching a Japanese busker play the cello. She'd smiled at him and walked away, heels clicking. Ghislaine. He shrugged away the thought of her, signed and took the money. André shook hands with Gaspard, kissed Ghislaine chastely on both cheeks. He'd trembled with cold on that first ride and she'd rubbed his arms to warm them.

– Be careful on that thing.

Gaspard was pumping his hand.

– Yes, be careful.

She said it wistfully, as Gaspard turned into the house, her voice clotted.

André started the bike as they watched from the doorway. Man and wife. He thought of the wine in the fermenting vats, its smell of fruit and carbon dioxide, its subtle chemical changes. André made the sign of a telephone with his gauntlet.

– I'll call.

– Relax. Don't worry. You've earned a rest.

Gaspard had his arm around Ghislaine's shoulder as he pulled away. She gave an apologetic little wave and he gunned the bike.

He rode for twenty minutes in a daze of tiredness, sunlight strobing through poplars. It felt good to have the bike under him, to be alive, to have the future. Sun struck against his visor burnishing its tiny scratches. The road ran down steeply to the river, coiling into a series of bends. In half an hour he'd be on the motorway. In three hours he'd be having a beer with his father and uncles, discussing the harvest, talking about football, the new wine. André changed down, feeling the heat from the cylinders against his shins. A lorry laden with grapes was coming up the hill, two young women seated up behind the cab, the breeze fluttering their tee shirts against their breasts. He changed down again, pressing the brake lever. The handbrake felt soft, then it was pulling against nothing. The bike kept going. Too fast. He tested the brake again and looked down. A spray of fluid shone across his right boot. He pressed the footbrake hard and the back wheel slewed on the slick, throwing him into the path of the lorry. A girl's hand went up to her mouth as the bike bucked and he hit the road.

André fell into the taste of berries breaking against his tongue. There was the scent of Ghislaine on his jacket, the heat of her body, her knees against his thighs, the swart stubble under her arms. Then the woods at dusk: blue shadows cooling like molten iron poured between the trees, a silence that howled and tore at them. He remembered long notes drawn from a cello, an echoing subway, footsteps, a man's black hair swooping over his face.

When he rolled into the road, gravel scarred his visor, blinding him. The bike slid away, a spray of sparks into the long screech of the lorry's brakes. He knew the meaning of *terroir*. It was the land and everything that had happened to it. Present, past and future. Everything that had and could happen. Everything that might come of the land, its fruits, the labour of human beings on it, their generations. Then there was no more to remember or to do or say. His mouth was numbed. No pain, but something beyond. The bike shimmered in petrol vapour, evaporating. There were footsteps and voices fading towards him. A blur of wild flowers on the verge. Convolvulus, pale as the smocks of choirboys. And there was life bursting in his mouth, its brief aftertaste. *Terroir*.

LEVERETS

Ellen ducked into the church porch, out of the rain. There was a dead starling on the bench, its wings folded, its plumage dulled. It looked like a knight with folded arms carved in stone, a sepulchre. She remembered starlings in autumn, how they gathered over the shorn meadows in their thousands, darkening the sky and thrumming like war. Then landing to pick over stalks of barley so the fields looked as if soot had fallen over them from the sullen chimneys of the village.

The headstones in the churchyard glistened with rain. Her mother and brother were buried under green humps at the east wall. Paupers' graves. Her mother had died of consumption and her brother, Ben – a beautiful boy with brown curls and freckled skin – of next to nothing. A rash that had started under one ear, spread to his throat and become a fever. He'd burned under her hands as she bathed his face and as her mother coughed her own life away in front of a damp fire in the room below. The doctor had stood in the doorway shaking his head, refusing the shillings she'd raised from the miner's fund her father had paid into. *Try to keep them warm.* That was all he'd said, as if he knew it was hopeless.

That's how they were taken, their kind. Killed by next to nothing. Flux, consumption, syphilis, scarlet fever, measles, influenza, typhus, mad dogs and hunger. And tetanus. Their uncle, Tom, had scratched his wrist baling hay for Terry Hoad and it had gone bad ways. A week later he was dead. He'd gone rigid from the arms downward, staring at the bare boards of the bedroom ceiling in the infirmary where they'd taken him in case it was catching. There were so many ways to die and so little ground to house the dead. She turned the stiff bird with her finger, feeling the child in her belly, its pressure against her skirt band.

The cottage stood at an angle to the churchyard where she waited, separated by a line of flagstones and an iron fence. A few crocus shoots were pushing through. A billy goat was tethered to a stake, its rank stink mingling with sulphurous rain and the wet wool of her shawl. The goat's eyes were pale yellow, like brimming chamber pots. Its horns curled outwards, its balls dangled from matted wool. Ellen made a run to her front door, squeezing through the stone stile to shoulder the swollen timber inwards. A grey spiral of smoke twisted up from the fire. She took the loaf from under her shawl and put it on the table, throwing some sticks from a broken skip onto the coals.

The cottage was one-up, one-down, just like any other in the village. It was in a row of eight and backed onto a yard with a line of earth privies, a midden, and an iron pump. In fine weather you could hang your washing there. In wet weather whole families took to their beds to keep warm. If the rain persisted, which it usually did, the drains backed up and the yard flooded. In summer, heat brought the same persistent stench. She'd seen the vicar's teenage daughters cover their faces as they went by, ducking their heads in a kind of furtive distaste whilst trying not to. No doubt that was their penance for the day, how they learned humility.

Ellen went to the coalhole out back, cracked a cob of coal with the hammer and tumbled it into the bucket. The coal broke open easily, showing a glossy face with the faint imprint of a fern. Someone explained that to her once, her father probably, but she'd forgotten how the fern got there. She clumped into the house, pushed the door to and set about re-making the fire. Beyond the window the village was crouched in mist, smoke coiling from chimneys, rooftops steaming as their heat escaped. A brewery dray came up the hill to the King's Head, its two shire horses stepping high, the driver hunched under his oilskin cape.

Ellen re-built the fire, pushing the sticks into the glow of the inner coals. She waited, watching the wood smoulder. She leaned in to blow, feeling her belly tighten. A few sparks crackled from the wood, then smoke, then flames licking, caressing, consuming. She let it catch then stirred the heap of flame until the coal sputtered, sending out plumes of smoke that caught fire like tiny volcanoes. They'd learned that at Sunday school, how the earth was hot at the core and how molten rock could burst out through a crack as if hell had broken free. She could read and write and do her sums. Not much more. And not that it had helped. But the Bethel lot were good for something. They stuck together and they liked to get ahead.

When her father was transported – seven years under the Night Poaching Act – the Seddons became disreputable. Though even some chapel folk were glad of the rabbits and pheasants her father brought by when the mine owners had laid them off. They made them shareowners in the mines so that each man was entitled to a part of the profits. But when the lode ran out and they were drilling bare rock, there was nothing for them. *Bloody simpletons,* her father called them. *A share of nowt is nowt.* He couldn't read and write, but he knew that much. He'd been gone four years.

She'd worked since she was twelve years old. Scullery maid, cheese presser, drudge on a local farm. The poorer your employer the harder they rode you. She was nineteen now and on the Parish. She'd given away the only thing she had that was worth anything. Call it virtue. Call it love. Some did. Michael had liked her though. She knew that. He'd have wanted the child. She knew that too, or thought she did. She wasn't stupid. Men were men in the end. They were made a certain way and it couldn't be helped.

Ellen sat in her father's chair, kicking off her clogs, watching water pool on the flagstones and darken them. In winter they gave you wicked chilblains. She placed her hands flat on her stomach, watching the fire wax into flame, feeling the child. She was four months pregnant. For the first three she'd been sick as a pup every morning, emptying her guts into the midden under the hard eyes of her neighbours. They'd know why, where, when and with whom. She was a dirty little slut to the chapel-going Methodists and teetotallers. She didn't care. She'd been kissed and fondled by Michael Simpson out back in the pub yard with drunken miners stumbling past and pissing up the wall. And after three gins and a plate of hot peas, she loved it. Loved his beery kisses, the tickle of his beard, the warm feeling of him inside her. Fingers at first, their tips rough from work, working their way towards her. Then they found more private places to meet and he'd grown bolder. He liked her as well as wanted her, she knew that. He died under a ton of rock in Swinton Level. Never uttered a word, just sputtered blood and broken teeth and gave up the ghost. The brass band turned out for his funeral and the mine bosses paid for a barrel of beer. Another life bought cheaply. *Tha'll do me, Ellen,* was all he'd said, after that first time, kissing her nipples and closing up her blouse. *Tha'll do me.*

When they took her father away to Richmond assizes they searched the house from top to bottom, but they hadn't found his gun. He'd made a special hiding place for it under the roof beams in the bedroom so that it was pushed between the plastered lath and the slates. They kept him in the stables at the Hall, word spreading that he'd been caught red-handed. She'd fetched him some food and spare clothing. He winked at her, putting a finger to the side of his nose as they took him away chained to a farm cart, expecting a few days in jail. He'd heard of the new game laws but taken little notice. *Nay*, he'd said, *they'll never thank us for tekkin' what's there's. Though what's theirs is ours by rights.* They'd expected him back within the month but he never came. It was Billy Crapper the carter who brought the news. *Transported*. Van Diemen's land, he reckoned, though he wasn't sure where that was.

Her father had taught her how to catch pheasants with raisins stuck through with a bristle to choke them, how to peg a wire snare, get rabbits with a purse net and ferret, and how to shoot his little rifle. They'd caught him snaring hares on the squire's land this time and they'd fought

43

viciously in the dark. It was winner take all. He laid out two of the under keepers with his fists, but the head keeper produced a lantern and a pistol and put it to him plainly. *You come quietly now, Seddon. Think of your children. You'll take no more game if I send you to hell, and that's where you belong, you thieving gypsy bastard.* Her father cursed him as a craven arse-licker, but had gone quietly in the end. Billy heard all this from a weaver who'd shared a cell with her father for a few days before being released. He spent his first day of freedom playing his fiddle for the soldiers and whores who plagued Richmond town and getting shit-faced drunk. Billy got the whole story for the price of a pint. Her father was no gypsy, but he'd learned their ways. Night skills, a gentle stealth.

A woman stooped into a plaid shawl went past the window. Susan Darrent, toothless, sick with age and consumption. She'd not last the winter. After days of rain the village was sodden and dark-stoned. Hillsides across the valley were streaked with white water where streams had boiled to the surface. Ellen went to the window nudging the fire with her clog as she went. There was hardly any coal left. She stood looking out, hands across her belly, feeling the warmth of the child inside her, remembering Michael's body heat, the little sigh as he came into her and then released himself. She hadn't known what was happening at first. But after that she enjoyed the power she had over him, the way a grown man would set his pleading eyes on her, bring her food and drink. He never forced her. He was never rough like the other men, not Michael. He had his eye on her ever since she took up as a maid at the King's Head and began

44

stopping by after work. As soon as the landlord found out she was pregnant he felt her belly, gave her a sovereign, grinned wisely and sent her home. Sour breath, white bristles, black teeth. She'd never seen so much money. He couldn't have her moping around the place with a full belly when there were guests to tend to.

Earlier that summer they got away from the village, racing each other down the lanes together to make love in the hayfields amongst the meadowsweet and clover where the river made a loop of silver against the land. That's how she got pregnant. Lying down to take him instead of being had against a wall. Or maybe because she told Michael she loved him. He'd not known what to say. Not being good with words. That last time she lay down for him a moth had blundered against her breast. When she brushed it away it left a faint powder on her skin. She ran her hands over his arms, marked with scars, where the hairs grew thick and blond and he watched her with a kind of wonder. As if he'd never been touched like that. When they made love it was tender and slow. He let his lips graze against her neck and ear lobes as he came deeper in. The lids sagged over his green eyes and the lock of straw-coloured hair flopped over his face. Three days later he was dead. It'd crushed her as sure as if she'd been felled by that same landslide of stone and darkness. Then her monthlies had stopped and the sickness began as if sin had curdled in her. Except she never believed that. How could love be sin when they lived under the love of God?

Her father had shown her how to take the gun apart and clean it. It was a small-bore rifle, specially made so that the

45

barrel unscrewed and could be easily hidden. Seddon got it from a gun-maker in Knaresborough. He showed her how to clean the barrel with the pull-through, how to oil the hammer and trigger, then how to load it, tamping down the powder and ball with wadding and priming the pan. A time or two he took her up in the moor for target practice. She was a good shot, he said. She loved the feeling of the rifle in her hands, the way it was warm from her father's hands, the way it cracked and jumped against her shoulder and a bottle flew into pieces. They lay next to each other in the heather in his smell of sweat and gunpowder and oil. Her father had been a soldier – *the King's bloody fool* – then mended shoes for a living, a trade he'd learned in the army, then travelled the country from north to south. He'd been a sailor for one God-forgotten voyage. Then he learned his real trade – *the taking of hares that is* – and here he'd wink and put a finger to his nose – from gypsies in Kent when the hop-picking season was on. They taught him to walk on stilts to get the highest flowers. They showed him the art of mole trapping, and that earned him extra cash when the farmers were plagued. And it gave him a chance to spot where game was being raised. What he brought home from the woods and estates around the village had kept them from hunger – though not from harm.

A few times he took her out with him. Usually when the moon was full and there was a high wind that tore the hems of clouds and drew them over its glare. The more noise weather made, the better. One night they climbed up to Reys plantation and went a few yards in to wait. The trees were mainly oak and beech with some elm and hazel. Her father taught her their names by showing her the shapes of their leaves. A ride was cut through the trees, strewn with straw. There were some feeders made from half-sawn barrels. It was here that the keepers put down grain for the pheasants to feed. They came out in the late afternoon as the light was fading, then roosted in the trees. The cock pheasants gave out a brazen clucking cry if disturbed, leaving their perches to crash through the branches. She loved their princely colours, like the pictures of Mughal emperors she'd once spied in a book at the Manse when she'd been helping to keep house for the vicar. It was hard to imagine they could belong here in the grey Yorkshire dales when their colours were so rich. *Brought from beyond*, her father reckoned, and regarded more than starving women or children. They were living brooches for the land – and as stupid as the lords were rich. ·

He took them with a loop of snare wire attached to a stick, guiding the noose over the bird's head as they rooted for the grain he'd dropped. Then a sharp yank and the bird was choking, all feathers and commotion. You had to snap their necks quickly then. He taught her to kill quickly and mercifully; never to be greedy, to take only what you could carry, to carry only what you could eat or sell or give away. How to wear a cap and beard or blacking to take the glare off your face, to wear boots not clogs, to work alone. Long netting in gangs was a fool's game for you could trust no one. The other man will always let you down in the end. He never poached for profit. Hares he killed on the ploughed land, or after hay time, catching them silhouetted against the sky and bringing them down with a single shot. He said the moon mesmerised them, that the man in the moon was really a hare if you looked properly. That's why they got drunk on moonlight, standing up on their hind legs to give him a clear shot through the heart.

Her father told her stories about his one time at sea. How he got drunk in a quayside pub in Bristol and got tricked onto a slave ship that was trading beyond the law. Not that he knew. They'd taken a hold full of brass pots and pans to the Gold Coast in Africa, then on to El Mina fort where pirogues rode the breakers all around them, and the natives cast out nets, their boats rising and falling, appearing and disappearing in the high seas. There, they took on a cargo of slaves. Her father described how a line of negroes covered in sores from their chains stumbled down the ramp, dazzled by the sun after days in a dungeon. They'd never seen the ocean or a great ship before. Next minute they were being roughly doused in the sea, then taken up and chained in the hold. He told her how he'd lived a life of shame to see them suffer in their own filth and blood, men and woman alike. Every day started with dropping the dead overboard. They lost seven sailors and twenty-two negroes on that trip.

Her father said things that she'd heard no one else say. How all men were born equal until they were made unequal, black and white alike. How 'nigger' was no name for a black man and how he'd not bear it said. He'd fought men over that, because God was everywhere and nowhere, in everything and in nothing.

One day they brought the negroes up on deck for air, chained at the ankles in groups of five. One group started to sing, doing a kind of war dance, stamping in their shackles. When the mate brought the lash to tame them, they jumped over an ill-rigged rail into the sea, dragging each other down. He watched them sink through the clear upper waters into the gloom below, their arms and legs still moving in their chains, air bubbles bursting to the surface. *Aye, that's how much freedom means, Ellen. Freedom is everything to a man.* He told her how he'd wanted to join them, to jump for liberty, even if it meant certain death by drowning or sharks. He told her how huge and restless and bright the green Atlantic was, how he'd seen coconuts and pineapple trees in the Indies and women walking around naked to the waist. How the island been set in the sea like a jewel in a crown. As soon as they'd docked in England he'd taken his pay guiltily and stayed sober, slinking past the press gangs, heading north to Yorkshire by country lanes and hedgerows. How he met her mother was never told. She wondered if he'd lain with black women before that. She didn't care.

After marriage, he became a lead miner, walking three miles to work and back. Starting at five-thirty and getting home at seven. When she lay in bed between her mother and brother she liked the peaceful feeling of him moving about the house in stockinged feet. She'd hear him taking the bowl of oatmeal from the hearth where it had soaked overnight, then putting on his clogs at the back door, trying not to make a noise. Easing the privy door because it creaked on its hinges, then lighting the lantern he had to carry in winter and greeting the other men of his gang in whispers as they tried not to wake their women. If times were good, they came down to a fire he'd got going from last night's embers. A cold hearth meant things were bad, even though they were never spoken of. When the hearth was dead you learned not to ask for more than there was.

It was mid-March now. Fells and fields were still pale brown. Winter had been hard, freezing the pump in the yard. The sheep were almost starving for lack of new grass, though she'd seen ransomes and dog's mercury spearing through in the woods. The weather was so cold that rabbits had gnawed the bark from the young trees, leaving bare white trunks as high as they could reach. The farmers had come out in gangs to shoot them. Sometimes they put turnips out for the cattle and sheep and she'd sneak down and bring a couple home under her shawl. She roasted them over the fire until they softened enough to eat. Then she'd get the wild shites and spend hours freezing in the privy, emptying her guts.

There was a crack in the thin window glass where droplets of rain were coming through. Mist blew over the fields below the church and the river had disappeared. The dray horses passed again, dragging the cart away with its load of empty barrels and firkins, the driver hunched into his cape, dangling the whip over the team as if he hadn't the heart to use it. She wondered where her father was. Van Demons land. The curate told her that was near Australia in the world's southern half. All she knew was that it would be hot. When her father had pleaded to the court that he'd served his country as a soldier and a sailor, the magistrate joked that the voyage wouldn't make him seasick then. He was a known poacher and would be made an example of. He ought to be grateful that he wasn't to be hanged. That was what Billy Crapper had said. Not that you could trust much that came from his mouth.

When her mother and Ben died, she wrote him a letter, telling him everything, saying that surely they would send him home now? She'd sent it care of the magistrate's court, but she heard nothing. He had three more years to serve. He'd come home to a grandchild and two graves, if he came at all. That thought of the child eased her grief sometimes, allowed her to go on.

Ellen was hungry now that the pangs of early sickness had passed. She took a knife and cut the crust and a thick slice from the loaf. The fire had just enough heat in it. She took a long fork from a nail on the wall and held bread over the glowing coals. She had a scraping of beef dripping from the butcher to spread on it. It was delicious – bread and dripping and coal smoke all mixed together. The bread would last her two days. After that, she didn't know what she'd do. The Poor House was always a risk for pregnant girls, but they'd never take her there. She was determined of that. She had her father's gun and knew how to load and fire it. There was enough powder and shot to see to things. She'd rather end it now than live as a slave, just as he'd said. Then one sin would be taken over by another.

Ellen dozed and woke and dozed again in front of the fire, only half conscious of the ebbing day, slipping light, of rain ceasing against the window. She dreamed of dark mine shafts where a scaled beast was turning under the earth. Then of a great sea, bright as scattered emeralds and black men casting out nets from tiny boats. Then Michael and Ben were in the nets, fighting for air, their hair stuck down with salt. Then her father helping sailors pull the bodies to shore. Her mother weeping and wringing her hands because her father was taken. Everything broken and mixed together and broken again, sense and nonsense both.

She woke hungry to an ashen fire. The church clock was tolling seven o'clock. She'd taught Ben to count that way when they were children. The rain had cleared and a big moon was pushing its face between clouds that were scattering and blowing away. She stood at the window, watching the moonlight come and go on stone walls that separated the fields, then opened the door to feel the air. Winter was on the turn at last; the night was warmer than most. She thought of the dead bird in the porch of the church, of her mother and brother buried under low mounds at the far side of the graveyard. A line of lanterns passed on the road below, bringing the heavy tread and low voices of miners on their way home.

Ellen closed the door suddenly and barred it. She climbed the stairs, changed from her dress and shawl into a shirt, then rooted out her father's canvas trousers. She'd washed and dried them, but they were still stiff as boards. She had to leave the top button open where she was swelling. She managed to push her feet into his boots and fasten the leather laces. Next she stood on a chair and pushed up the hidden flap of wattle in the ceiling. She reached inside to find the rifle wrapped in an old singlet. The powder and shot were in a tin close by, still dry. She drew them out and let them fall to the bed, then stepped down and took them into the room where the fire was glimmering. In the tin were flasks of oil and powder, a paper packet of ball shot and wadding and some flints. Wiping the rifle on the singlet, she screwed the barrel to the stock. Then she oiled the hammer, smearing oil on her hand which she worked into the walnut stock until it gleamed. She cocked the hammer and pulled the trigger, watching a spark jump at the pan. Then she took the gun apart again, hanging the barrel in a special loop in the trouser and concealing the stock under her father's thick cotton jacket that he'd brought back from sea.

Before Ellen left the house she pulled on her father's cap and tucked in her hair. Dragging the door to, she noticed stands of snowdrops beside the path. The moon was hidden now and she made her way through the churchyard limping slightly, the cold metal of the gun against her thigh. At the road she turned right and down the hill to the river meadows. There were cattle gathered there where the farmer had put down beet or swedes the day before. There was a chance the fodder would bring out hungry hares and rabbits.

In the field she could hear the river singing beyond the broken willows that lined the bank. In summer it was a good spot to see kingfishers, their blue lightning blinding the eye with speed, as if they were never real. She pulled out the gun and assembled it, fumbling in the dim light, working by touch. She loaded it with ball and a measure of powder, then tamped in the wadding, then primed the pan, pulling back the oiled hammer. Then she crouched behind an iron roller that had been dragged and left there. The moon peeped and glimmered and disappeared again, showing the gnawed swedes scattered on the grass like golden skulls. There were beasts gathered in the far corner of the field, a mass of shadow. She could hear them, not see them. Their guttural breath shunting the air, their heavy tread, a hoarse cough, sometimes a lowing moan. They moved at the edge of her vision like the beast in her dream. Ellen slipped her hand under the shirt to feel the small swelling in her belly above her pubic hair. She moved her hand lower, shivering with pleasure and with cold. She remembered Michael's breath on her neck, his tongue at her breasts, then the heavy sigh as he came into her. She rested the barrel of the gun on the roller and waited.

The hare appeared at last from the dark end of the field, coming through the scattered cattle towards her. They ignored it as it slunk and hopped, pausing to lower its ears then raise them again. The breeze was blowing away from her, carrying her scent back to the village. The moon glowered through a gap in the clouds and the hare came on, bounding easily over the cropped grass. It stopped to sniff at a swede and then another. It seemed to disdain them or perhaps had already eaten its fill. The hare came within ten yards of her and sat with its ears pointed and swivelling. She could see the dark marking on its face, the gleam of its whiskers. Its eyes were treacle. The gun was already balanced. All she had to do was slowly swing it around so that the hare was in her sights. She squinted down the barrel, remembering all her father had said. How she must squeeze, not pull, how to keep her elbows close to her body. The rifle cracked and the hare's face lit up in the spurt of flame. There was a smell of black powder. A drift of smoke obscured things for a moment and she thought she must have missed when the hare took off. It ran for twenty yards and then collapsed onto one side and lay still.

Ellen hid the gun under the roller. Her father had taught her never to take it to the kill. A dead hare was one thing to be found with, but a hare and a gun couldn't be explained away. The ball had gone through the hare's chest and out through its shoulder. Its fur was dark with blood and its face was resting on the grass. She could see a tiny white moon reflected in its eye and was glad when the clouds gathered to hide that. She took up the long body and wiped its face gently with her hand. Then she put it inside her shirt, around her waist, and buttoned it there, feeling its heat next to her own, next to the child inside her.

Ellen walked home awkwardly with the dismantled gun and the dead hare lolloping inside her clothing. She could feel it oozing against her ribs and caught the thick scent of its blood. She clicked the catch of the cottage door quietly and dropped the hare into the stone sink where it could drain. Taking off the smeared shirt, she shivered with her feet on the flagstones. She lit a candle and washed her belly clean, using a rag and the bucket of water beside the stone sink. Her body was pale in the flickering light of the candle. The hair under her arms and between her thighs dark. *Tha'll do me, lass*. She remembered Michael again, how he'd kissed her and caressed her neck with his calloused hands and put himself into her and released the seed that had made this life that burned in her.

When she was dressed, Ellen cleaned the rifle and stowed it back in the eaves, then drew the curtain at the back window and took a candlestick and a knife to the sink. She held the hare and made a long incision from just under the ribs to its anus. It was a doe. When its guts fell away she saw that it was carrying three leverets, tiny pale ghosts that spilled from its womb. Ellen cut off the intestines and ran her thumb down the bowel so that

55

pellets of dung squeezed out. She reached under the ribs and pulled away the lungs and heart, then cut off the head and paws, pressing the knife though bone that crunched and gave. Then she pulled the skin away from the neck and body until it was naked. She took the guts, the head and paws and the tiny foetuses and buried them in the midden where they couldn't be seen. The fur would make a cap for her baby. She left it on the hearth to dry. She poured water over the carcase to rinse away the blood, then quartered it and dropped it into the cooking pot for tomorrow's fire. She poured water in, salted it, dropped in some sprigs of thyme that were hanging from the roof beam. Then washed her hands, smelling the rich, earthy scents of the hare, half sick at what she'd done.

Ellen climbed the stairs and changed into her mother's nightgown. It was white cotton with tiny violets embroidered over each breast. A wedding present from her father that came with the bed and three copper pans. She took the candle to the window that overlooked the graveyard and the river. Lead on the church roof showed as a dull gleam. The clock struck ten. She'd been a long time in the fields. Now she saw herself in the cracked glass, cupping the wavering flame, pale skinned, dark haired, shadows smeared beneath her eyes. Her hands and wrists had grown thin and were red from the cold water. There was blood under her fingernails. She'd done what had to be done to live. Her father would have been proud of her, the way she'd known how to load and shoot. And she'd been quick, merciful. She thought of the bullet striking the doe, the way it had drowned in its own blood and died running. Died making for freedom.

Remembering the way the day had started with rain, the church porch, a dead starling with folded wings, she pinched out the candle so that her reflection disappeared, then put her face to the cold glass. Her brother and mother were huddled under green mounds close to the churchyard wall, without headstones or words to mark them. In the flat valley bottom the river was coursing over stones and strands of weed to the sea. The sea she'd never seen except in dreams and probably never would. She thought of her father in chains and where he was and whether it would be night or day. He'd lost his freedom to the Queen's pleasure, to the might of an empire where all men were born equal then rendered unequal. He'd been made an example of and so would make his way home to grief and sorrow. She knew that. One day, not too distant. One day where the future lay, waiting to happen.

Someone sluthered across the flags of the square in clogs, then coughed, retching their way through the yard. A door slammed and there were raised voices for a few minutes. The man's slurred and drunk, the woman's shrill with anger. Then her voice stopping halfway through something she was trying to say. That was the way of it. Man and woman. Fist against tongue, tongue against fist. Silence trickled back to fill the space the woman's voice had left. Ellen put the candle down and sat down on the empty bed, hugging herself, feeling the chill on her legs, letting her cold fingers stray to her belly. She put her hands together to pray and the light of the moon brightened again, casting shadows from the headstones in the graveyard, tearing clouds open, looming, unstoppable.

THE SHOEMAKERS OF NAKASERO

The call of the Imam woke me. His voice was distorted by the speaker system, like the bit on that single by Cher where she sounds like she's singing down a drainpipe. What was it called? Another blank one. I lifted my head. The pillow was damp. *Jesus.* No aircon in the university guesthouse but the room was pretty cool. My tongue felt like last night's pit latrine. I couldn't remember much about how we'd got home, just the taxi lurching over potholes and someone spewing out of the back window. *McKenzie.* My clothes were crumpled on the floor like a man hunched into a foetal position. They looked how I felt. I took a swig from the bottle of water beside the bed and dozed off again. When I woke, my head was banging. I searched for my watch, but I was still wearing it. The hands glowed in the light that filtered through the mosquito netting. Eight-thirty. *Fucking hell!*

This was supposed to be a rest day. Saturday morning in Kampala. I wondered what Helen and the girls would be doing. It was still early in the UK. They'd probably have breakfast then pile into the car to see her parents at Saddleworth. Her parents who'd never liked me. I wondered if she was still seeing that guy from the Building Society. Gary? Gordon?

When I tilted my head, a pain shot from side to side as if I'd just touched two wires together. I let it sink slowly back to the pillow. *Believe*. That was the name of the record. Weird, how things come back.

I must have dozed for another hour and was woken by the sound of a croaky American voice using the phone in the guesthouse lobby. *I love you too honey. Give my love to the kids. Yeah, yeah. Love you too*. Sometimes he was on the phone at three in the morning, calling his family in Colorado, driving me nuts. Always the same droning accent. And love, love, love. He'd been out here for a couple of months fitting a new X-ray system at Mulago Hospital. Long enough to get lonely. I was just back from three days up country with McKenzie and we'd got wrecked at Al's bar, firing down Nile Specials and playing pool with the young prostitutes. I had a vague memory of McKenzie dancing on the table to Queen with his arms round a nineteen-year-old called Grace who had a bare midriff, small breasts, and was high on ganja and free beer. *Another one bites the dust*.

We'd been taking readings and rock samples from the river below Jinja where they were planning a hydro-station a few miles down the White Nile to sort out Kampala's knackered power supply. There was already a dam at the Owen Falls, but that wasn't enough any more. We'd spent three nights in a tent, McKenzie moaning about the heat, mosquitoes eating us alive. I told him how the crocs crawled out of the river at night and could take a young antelope in one lunge. How they dragged and drowned their prey before eating it. That quietened him a bit. I saw his wind-up torch flickering at night through the tent fabric. Fortunately we had a tent each – me, McKenzie, and James. James was the driver and cook: tall, elegant, and a genius on pot-holed roads. He was from western Uganda, near Mbarara. Cattle country. He spoke Runyankore, Luganda, and Swahili and three or four other dialects, including English of course, so he was pretty useful.

We'd got stopped at a roadblock on the way back to Kampala: boy soldiers in camouflage fatigues and maroon berets looking through all the boxes of rock samples in the back of the truck. The corporal looked about eighteen and the kid who swung open my door had his worn-out AK47 slung and pointing at my thigh. They wanted me to unpack my theodolite. Christ knows why, but they were good-natured enough. James chatted away in the corporal's own language. It turned out he was a westerner, too. We gave them a crate of warm beer – *something small* – and after shaking hands they let us bounce back to Kampala past the tea and sugar cane plantations spaced out along that fucked-up road. Back to running water and flushing toilets and clean sheets. McKenzie had got bitten by mosquitoes all over his arms and he sat behind me in the truck scratching away and hissing through his front teeth. I caught James' eye once or twice and could have sworn he was smiling as he drove, humming gospel songs. McKenzie was new to Africa, all freckles and ginger hair and blue-eyed naivety. But I'd worked with worse. I'd worked with Armstrong for almost six months and he was an arsehole. Pure and simple. I wondered where Armstrong was now. Last thing I heard he was checking out an irrigation scheme in Zambia, but who knows? I liked to think that worse things might have come his way.

I got up and took a shower. There was a trickle of warm brown water and I washed the soap off carefully. There was no shortage of cold water and it cleared my head to have that sheet of ice gushing over my face. Africa could be dangerous in unexpected ways. Once I'd slipped in the shower and shot out like a greased pig. There was more chance of dying from a broken electrical socket when shaving or in a shagged-out taxi after a few beers than being eaten by wildlife.

No shave today. I dried myself off, pulled on some clean clothes and dropped last night's shirt into the laundry basket. It stank of sweat, mosquito repellent, smoke and dope. Swigging water and remembering to take a malaria tablet, I checked the fridge. A row of Bell's lager bottles gloated. The pain in my head pulsed. I swung the door shut and pulled on some shoes. Yesterday evening we'd stashed the gear at the company compound, drawn some cash – a satisfying wad of Ugandan currency in ten thousand shilling notes – then cleaned up at the guesthouse where we were staying this visit. I hated the Sheraton and the tourists who frequented it. There was something down to earth and unpretentious about Makerere University and its accommodation. I liked the staff too; they were attentive without being obsequious. It was James' idea to go to Al's, which, for a born-again Christian, was pretty cool. After a steak and a couple of beers and a quick spray of Jungle Formula we were ready for the night – which turned out to be more than ready for us.

I went down the corridor towards breakfast. CNN news was on the television in the dining room. The usual stuff: an earthquake, a financial crisis, diplomacy in the Middle East. I took bacon, sausages, and two pale yellow eggs from the tureens. Then plenty of strong coffee. A sign above the picture of President Museveni advertised Bell lager with the stylized rays of a rising sun lighting up one customer's happy face. The idea seemed to be that you woke up feeling good. The waiter, Moses, took my plate.

– More, sah?

I shook my head. No way. He'd worked here for years and never seemed to find anything better. I nodded to Sister Agnes who was talking the hind leg off the guy from Colorado. He had a grey moustache and the sagging features of a Bassett hound. She was in full rig. I got up quickly before she caught my eye. Having breakfast with her was like sitting down with the headmistress to talk through your school report.

McKenzie would be spark-out half the morning, so I decided to walk through Wandegeya and into town. I picked up my bush hat, stuffed a roll of bank notes into my pocket, and took a bottle of water from the fridge. The power had failed again and the water was at blood heat. I walked out of the compound. Past the acacia trees at the entrance. Past the guard with his ancient bolt-action rifle. Past the mosque where a row of slippers was lined up at the entrance. Then down the red dirt track that ran beside the road into town. The air was sickly with diesel fumes and charcoal smoke from the braziers where women roasted maize cobs and sold them to the students on their way to Saturday classes at the university. They came in a steady stream in freshly pressed clothes, smart and eager to learn.

The track was uneven, rutted with rainwater. Open storm drains were clogged with rubbish beside the road. I saw a dead lizard curled in the dust. The kind that were supposed to cast a spell on pregnant women. I stubbed my foot and scuffed the toe of my shoe. They were pretty shot anyway. My dad always used to say that he couldn't afford cheap shoes. When he died I found boxes of them stored in the pantry at home, never worn. Grensons, Loakes, Crockett & Jones, Cheaney's. He must have combed every charity shop in town. Some were brand new and all were two sizes too small for me. Towards the end he'd developed bunions. His big toes had crossed over and he'd only been able to wear trainers. When I went to see him in the hospital his feet were yellow and twisted like roots.

It was about that time when things in the UK had gone wrong for me. I'd been made redundant when my firm downsized, so I'd gone freelance. First a pipeline in Cameroon, then Kampala, Nairobi, Llilongwe, Accra, Harare, Joburg, Kano and Lagos. I had this dream, that somewhere in one of the marketplaces – maybe in Kano or Nakasero – I'd find an old man making shoes by hand. He'd be a product of empire, crafting the finest veldtschoen from buffalo hide for army officers who sought him out from their retirement homes in the UK. Each would have his own last, carefully numbered, and the shoemaker would store them in the shady back room of his shop, even after the ex-colonials had died out, one by one. Every year he'd send a few pairs of hand-stitched shoes to the UK and a cheque or bank order would come back by return.

My dad was a wrought-iron worker and could make anything out of metal. He used to belt us and his hands were as hard as ingots. You learned never to let him come up behind you. Once he smacked my brother's head so hard that it hit the plasterboard partition between our bedrooms and cracked it. He got another smack for that. In those days most men had a trade and in our row of terraced houses we had a joiner, a painter and decorator, an electrician, a mechanic, and a violinist. And my father, of course. Together they could have built the Ark and entertained the animals.

My father liked to walk when he had no work – which was most of the time as he got older and more cantankerous. He'd stump angrily into Manchester and back, placing small ads in newsagents, saving on bus fares. He liked those metal pieces nailed to the heels of his shoes – *segs* – so he rapped his way down the pavements. When we were little, my dad *was* the creak of leather. You heard him before you saw him. Luckily. Once he had a pair of shoes repaired and the leather wore through in a few weeks. *I asked for bullhide on these not bullshit,* he told the cobbler, slamming them down on the counter. He had a nice turn of phrase when it suited him. For a man of five foot two, he was the most intimidating person I ever met. But then, he was my dad. Enough said.

I waited at the only working traffic lights in the city. The sun was melting the sky. An amputee went by on a hand-operated tricycle, his face shiny with sweat. This was my fourth visit to Uganda – a six-week stint in Kampala, with occasional visits 'up country' – as the Brits call it. Up country can be pretty much anywhere, even down country. I never really figured that out. McKenzie was the geologist and would be with me for this last two weeks of the survey. The heat was blistering now, the sky almost white with heat. A few black kites soared in thermals above the shantytown to my right. I passed a group of boda-boda riders straddling their Chinese motorcycles and hoping for a fare. Then down Kampala Road, slackening my pace a little. I'd had to learn to walk slowly. Heat shivered on the tarmac like white spirit evaporating. There was a dead dog at the kerbside, bloated with heat. The stench was a stifling muzzle of decay, sickening. A few years ago the same road had been strewn with human bodies.

I walked past the area they called Bat Valley where thousands of fruit bats roosted at night. I'd watched them earlier in the week from the guesthouse terrace, flying in their thousands, flapping into a yellow tropical storm. I passed a half-built hotel clad in bamboo scaffolding that never seemed to get any bigger. Then a Shell garage where security guards in blue tracksuits and baseball caps lounged in the shade with cheap, pump-action shotguns. I saw a woman with dust in her hair, blinded by cataracts, sprawled under a blanket, too weak even to beg. I put a few coins into her hand and she stared through me as if I didn't exist.

The sun was really bending my head. Usually I made a point of never getting drunk in Africa. For obvious reasons. One was to avoid doing something stupid. The other was feeling like shit. But that would pass. Hangovers do. There were worse things here and you didn't have to look far to find them. I bought some more water from a boy lugging a box of Rwenzori Spring and walked on past the tennis courts where two Brits were playing a feeble game of doubles with a couple of local girls. They didn't look as if they knew one end of the racquet from another.

I bent down to tie a lace and saw the leather was cracking on my shoes. I had an idea that this visit I'd find what I was looking for.

I turned off the main drag to the market at Nakasero, teeming with Saturday shoppers and piled with cheap household goods: bolts of cloth, clothing, electrical plugs and sockets, pots and pans, plastic ware, knives, fruit and vegetables. The food was piled up neatly in pyramids – oranges, peppers, pineapples, watermelons, eggplant, cassava, passion fruit, tomatoes and Irish potatoes. Then an open-air butchers where goat meat darkened in the sun. Then a whole area dedicated to plumbing and tiling, its chrome and enamel gleaming. Coils of copper and plastic piping. Baths and toilets and bidets lined up against the pavement. Bidets? It was hard to find a bath plug in most hotels. The marketplace was pure sensory overload. A press of humanity from all over Uganda and beyond. A daze of sweat and heat and talk. Muslim. Christian. Poverty-stricken. Laughing. Proud. Abject. Above all, on the move. It was Babel. It was Kampala. It was the pulse of Africa. The pressure of life; the pull of death.

Beggars reached out from where they lay, twisted legs on the stained earth. There were skips piled with rotting vegetables, marabou storks picking over the rubbish. A stench of decay and diesel fuel. Charcoal sellers laboured, grey with dust. I passed a group of women cooking matoke and beef stew in huge aluminium pans. They were laughing, eyeing me up as I went past. *Mzungu*. The only white man walking in the market. *Mzungu*. Sometimes they called it out as a joke. *Hey, Mzungu!* At the heart of the market was the bus station, glittering with glass and steel under hoardings advertising Guinness and Nokia where hundreds of mini-bus taxis – *matatu* – gathered like a migratory herd. Their touts were busy doing business, soliciting passengers, heaving their bags into place. From here to anywhere.

Beyond Nakasero and the bus station lay Owino market, equally vast and equally hot and tumultuous, where you could buy anything from clothing to crockery, baskets to bicycle parts. There were sacks of maize meal and rice, bunches of plantain, sugar cane, soap, woven mats, baskets, tools, tapes of Congolese music, leather belts and cheap shoes. There were cheap shoes everywhere. Clever imitations of Reebok trainers and Italian style shoes with pointed toes and plastic soles. In Owino the light was so bright it was like walking into polished blades. There wasn't a stitched or welted shoe anywhere, not even above the markets in the commercial district around the Crane Bank, where our office was. Where men in smart suits mingled with the crowds and street hawkers. Where the same man lay asleep every day on the pavement – barefoot, drunk, drugged or dying from Aids – his skin gleaming like oiled wood.

All the time I was in Nakasero I thought about the mill town of my childhood. The factories were still there but King Cotton had died, as all dictators do in the end. The mills were mostly empty hulks staring into algae-infested lodges. *The cradle of industry.* That was the cliché they'd fed us at school. Now the factories were rented out to engineering outfits or catalogue sales companies that went bankrupt after a couple of years. Or they lay empty, giant nurseries for the rats that took to the town's sewers and culverts at night.

All through my childhood the chimneys came down, one by one. A red brick forest became a clearing. It was strange to think of that in the centre of Kampala. Well, maybe not so strange, here in the old empire where the Nile rose a few miles away and flowed north to water the plains of Egypt. I remembered old Mrs Stead, our next-door neighbour, speaking lovingly of the Sea Island and Egyptian staples that she'd spun with my grandfather. Purple veins stood out on her crippled hands.

It was only a brief flare of synapses, a blush of memory in the chemical brain, to connect Nakasero or Owino market in Kampala to Tommyfield market in Oldham, or the little market behind the swimming baths in Chadderton, or the famous market in Bury where you could buy black puddings and yards of worsted or cotton cloth.

After their retirement my parents had loved to take a day-trip to Skipton or Halifax, wandering through the markets in search of bargains, buying a nice piece of rolled brisket and having fish and chips for lunch. Every so often my father would return home with a pair of shoes, a bargain from the Age Concern or Oxfam shop. Those shoes had the scent of death and decay about them, a coolness to the touch as if body heat had just evaporated. Once he bought a mobile phone, a year or two after my mother had died in Crumpsall hospital, but he'd never learned to use it. Another gadget – like the TV remote – he never got the hang of. A problem he attributed to things that were *fucking rubbish*, rather than to himself.

Now here I was in Owino, a sweaty mzungu among thousands of Africans, wandering towards Nakasero in my bush hat and cargo pants, thinking about the dark little cobbler's shop I'd visited as a child.

Where I grew up there were four spinning mills, built at the turn of the century when cotton really was king, and money was still spewing from the frames and looms for the mill owners. My grandfather had been employed in King's Mill as a mule spinner until he'd lost three fingers from one hand and worked out his days on the roads for the Corporation. He died six months before retirement, leaving a sweet-jar full of sixpences he'd saved. He didn't even live long enough to see his son buy his first car – a Morris Seven with a second-hand prop-shaft and differential. We had some old photographs of my dad with his mother on the front in Morecambe – a stout woman in a beret leaning on the bonnet and licking an ice cream in the wind.

The cobbler's shop was below the mills. Below the fishmonger's and the corner-shop butcher's and the Co-op where we bought ammunition for our peashooters, where my father had begun work just before his fourteenth birthday. In the window was a pair of clogs and on their soles a pair of flamenco dancers had been picked out in nails and hand-painted. I remembered how the woman wore a crimson frock and the man tight black trousers. The clogs had brass toecaps and were made of oiled leather.

As a child my father had worn shoes rather than clogs, a fact he'd always been proud of, as if it marked him out as special. The other kids had clogged seven bells out of him and, despite the shoes, labour had stuck to him all his life. The cobbler's shop had a doorbell that jangled over your head on a metal spring, bringing Carson limping from the back room in his grey apron. He'd lost a leg at Monte Casino. The shop counter was dark mahogany and the shop smelled of tanned leather, neat's-foot oil, Dubbin, heelball and brown paper. All the accoutrements of the cobbler's trade. Bullhide not bullshit, my father had said right there at the counter, with a light in his eyes that was the blue flash of thunder. I'd always wondered what Carson's artificial leg was made of. As far as my father was concerned, he had a job where he sat on his arse all day.

– Sah?

You're right that it makes no sense – harking back to a mill town in the 1960s when I was walking through an African marketplace in the twenty-first century and mixing it all up together. As if Carson might limp from one of the shop doorways or leap up from one of the treadle-operated Singer sewing machines that were everywhere. Just like the machine my mother had used to make our clothes when we were children.

– Sah?

A meat fly landed on my arm and I brushed it away. Maybe it was those black enamelled machines with their gold lettering that had sent me back, recalled my mother sewing clothes for the neighbours, or pinning up my father's trousers as he stood on a chair and ranted. My mother who could make any garment with her hands. My father who could shape even the most recalcitrant piece of metal. The cobbler who turned over a freshly repaired shoe in his hand to show the new leather gleaming. *Good for a few more miles.* It made no sense, admittedly, but then maybe that's all the sense there is. To be everywhere and anywhere at the same time. Somewhere and nowhere. To be outside yourself.

– Sah?

The man's voice – a soft, insinuating voice – startled me. When I did look up I saw a small Ugandan man in a ragged tee shirt and khaki pants. He looked about thirty, but it was hard to tell. He had a wispy beard and his skin was paler than that of most Africans. His eyes were the lightest brown eyes I'd ever seen, like honey poured over almonds. Beautiful eyes that slanted down with slightly hooded lids.

– Shoe, sah?

He was holding out a pair of refurbished casual shoes. You saw them all over Kampala. Dead men's shoes re-cycled. They were made of tan-coloured leather and had plastic soles and had been polished until even the scuffmarks gleamed. They were shit. You needed good shoes in Kampala where the roads were broken and gave way to red dirt and pot-holed tracks. I shook my head. The man held the shoes closer, as if I hadn't looked at them properly.

– Good shoes. Try them. Try them, sah?

A marabou stork flew over the market and its shadow crossed the man's face. Darkening those amazing eyes for a moment. His arms were sinewy and the veins stood out on his hands.

– Not for me, thanks.

– Not for you? No shoe? They your size. See?

The man smiled incredulously. He thrust the shoes at me again, then looked down at my shoes, a pair of knackered brogues made in Dundee. Good shoes once, they had a coating of dust from the market and were stained with salt. Sweat was trickling from my hatband and down my neck.

– Sah, you come!

He tugged my sleeve and dragged me into a gap between two stalls.

– Come! Come!

We ducked under a carousel of leather belts, past a stack of watermelons with their sweet, sugary smell. Then we were in a narrow alleyway between buildings, catching the tang of human shit. A beggar held up his fingerless hand, but we brushed past and turned left into a narrow street and into a shop doorway that gaped under a blue and white striped awning and had yellow cellophane in the widow.

– Come sah, come sah!

The shop was piled up with fabric, saris and shalwar kameez and made-up suits hung from mannequins, the glass-fronted display cabinets were piled with ties and collars and socks and – yes – shoes, though of a kind I'd never buy. We entered a gloomy back room where an elderly Sikh gentleman with a white beard and a maroon-coloured turban was watching a black and white television set. Gentleman? There seems no other word. My Ugandan guide spoke to him in Swahili and the Sikh eyed me carefully. He held out his hand to shake mine.

– You are welcome.

– Thank you.

– You are looking for shoes?

I shrugged, slightly helpless and more than slightly intimidated. The Sikh gentleman bent down and examined my brogues carefully. He drew a finger across the toe of one, making a line in the red dust.

– I have. Come.

The Ugandan man had taken the Sikh's place and was screwing up the volume on a Kenyan soap opera. I felt a tug on my sleeve and followed the proprietor into another room at the back of the shop.

At first glance the room seemed to be draped with curtains but as the Sikh pulled the curtain back I saw that the walls were lined with shelves and the shelves were filled with boxes. Shoe boxes. I remembered the sharp smell of my father's pantry – a mixture of shoe polish, turps and Swarfega – where he kept his shoes neatly stacked on shelves made from old fruit boxes. The old man stooped in the gloom and pulled out a box, pulling down his spectacles on his nose to check the label.

– You are a nine?

It was a good guess.

– Yeah, nine.

He straightened up and handed me the box.

– Here. You try. Very good shoes.

I noticed that he was wearing light leather slippers that allowed him to shuffle almost noiselessly from room to room.

– Come. Come to the light.

He led me back to the room with the television where my Ugandan friend was now eating from a Tiffin tin of matoke and tilapia stew. He ignored us both. The food reminded me I was hungry.

I took a seat and opened the box. Inside was tissue paper, then two velvet bags and inside each bag was a shoe of unmistakeable quality. Dark brown stippled leather, richly oiled. Double-welted soles. The tongues were stitched into the shoe at the side to form waterproof webbing. Genuine veldtschoen.

– I am Nayanprit Singh.

The proprietor smiled at me a little shyly.

– These are good shoes, eh? Good shoes. You like them?

The shoes were kid-lined and the soles were solid leather, each heel laminated from thin sheets. They had that old smell that brought the ringing of the bell of the cobbler's shop in my hometown to my head. Flamenco dancers and the smell of lamp oil sold from a big metal drum under the counter. The stump, stump, stump of Carson's artificial leg. When I put my hands inside to feel the linings, they were soft and supple. There was no name inside, just the number nine hand-written on each tongue in black ink. They were probably the most beautiful shoes I'd ever seen and when I slipped them on and tied the laces, they fitted as if they'd been made on my personal last. I reached for the roll of cash in my pocket.

When I woke on Sunday morning, after a quiet night sipping tonic water on the guesthouse terrace, it was to the smell of new leather. No hangover after a quiet night. No work until tomorrow. I'd grown to love Sundays in Kampala when the city took on a sleepy quality, like a 1950s English suburb. Well, like I imagined that to be. No wonder the British had loved it here. I pushed on the curtains and caught the scent of cut grass where the gardeners were busy with sickles. A woman in a bright yellow gomesi was brushing fallen petals from the path with a broom. It made a soft, sifting sound, repetitive and soothing. A couple of cattle egret pecked at the lawn and a pied crow was mithering something that had died in the night.

After breakfast I walked down to the gate to buy a newspaper from one of the boys who gathered there, working the traffic and passers by. I hadn't seen much of McKenzie since Friday night. I wasn't surprised after his performance at Al's bar. All that beer and brown sugar. My new shoes felt good. Supple yet strong. They already had a layer of red dust. A woman passed me carrying a fat little girl in a frock made of pink gauze. She was sweating and cross. I could already hear hymns rising from the university chapel. One day I planned to give up fieldwork and teach somewhere. Maybe here where they needed engineers and surveyors and you could live cheaply. There was nothing for me at home now. Not since Helen had left me and taken the girls. For no reason, actually. I'd been faithful, but she didn't think so. I missed Emma and Tracey. Every Christmas I got a letter from them as if she'd stood over them with a whip.

Emma was the youngest at seven. Tracey was just nine. Emma had a harelip and cleft palate which had been repaired after a couple of operations. The surgeon had done a pretty good job. Helen even blamed me for that because it ran in the family as far back as my dad's uncle. I don't know what Helen thought I got up to when I was away. Not much but work, actually. I suppose you couldn't blame her, stuck with two kids when my job was a whole continent away. The guys I met who worked out here were mostly fucked up and mostly divorced. A lot of them went with young black girls. But I didn't want to be loved for money.

My new shoes felt good against the crumbling footpaths and pavements of Wandegeya. *Nayanprit Singh.* That was his name. A gentleman. A gentle man with a shoe emporium. His breath had smelt of peppermint in that dark little back room. I'd tried to memorise the location of the shop, the alleyways that my Ugandan guide had taken me through. It wasn't easy, though I remembered the touch of the old man's hand against mine, soft and insistent.

When I got back to the guesthouse I found McKenzie, still looking sheepish, sitting over a late breakfast on the terrace, watching two African boys play tennis on the clay court. They ran like deer, retrieving the ball from impossibly angled shots with vicious topspin. I tossed McKenzie *The Monitor* and ordered some tea. Then I stretched my legs and leaned to wipe the dust from my shoes. My father would have loved them. Maybe shoes were the only things he had loved. Not my mother, not me or Steve. Certainly not sheet metal or iron, which he beat with deepening hatred.

I looked across town to where the tower of a mosque leaned against the sky. It had never been finished. It needed pulling down before it fell down. I'd done some calculations once and worked out that it shouldn't be standing at all. But this was Uganda, where the impossible happened every day, where red tape could be finessed with something small.

A couple of brown parrots were quarrelling in the bushes. The leather of the shoes had a deep burnish where

I'd wiped the dust off. I thought about Nayanprit Singh, serene in the depths of his shop. I thought of the shoemakers of Nakasero and of my father. The last circle of hell would be an everlasting absence of good footwear. I thought about Helen and the girls and how I could have tried harder. Maybe. I'd call her when I got home, get some presents for the girls in Wandegeya where they sold banana-fibre dolls, hippos and giraffes carved from wood.

McKenzie was smiling at something in the paper. Moses appeared at my elbow carrying a tray. I'd forgotten to order English tea and there it was, African tea with the milk already in the pot.

– Tea, sah?

It didn't matter. Nothing did. Kites turned in thermals above the city. White clouds puffed up at the horizons. The voice of the Imam sent a pair of doves fluttering from the trees. It was going to be a beautiful day. Tomorrow we'd clear some emails then load up the truck and James would drive us to another river. Up country. Later on today we'd get the maps and plan a route. Then James would change it, the way he always did.

A dragonfly hovered by the toe of my shoe, a blue rod of iridescence. What was that song I kept remembering and forgetting? It was on the tip of my tongue. *Believe*. That was it. McKenzie looked up, surprised. I must have been thinking aloud. He raised a ginger eyebrow. I shook my head.

– Nothing.

– Didn't sound like it.

He folded the newspaper then cracked his knuckles. Which reminded me of Armstrong in a way I could have done without. Then the gate of the tennis court clanged shut and the boys were walking past us with their racquets. There was something vacant about McKenzie in the end. As if he had no imagination. As if he was just here, now, and nowhere else.

A GLASS OF WATER

She brings him a glass of water. A tall glass beaded with droplets that sweat against her hand. He's crouching in the garden, a heap of stone piled up, a string stretched between two beanpoles. A spade against the cherry tree, the lump hammer set aside. He waves away a wasp, pulls off the leather gauntlets and takes the glass. Zoscia touches his arm. His skin is brown from a long summer, his hair faded blond across the line of muscle.

– It's looking really good!

Sunday morning. The bell is ringing at the new church, a single repetitive note that blurs with distance. He's looking beyond her. A flycatcher is working the air between a telegraph post and a crab-apple branch bright with fruit. In the war they shot three partisans against the old church, then burned it down. Carl pulls his shirt from his armpits. The sun is still hot, even in September. Zoscia tries again.

– It's going to be nice.

– It'll do. It'll have to. The stone's pretty useless…

He's taken down an ornamental flowerbed and is re-building it against the boundary wall as a long border. That way they can get the mower in and things won't look so fancy. Instead of marigolds and violets they'll grow tall poppies, St John's wort, mint and sage. Borage maybe.

– We can have lunch soon.

– OK. Bring my testing kit would you? Before we eat.

He watches her saunter back to the house, picking some leaves from the rosemary bush, rubbing them between her fingers. She's let her hair go grey. Once it had been golden brown. But it suits her, cut close to the nape. There are buddleia flowers turning from purple to brown. A few butterflies linger there, dabbing and retreating. Cabbage whites. Peacocks. He pulls out more stone, finds snails that have died in the wall, their nacre like dried sperm.

The stone's all wrong, river boulders that have been rounded by the current. Slabs of shale that have started to rot in winter rain. Hardly anything flat or square. It's a bodged job. No through-stones to tie it together. He's got a bucket filled with smaller stuff to fill in with, but it's not the way to build a wall. There's no rear access to the garden, no way to bring in more materials. When he's out and about in the car and sees something suitable he stops to haul it into the boot. He's heard of a farm worker in the next village who did that, building a house for his old age. They said he could tell where every stone came from. Every one had a story. One of these days, Zoscia says, he's going to get caught and they'll all end up in court. For what? And who cares? Good stone is hard to come by. It's hardly stealing.

Zoscia's stepping across the lawn, the muscles in her calves broad and tight. She's bringing a tray of sandwiches now, a bottle of Pilsner, a bottle opener next to the black pouch. There's a packet of crisps, sliced cucumber, gherkins, baby tomatoes from the greenhouse. The tomato plants are turning white with mildew. They'll need clearing soon. Carl cracks a stone in half with the hammer and a splinter strikes his face.

– Shit!

– You ok?

He shakes the gauntlets off and kicks fragments towards the wall.

– Ach! Bastard thing!

– Come for your lunch ... come on, you're tired.

Carl walks away from his work, rinses his hands under the garden tap and dries them on his polo shirt. Zoscia watches him, a little stiffness in his movements. His hair is cropped close and his head is tanned. His stomach is still taut and lean, his legs slightly bowed. Footballer's legs. Though he hasn't played in twenty years. Zoscia pulls a chair away from the table for him. He sits down, letting his shoulders sag for a second, dangling his hands in mock exhaustion. His grey eyes flicker towards her. He's still handsome when his face catches a smile.

Carl unzips the black pouch and takes out the meter. He puts in a new testing strip and sets the symbol: an unbitten apple. He fiddles a needle into the lancet, twists off the plastic cap, then shoots it against his little finger. Zoscia watches the droplet of blood squeeze out. It's like a ruby or rowan berry. Carl touches the strip to it and the blood is drawn away.

– What does it say?

Digits are counting down from five to zero. Then a new number appears.

– Five-point-eight.

– Is that good?

– Pretty good, I guess. Anything over seven is high.

Carl shrugs and packs the kit away.

– I'll live at that.

Zoscia takes a crisp and holds it for a second.

– Anika rang, by the way.

– What did she want?

– Just to Skype us with Michal. I said we were busy. Maybe tomorrow.

– Are they ok? She usually wants something.

– They're fine. She said so.

Carl sucks his finger clean and for a moment they sit with their faces turned to the sun, soaking in the heat. It feels like a dimming ember, slowly sinking to autumn. Winters are cold this far inland. It's a good feeling when the leaves fall and the days turn crisp and the lawn glitters with frost in the morning sun.

Under the table, her open-toed sandals and brown ankles; his work boots and frayed cargo pants. Against the garden wall, sunflowers, espaliered fruit trees heavy with pears and plums, a hollyhock still in full bloom. There are foxgloves everywhere this year. Bees are working the purple and white bells, crawling along the stems of lavender, brushing stamens on the ragged pink flowers of the dog rose. Their low thrumming and the clanging of the bell meld together. The partisans' names are cut into a slate plaque with a line of poetry. Once a year there's a ceremony with a wreath and the local scout group. It's said the priest gave them away. But that hadn't saved the church. The bottle hisses as Carl pours it, catching the excess with his mouth as it overbrims the glass.

Carl sits for a moment, feeling the beer cold in his stomach. Cold like metal. Then he puts the glass down and massages his neck, rotating his head from side to side to stretch the tendons. Zoscia is watching him, the way the skin tightens and slackens around his jaw.

– Is it still sore?

– It's going to be.

She stands behind him and massages the sides of his neck and he groans with pleasure.

–You should take it easy.

–This is taking it easy.

–You know what I mean, after what happened.

Carl shrugs her off and reaches for the glass of beer. He stretches his toes and calves, sending a wave of tension through his spine. His neck still feels tight after all this time.

He'd been driving through wads of early morning mist, leaving the hotel in the company car to get to a sales meeting. He fumbled the keys into the ignition. The engine turned over then died. Carl tried again, watching white smoke fan out behind as it fired. The clutch retracted smoothly against his foot and he pulled away.

He was tired, even though he hadn't had a drink with Jonas and the others last night. If he went to the doctor it'd mean more tests. He just needed to slow down a little. The news presenter's voice filled the car, smooth and reassuring. Syrian refugees were flooding into Iraq; suicide bombers in Pakistan; an attack on a church in Kano. He'd been there once, before he met Zoscia, working in pharmaceuticals for a British company. It hadn't lasted long, just three months or so. Then he'd had enough of backhanders, of never knowing where you stood. And that was just the Brits. The voice went on to the exchange rate, the FTSE 100. Then the weather, which was supposed to be mild when the mist burned away. It thinned and gathered again like cannon smoke from a movie.

Carl switched on his fog lights. Then the headlamps, dimming them as they bloomed against blank air. He drove down the slip road to join the motorway. Something moved in the corner of his eyes and he braked. A family of fallow deer crossed the road ahead. First a stag with small pointed antlers, testing the air, then a dappled doe and her foal following, stepping with dainty footsteps across the tarmac. Sometimes he surprised an early morning heron or caught a hawk working the verges. He never tired of that: nature was out there, going on despite everything. Carl watched them leave. They seemed bewildered for a moment then made a way through bushes that lined the slip road, finding a way to disappear.

Animals had senses that humans lacked. Dogs had some organ that mingled taste and smell, but was neither. Maybe deer, too. It was hard to fathom stuff like that, things there were no words for. He slipped the car into gear and pulled away, picking up speed as he swirled into sparse traffic. There were container lorries heading for the ports. Guys like him in ties and pressed shirts, risen from hotel rooms to shower and shave. Now they were moving on to the next thing, their faces grim and tight. Six-thirty. Zoscia would be just waking up now, pressing down the lever on the kitsch alarm clock that Anika had given them one Christmas. She'd be pulling open the curtains to look across the fields and they'd be lost in mist. He'd been away for three days already. One more meeting, one more PowerPoint presentation, then home to decent food, his own bed.

Zoscia lay in late, deciding not to go into the office that day. She'd work at home on her laptop. It made no difference in the end, whether you were in your office emailing the colleague next door or emailing from home. They all existed as pixels on a screen now, text messages, scraps of thought, binary code pulsing through fibre optics. Disembodied, as if their flesh and muscle and blood had been superseded. Before you registered on the system you were a non-person. Username. Password. Then you existed through your virtual self. You were your own avatar. Though that was to do with something else. *Vishnu?* Some god or other in human form. She pulled the sheets back and stepped into the shower, letting the water fall against her breasts and tighten them.

She could use the time she'd spend driving to the office doing jobs around the house or just relaxing, taking a few minutes to herself. She towelled herself dry and dressed in casual clothes: slacks and an old shirt of Carl's, washed but not ironed. She didn't bother with a bra and the soft cotton seemed promiscuous against her skin. She caught its faint scent of detergent and fresh air where it had dried on the line in the garden. When she opened the kitchen blinds the lawn was covered in bluish dew and there were jackdaws hopping across the turned earth of the flowerbeds. Beyond the garden were fields of maize and barley, cabbages spreading to the flat line of the horizon. Last year it had been sunflowers. *Turnesol.* The mist had almost cleared.

She made coffee, poured breakfast cereal into a bowl, plugged in the laptop at the kitchen table and piled up a stack of case notes with the report she was working on. The house was at the edge of the village and it was quiet, just the odd farm vehicle moving on the lane outside. It led nowhere, to a farm gate, to those fields of drilled crops. She ate the cereal walking barefoot on the lawn where there was no one to see her except the jackdaws squabbling in the ash tree now. The dew was numbingly cold, like needles against her toes.

Zoscia dried her feet, dropped the dishes into the sink, found her spectacles and set to work. She thought about Carl waking in a hotel room, finding a crisp shirt from his luggage, shaving, fastening cuff links, pulling the lapels of his suit jacket tight. She frowned at the dry air of a hotel, anonymous rooms, air conditioning, the breakfast queue. Malaysian and Filipino maids moving between tables in tight uniforms. The way Carl would watch them. All that smiling politeness, their real lives somewhere else.

Zoscia worked all morning, stopping for coffee and a cigarette which she smoked sitting at the garden table on the iron chairs. Her mobile rang a couple of times but she saw it was the office and let it go onto answerphone. She'd pick up the calls later and deal with them in one go. She could always blame the signal, which came and went like a ghost here. Their phones worked almost everywhere but at home. That's good, Carl said when they found out it was the downside of their new house. No signal, excellent. Fuck them. Downside was upside. To hell with it. Peace. Until a new radio mast went up and one bar became five. Not yet. As she pulled the smoke into her lungs, she remembered her mother tying up her pigtails before she left for school. Her leather satchel with the broken strap. She was in a home now and didn't know them. Zoscia stubbed the cigarette. She cleared the dirty cups and plates into the dishwasher and ran a cloth over the sink, spattered with coffee grounds from the cafetière.

Carl entered the main stream of traffic. The sun was trying to burn away the mist. It cast a yellow glow onto the windscreen. Each time he passed into a zone of cold air – a temperature inversion – there was a thicker band of white. The radio news was followed by one of those arts programmes where the guests had done supposedly interesting things and written a book about it. An actress writing about her father who'd been a wall of death rider; an ex-gang leader who ran an NGO in the Sudan; a mother who'd published a diary about her son's autism. Carl switched the radio off. In the silence, he though about Anika. He thought about Michal, the smell of his baby head, his tiny fingernails, the creases in his skin. Fat thighs buttoned into a striped baby suit. The way he'd bang a wooden spoon against this highchair or patter across the kitchen floor, pulling himself upright against the fridge or kitchen cabinets. He'd be walking soon. Into the future, into whatever lay ahead.

The car appeared to glide, entering another veil of mist that thinned momentarily then seemed to clear. He'd got the climate control on so it was warm. The heated door mirrors stayed clear. Carl pressed the accelerator and gathered a little speed. The turbo was almost silent. He liked that relaxed sense of speed. The scent of leather upholstery that creaked faintly as he shifted in the seat. The leather steering wheel and gear shift. His hands were freckled, the skin softly wrinkled. But the car was almost new, renewed every three years, mocking him.

The banks of the motorway were wooded with birch trees, their pale bark spectral in the light. He thought of the deer fleeing, the little stag breaking through the trees with the foal following, then the doe. Everything in the air was a message to them, every molecule of scent meant something. There was a soft crump ahead, then the glow of brake lights through mist. Carl hit the brake and then was thrown back by the airbag as the bonnet crumpled and was flung open. Just a second later he was thrown back against the seat as a car smashed into his and then span and slewed alongside.

Carl was cursing softly. He pressed the button to open the window. Cold air. The taste of fog. Voices shouting. The smell of petrol. From behind him the squeal of tyres against a wet road, as car after car joined the pile-up. The sound of tyres and tearing metal was softened by fog. Carl needed to run, his body drenched in adrenalin, but he was afraid to step from the car. Then a woman staring in at him, shouting something over and over, blood pouring from a gash in her cheek. He felt stupid, paralysed, the airbag pressing against his face, thinking of Michal, of deer streaming through trees, panicking onto the ploughed land, their breath streaming.

The kitchen was open-plan, joined together with the living room with its big brick fireplace and wood-burning stove. The log pile was at the side of the house where Carl loved to split and stack a load for the winter, piling them in some scientific way so they'd dry in the airflow. It was a good feeling that, being prepared for whatever lay ahead. For those winter days when snow might pile against doors and windows, though it hadn't snowed that hard for years. Mainly it was grey skies and a sniping wind that hissed over the farmland.

When Zoscia glanced up from the screen she could see through the lounge to the track outside. A tractor passed, towing a harrow. A jeep spattered in mud and dung, rocking over potholes. Someone went by on a mountain bike, passing the window and glancing in to where she was working in the shadow, behind curtains. A blue top, black shorts, grey cycling helmet. There was no through way and she wondered if they were lost. She half expected other cyclists to follow, riding in a posse, the way they did on the main road.

The lone cyclist reappeared a few minutes later outside the window, leaning his bike into the hedge, unstrapping his helmet, reaching into his backpack. Zoscia stood up, went to the window, then the door. When she opened it she saw it was a young man, thick curly black hair spilling from the helmet. He was short for a man – about her height – broad, with strong legs. His sleeves were pushed back where dark hair grew thickly on his arms. The bike looked technical, all cables and levers, like the one Carl kept in the garage with its gadgets for measuring things. She noticed that he didn't wear a wristwatch. Zoscia smiled and he smiled back, open-faced, showing teeth that lapped over slightly at the front. His eyes were so dark they seemed almost black, the pupils absorbed.

– Are you lost? There's no way through here.

The young man nodded and smiled and pointed to the map. It was under control, it was all in hand. He unstrapped his helmet and sat it on the saddle.

– Where are you trying to get to?

He didn't answer but raised his head and tapped two fingers to his throat. She must have looked absent because he shook his head and made the mute gesture again, more urgently. Zoscia felt something melt. Her belly was a soft fruit, her blood effervescent, washing her away, drenching her. The dark eyes were watching her. He smiled an apology and held out the map.

Zoscia traced the route he'd taken with her finger and he showed her where he must have gone wrong. They were laughing. Standing this close, he smelled of grass and hedgerows and fresh sweat. Then he was in her kitchen drinking a glass of water. Then her hand was on his arm, brushing the dark hair. Then he was tasting her mouth, like the water, like the fruit that had seemed to melt inside her at his muteness.

Zoscia found a fresh towel and led him to the shower. When he emerged she tugged the towel away and led him to bed. His hair was tousled and wet. Zoscia guided him, his eyes widening then closing. She pulled him towards her, into her, feeling his urgency and heat, his arms still faintly damp from the shower. He was gentle as he quickened and they came together in a little tremor that she knew might be the beginning of remorse. Then they lay in a band of mild sunlight that showed up motes of dust turning in currents of air. A dog was yapping faintly at the nearest farm.

After a time he kissed her shoulder before rising to get dressed, smiling at her, pointing to where his watch should have been, that pale stripe on his wrist. When he left, Zoscia watched from the upstairs window. He looked absurd with his curls spilling, peddling down the lane towards the main road. Vishnu in a cycling helmet. Zoscia showered, then dressed in Carl's old shirt, changed the sheets, and carried on working as if nothing has happened. She didn't even know which language he might have spoken. She'd stroked his neck like a child's when he came and sagged against her. She wondered when he'd last had a woman. Her phone beeped and she saw a line of messages from Carl.

Zoscia collects the plates and the beer bottle and bottle cap and glass and neatens them on the old tin tray. It'd been her mother's before her mind had flown away. She goes to the trellis where the fruit trees are espaliered and brings two plums, dusky with bloomed yeast, and rinses them under the tap. They're sweet and warm from the sun. Carl takes one and bites into it. She thinks of the boy's eyes, how dark they were.

– Will you get it finished today?

Carl squirts the plum stone between his finger and thumb and it shoots into the shrubbery where verbena is fading and dropping its leaves.

– Maybe.

He'd worn a surgical collar after the crash, his neck stiff from whiplash. They'd waited in the mist, listening to what was happening on their car radios as the fog gradually cleared. Over thirty cars and lorries had piled together. No one was killed, which seemed a miracle. A white horse had galloped past them in the field beyond the hard shoulder, snorting with terror. That had been two years ago, yet his mind still went back there to the bloom of

91

brake lights, the soft crumpling of metal, to that woman's face, and to the deer stepping across the road as his engine panted smoke.

– What about dinner. We could go out?

– We could. Is that what you want?

They could walk to the new restaurant in the village. Paulo's. It was owned by an Italian guy and his wife. He did the cooking and she looked after front of house. The food wasn't bad and they could drink decent wine, find something to talk about, then walk home arm in arm. They'd pause to read the names on the war memorial, think about those three boys waiting to die, white-faced in the sun. They'd regret the new church, all concrete and stained glass. As if God would mind. The village would be settling down to sleep, curtains drawn, dogs calling from the farms. Then cities lighting up the horizon, shutting out the stars, reminding them how the world turned from sleep to waking, from waking to sleep.

– What do you think? Dinner at Paulo's? My treat...

Carl shrugs and stands up, stretching his arms, massaging the tendons behind his knees.

– I don't mind.

– Don't mind?

A little cloud drifts into her face to darken it.

– I meant it would be nice.

He smiles a little ruefully and she dips her head, remembering to call Anika in the morning, wondering if Michal will recognise them on the computer screen.

– OK. We'll go out, then. I'll ring to book a table.

– Do you need to do that?

– Might as well be sure.

– OK. I'll get on with this.

Carl looks to the wall he's building. Once it's up and planted out and the moss has grown back no one will notice its flaws. It'll blend together with time. Zoscia lifts the tray with its glasses and plates. The bottle overbalances and she steadies it.

It would be a nice thing. Dinner, with Zoscia then the walk home, a bed made up with crisp sheets and nothing much to do next morning except a slow breakfast and the Sunday papers. Carl pulls on the gauntlets and leans down to kiss the nape of Zoscia's neck, remembering how her hair had glowed once, fierce and tawny. Like a lion. Like a hawk. He picks up a stone and taps it into place.

IN THEORY, THEORIES EXIST

The air above the trees vibrated to the sun's rising pitch. It looked like ice or flawed glass skimmed by water. The sky was pale, empty of birds, though swifts had flickered over the roofs earlier. To his right, the rocky coastline simmered in foam where an acid-blue sea met burned volcanic rock. To his left, the Pyrenees stepped away, gaunt as caried teeth. Directly behind him, the church glared. From here it was tiny, almond white. Yachts glinted in the marina and a few windsurfers were glittering across the bay on fluorescent blades. He loved the way the headland dropped to the subtle blues of the Mediterranean: earth, sea and sky colliding. Though once the early mist cleared. The land flowed around her: west to the North Sea, east to the heart of Europe.

If you squinted hard, or looked through binoculars, you could see a red fishing vessel moored at the quay where a group of fishermen in yellow overalls were unpacking the night's catch or mended their nets. A few workmen and tourists were taking coffee in the quayside cafés, reading the newspapers, thinking about what to do with another day. Down there was the stink of fish and chickens roasting in the butcher's *rotisserie*. Up in the valley, the air was aromatic with the scents of crushed lavender and rosemary where his boots laboured at the path and his legs brushed the tinder-dry undergrowth. Two years ago a fire had

94

scorched the hillside. The scrubby pines had exploded like fireworks. You could still see blackened bark on the parched cork oaks, the firebreaks where they'd cleared the trees and tried to stop the flames from leaping across.

Ralph was going to be fifty-four in three days. Fifty-four had been unimaginable once. An insect touched against him and he pushed his shirtsleeve from his forearm to see the bite. His grandmother was from Kashmir and his skin had a cappuccino tint, though no longer smooth and youthful. It had the look of aged vellum now. His grandfather had been a professional soldier and met her in the NCO's mess, the daughter of a famous silversmith. It had stirred things up a bit when he brought her home. Especially when she turned out to be more English than the English after being educated by the Sisters of Mercy. She was long gone, only this trace of her in his genes.

He was going to be fifty-four, so he didn't much feel like being told what to do. Not by Stella now that Simon had gone. Not by his shrinking circle of friends – half of whom Simon seemed to have pulled away with him. Not by anyone if he could help it.

Stella was flying out to spend a few days at the flat with him. So she'd be here for his birthday on the twelfth. Which promised to be less than glorious. He'd better do what he wanted to whilst there was still some vacation to do it in. After all, Stella couldn't help telling him what to do. It was just her way. Like her abrupt laugh, her tangle of auburn hair with its threads of grey, her stout calves and her addiction to Scholl sandals with wooden soles that made her feet look like hooves. She'd never had much use for gratuitous physical exercise and she'd think he was mad, climbing up to the monastery in this heat, in his *condition*. Maybe he was mad. Not bad and dangerous. Just a little *deracinated*. A good word for it.

He'd already been in the village for a few days and got pretty well acclimatised. Each morning he started with a swim in one of the rocky bays around the headland, bobbing out towards the opposite side of the bay and back again. He wasn't a great swimmer, but he loved the astringency of early morning water when a faint mist rose from the calm. Just as the first fishing boats were putting out to sea, before the beaches filled up with scuba divers and tourists. Yesterday a stocky young woman had stripped naked in front of him before pulling on her bikini bottom and lolloping into the sea clutching her breasts. It made him feel old. Wasn't he supposed to look for God's sake? She spent the next twenty minutes pretending to shriek at the cold for her husband's benefit. He was one of those Spanish guys with thick legs, soft brown eyes, a mat of chest hair and a broad, dark jaw. He was fond of her, his idiot wife, and didn't seem the slightest bit put out when she dropped her skirt. Ralph had grabbed his beach things and the novel he'd been trying to read and headed back to a bar for a *cortado*. At times like that he missed Simon. How they'd have laughed, Simon mimicking her cries with cruel accuracy and mocking the he-man act.

They'd holidayed in the village every year for the past five. Six? Well, they'd missed last year for obvious reasons, when Ralph had been recovering from the op. So that didn't really count. He felt conspicuous being here alone. Not as conspicuous as at the university, though, which was just another village with its rivalry and gossip and intellectual bitchiness. If *intellectual* was the word. The village here stank of hot stone, cat shit and fish. The university stank of mendacity and ambition. Thank God for Stella with her dirty laugh and her dependable cynicism. Though she'd always managed to do OK, somehow. When the shit hit the fan she never seemed to get spattered. *Finesse*, darling, *finesse*, she'd say to that, showing her wicked back-slanting teeth, lighting another cigarette, blowing out phantoms of smoke.

Ralph paused to pull the damp shirt from his back. The path he was walking led to a ruined monastery on the hilltop opposite the town. Each year the builders renewed a tower, patched a wall or fitted windows to the stone slits. There was a museum now and a café. The route started from the neighbouring village, which lay about a mile along the road, past thickets of bamboo that grew in a lagoon of fresh water where a stream met the sea. Then past olive groves and new holiday villas with swimming pools. Then into the twisting cobbled streets of the old village that went up past a tiny chapel and cemetery and eventually became a rocky path. He'd thought about the little cemetery when in hospital. That was the worst time. After the angiogram and the bad news, but before the tests had shown he was *viable*. A lousy word. It had reminded him of university management-speak. Undergraduate courses and avenues of research were viable, not people.

Years ago the same village streets had practically flowed with wine. You could still see the oak barrels rotting from their hoops in dark cellars. On their first visit he and Simon had drunk a local vintage in a restaurant that overlooked the village square. It came unlabelled, amber-coloured and dry with a hint of sherry, unlike anything in the supermarket and shops. But the terraced hillsides were going back to nature now. There were just a few acres of new vines at low level. Phyloxera had done for them, then war. Then tourism had offered an easier life: jobs on the checkout in the Bonpreau, waiting on in restaurants or behind the bar in the new discotheque deep in the thicket of bamboo that grew near the beach. They'd danced there once, chest-deep in pounding bass lines, half-blinded by sweat and strobe lights. A Spanish girl with huge dark eyes and short hair cut like a boy's had danced close to them and danced away, then moved inside again, sharing the frisson that ran between them.

The path led past the cemetery where the faces of the dead stared from ceramic plaques on the headstones. Then alongside an electricity sub-station that hummed like a wasp's nest in the heat. A line of pylons traversed the hill ridge to his left, but the path veered right, crossing a dry stream-bed, entering a grove of dwarf trees that somehow survived by sucking moisture from the friable soil and rock. Higher up, the old vine terraces spiralled, their drystone walls falling away in landslides of dust and rubble. The strata had been warped by volcanic heat and twisted from the earth, leaving awkward ridges and loose rock. It took about an hour and a half to reach the monastery by this route and there was hardly any respite from the climb. The path went up, up, up, zigzagging through the woods, following the terraces with only a few yards of level walking between here and the summit.

In hospital he'd thought about doing this walk again. He'd thought about it through the long nights of pain and hallucination, when he could hardly get out of bed to go to the toilet. He'd thought about it when he came round from the anaesthetic and the pain in his chest was deep, like fear itself. Something you lived at the edge of, each breath taking you closer in. The pain was held back by morphine. But only just. He had a nine-inch scar down his chest, still livid through his short-sleeved shirt which was unbuttoned as far as he dared.

He'd thought about this walk when Simon was leaving and when he had, finally, left. Then sleeping alone, breakfasting alone or with Stella – which was almost the same thing since she always had a book on the go. Sometimes when driving to work or when he chatted to colleagues by the photocopier. Colleagues who asked him how he was. How he was *doing*. All that time, the mountain drew him. Like a pilgrimage, a vision, a penance. Something he had to prove to himself by going back to … well, maybe. He heard a grasshopper call from the dry plumed grass. It landed on the path in front of him, armoured in dusty green, its wings folded, its head a mask of otherness. Ralph stepped over it, scaring a slim lizard with a long tail and delicate stripes that sprang away then pretended to be a twig.

Things had been going wrong for a long time before he was ill. Rows, silences, a mutual sarcasm. At least Simon had had the decency to hang on for a few weeks, to make sure he was OK. Then he'd moved in with his secret lover. That rising star of Sociology, Paul Kretzinski. Twenty years younger, already a Professor. A Californian boy with a chromed motorcycle, floppy dark hair and a predatory innocence. In twenty years at the university Ralph had

99

never made it past Senior Lecturer. He'd tried for a Readership twice but those bastards on the Faculty promotions panel had passed him over. Twice. He didn't have the guts or the heart to go for it again. Fuck it. Fuck them. *Fucked over.* That's what he'd said when he was still high on morphine, with Stella and Simon sitting anxiously beside the bed, when he'd looked down his tee shirt. Not that he remembered any of that. It had started there, the myth of his indomitable spirit. It was all bullshit. He'd felt more like Orpheus, so close to death, to the myth that would become of him.

Ralph filled his water bottle at the fountain in the village, then walked up through the last houses to the church. The oak door was locked and the rattle of the catch echoed inside. In the whitewashed porch the statue of Jesus with his crown of thorns was tilting on its pedestal. Someone had touched up his mouth with lipstick. The cemetery had a wire fence like a municipal tennis court. There was no shelter in it. Not for the living. No yew trees to offer shade like an English churchyard. Just tightly packed headstones, most bearing a ceramic disk with a photograph of the deceased. He stood by a grave where a man and wife were still dressed in the stiff clothes of the eighteen-nineties: dark cloth and winged collars and a starched white bodice. Their plump pasty faces were still alive back then, staring into the future they could never know, remnants of another age. Ralph thought of all the history that was absent from their minds. There seemed so much less to know back then, or maybe history simply seeped away into the soil.

He thought of the couple making love, their bodies still

warm and moist, alive with veins and glands and pumping organs. He thought of their children fed into the new century like so much unsuspecting meat. Then he thought of the blond hairs on Simon's neck, the curve of his chest, his shoulders, the way his buttocks met his upper thighs in a crease of smooth skin. The way he tanned so easily. His slightly crooked teeth bared in a grin. The turquoise-blue eyes that became paler as his skin darkened. And his smell, indescribably intimate and sweet, its salty tang rising after squash or tennis.

That was all too easy to imagine. Ralph stooped to tie his bootlaces, feeling that crease of pain down his chest. A reminder. A reprimand. There were still little areas without feeling where nerves had been severed. He pressed a finger to his wrist and felt the rapid pulse of his heart, blood spurting across bone. When he'd first got home his heart had beaten so hard it shook the bed and his breath had come fast and shallow. After ten days he'd made love with Simon. In retrospect that was probably some kind of betrayal on Simon's part. Taking pity. It had been gentle and loving and he'd felt healed. Blood had seeped out afterwards, where the catheter had hurt him inside.

He'd wanted to cry then. For the first time he felt sorry for himself, for his helplessness, for not being able to put on his own slippers or dress himself. It was only when he went back for a check-up that the consultant showed him an x-ray of his collapsed lung. No one had told him and it explained a lot. He'd lain awake hallucinating from the painkillers, watching smoke billow across the bedroom ceiling, trying to catch his breath, watching Simon being caring, Stella matter-of-fact. She never minded the bodily stuff; it just had to be done. But Simon made too much of a show of it. He moved in for the first three weeks or so, then went back to his own flat when Ralph could manage things better. The worst things had been trivial: chronic constipation; seeing how thin his legs were; the support stockings that constantly fell down. Mere indignities, maybe, but they reduced him. Whereas the pain was dependable. There was dignity in pain, in withstanding it. Stella must have known that Simon was seeing someone. Ralph could understand why she hadn't told him. Just about. It rankled. Hurt even, but life was too short to fall out with Stella.

Ralph crossed a band of exposed rock, clambering upwards. He took a swig of water, putting the bottle back in his shoulder bag. He'd bought it as a camera bag years ago. Now it was in style as a fashion accessory. Not that he gave a shit about style any more. A partridge emerged from the undergrowth to watch him, then flew off in alarm as he moved. His leather watchstrap was dark with sweat. The scar on his left leg felt tight where they'd stripped out the vein to repair his blocked coronary vessels. At least, that was the theory. Even when he went in for the angiogram he had a secret feeling that it would all be shown up as a mistake, or at the worst they'd fit a stent. Such stupid, self-serving vanity. Odd that he wasn't at all vain about his appearance but he was about his health. He'd lain there during the procedure with the catheter bumping inside his chest, feeling the hot flush of dye, hanging on as the x-rays were taken. It was the weirdest feeling, impossible to describe. Not painful exactly, more like an apple core bobbing inside him, but bad enough. And he was helpless. He'd lost control. He should have known then that it was serious. The doctor had shaken his head.

– I'm sorry, there's nothing we can do for you. You're going to need surgery.

– Surgery?

The knife. As simple as that. *Fuck.*

– A bypass. One artery is ninety percent blocked.

There'd been nothing to say to that. The doctor smiled and touched his arm.

– Don't worry, you'll be playing cricket again next year.

He was Indian, dapper and dark-skinned, his hand cool on Ralph's arm. Ralph thought of his grandmother, the silver bangles her father had made and that *his* mother had kept in her chest of drawers. Surgery. So that was it – the thing he had to face – and for the first time in his life. He'd never even been in hospital before.

They kept him in and operated six days later. In many ways he'd been lucky. If they'd sent him home he'd have been walking around like a time bomb. It was bad luck/he was lucky. Which? He'd always exercised plenty, eaten properly, was only maybe half a stone too heavy. His own father had lived to be ninety-two and his mother eighty-seven. But then they'd been looking in the wrong place for a long time. Denial wasn't just a river in Egypt, as Simon used to say.

Ralph took off his bush hat and wiped his forehead. The brim was soaked and dusky with sweat. There were white rings of salt where his sweat had dried, the tidemark of earlier walks. He was wearing shorts and hiking boots. There was the purple scar down his leg, there the scar on his chest where he was wired together with titanium. Nine months after the op, stitches still made their way to the surface and he pulled them out like stray hairs.

The path forked in front of him: the left-hand side veering over open hillside, the right-hand side entering a shady gully. He kept to the right watching blue and yellow butterflies and dark moths scatter up from pink flowers that grew beside the path. He didn't know the names of the flowers or the butterflies. They would have names in Catalan, names in Castilian, names in French and Basque. That was how the human tongue played over things, defining them until language itself died. He couldn't decide if it was good to be alive or not. Being close to death had brought him face to face with a vast ignorance. All the things he couldn't name and didn't know. The university was like that, too. What he didn't know seemed so much bigger than what he did, which at times merely seemed a lot about a little. Contemporary literature and theory. Saying that he was a doctor *but not a real doctor* had been a joke. It didn't feel like that now. Not after the real doctors had put him under the anaesthetic and renewed his heart and woken him back to life. He'd visited the underworld and returned, *knocked on the downstairs door*, as his friend Tariq had put it, translating from Urdu. Even his surgeon had been Greek, leading him on that journey through dark rivers where his blood pulsed and roared like a bull's in cavernous dreams.

Somehow Simon and Stella had got him through, even though they pretty much hated each other by then. After all, Simon had put her in an impossible position. He'd given her a secret that she didn't want and couldn't keep. She'd told Ralph one evening, on one of the rare occasions they had dinner together. Just six months after the op and he'd been about to return to work, part-time. Simon couldn't make it and Stella had cooked an Indian meal, which was surprisingly good. Ralph had got her to shave his head. She said he looked like Mahatma Gandhi. He'd quipped that he looked as if he'd had chemotherapy, not heart surgery. Cooking always took Stella hours and, unlike Ralph, she made meticulous reference to recipes, wore an apron that had arrived free with a case of wine, and used the kitchen scales to make exact measurements. Lamb cutlets with spiced rice and okra. Afterwards, she'd dabbed her mouth on a napkin and lit a cigarette, blowing smoke away from him.

–You know he's gone don't you.

–You mean to the conference?

– Don't be stupid, Ralph.

He had known. It was true. It was like pain arriving. First it circled and then it cut you in half.

– How long have you known?

– Not known, not really. Suspected.

– How long have you *suspected*?

– About as long as you have.

She pulled on the cigarette.

– Don't pretend it's all my fault.'

She was right, she was only telling him what he knew in sheepish glances, cancelled evenings out, Simon's hurry always to be somewhere that was somewhere else.

– I'm sorry.

She stubbed the cigarette out on a plate. A habit she knew Ralph hated.

– Shit! Now I'm really sorry.

She wiped away the ash with her finger.

– Forgot. Again…

Then, somehow they were smiling at each other. Ralph never knew how Simon found out he knew. It wasn't easy in the Department, but the place was deserted half the time anyway with central timetabling and colleagues on sabbatical. They'd never advertised that they were an item and they never told anyone it was over. Ralph met Stella a few times more than he usually did for lunch, usually in one of the bars around the campus, but that was all. Apart from pain of a different kind that kept him awake at night now. When he went back to work there had been a colossal sense of hurt. Visceral. As if work had hurt him. The first staff meeting had been difficult, when they'd ended up sitting almost side by side, looking up from the agenda and minutes to exchange wry glances. Ralph had felt naked then. But then it became easier. It became a fact of life, a *fait accomplit*.

The path left the trees now and reared up into a left-hand curve where the old vine terraces began. The low walls that kept back the hillside had collapsed and he had to pick his way over scree. In a few places prickly pears had colonised the land and he scratched his leg trying to negotiate them. A trickle of bright blood ran down his right calf. He dabbed it with a tissue, but the blood kept coming. Ever since the op he'd been taking low dose aspirin to prevent clotting. But if he cut himself the blood flowed. After the angiogram a big Nigerian nurse had leaned on the wound in his femoral artery when the cannula had gone in, pressing until the bleeding stopped, telling him about her kids back in Abuja.

After the first game of tennis they'd played together,

when it had all been new, Simon had licked the sweat off his chest in the shower. There seemed no going back on each other then. He had the gentlest hands of any lover Ralph had known, man or woman. Not that there had been many women. Though Stella had sometimes been a convenient front for them both. She lectured in Gothic literature and wore trademark black polo neck sweaters and slacks. On one arm she had a tattoo of a snake eating its tail in a figure of eight. That was considered pretty racy in academia, though Ralph often thought it was an image *of* academia. She was a Reader now, as from the last appointments round. He'd had the grace to feel glad for her. Her new book on the Brontës had been well reviewed. His own, one and only, book on the sonnet form and its links to Renaissance music had sunk like a stone into the usual dismal university libraries. No one else would want to read that. He'd be lucky to collect half a dozen citations. The Dean was already hassling about the next research excellence thing. *Exercise? Framework?* He couldn't remember. Bullshit, anyway.

Ralph was panting now. His hips and legs ached with the effort of constantly climbing. He could feel the steady bumping of his heart. There were a few yards of flat path as his route ran parallel to the hillside before climbing again. He came to a flat rock jutting out from the slope and sat down to rest. The sea seemed a vertical plane, a blue-grey veil. The town was fainter, the church a pointillist's dab of white. Scrubby trees spread out below him, khaki green. A pigeon or dove broke from cover and crossed the valley frantically, as if a predator was patrolling the tree line. He'd seen a sparrow hawk take a blackbird like that once, almost in front of his face on the south campus. So close he'd ducked. One minute gliding from the trees, the next an airburst of feathers. Then the hawk sculling away with the dead songbird in its claws. Oddly enough he'd found that invigorating, as if he walked on into the day more alive. When in fact he was on his way to the Emily Dickinson lecture theatre to enlighten Part II students about modern forms of the sonnet. All those bleak, hungover faces lined up in semi-circles.

Ralph felt in his shoulder bag for the bottle of water. He took a long swig, spraying the last of the mouthful into the dust. A libation. Droplets sparkled, then darkened like old blood. He set off again, already scanning ahead for the next resting place, feeling balls of sweat trickle down his sides under the shirt. He remembered Simon's tongue lapping at him the way a cat lapped a saucer of milk. For a theorist he was amazingly ... well, *immediate*. For someone who spent his time with Foucault, Derrida and Lacan, he knew the secrets of touch. *In theory, theories exist. In practice they don't.* Who was that? Latour? Ralph halted where the path widened a little, breaking some dried leaves from a sage bush and smelling his fingers. The herb was as pungent as wood smoke. He flexed his left leg and rubbed the scar where it ran deepest behind his knee. He had a little birthmark there that looked like a rabbit. Funny how those things stayed with you all your life, like having green eyes or the way your fingernails grew or the hair on your chest tapered. His chest had been parted with a saw, shaved, cranked open and then wired back together. Before the op, he'd asked the surgeon – *the Greek* – what the procedure would be like. *Invasive*, he said. Then, later with a smile: *It'll be traumatic, but don't worry, eh? You're going to be OK.* He was right, it was like being invaded.

He hadn't wanted anyone around when he went to the theatre. The anesthetist had been an Irishman, about his own age. Jovial. He'd had the pre-med, then waited as time dissolved around him. He'd slipped away from consciousness and they put him under and started work. Diverting his blood supply, cutting away diseased vessels, grafting new ones. Like the way they'd tended the vines he was walking through. Six hours of surgery. Death and resurrection. When he came to, it was evening. He'd been worried that he'd wake up shouting obscenities under the effects of the anaesthetic. But he felt at peace, and was being washed by a beautiful Malaysian nurse who had gold hoops in her ears. She was smiling at him, teeth glinting, eyes dark as occlusions in honey. His body, still painted with iodine, looked radiant, as if he'd been coated with gold leaf. His chest was seared with a bloody line and his pubic hair gleamed like copper wire. He had the sensation of floating in warm water, of a wide dark river with fire playing over the surface. A small apocalypse in which he felt like a river god with his bride, her hands light as tender flames across his body.

It must have been hours later when he woke again and Stella and Simon were sitting beside the bed. He didn't remember this, but they said he'd been in *good form*. Pleased to see them, genial, peeping down his tee shirt, smiling sardonically, babbling. That would be the legend back in the Department. He hadn't feared pain or death, but the end of life: the axe, not its shadow. He'd waited for days before the op to have the tests that would confirm him as viable. He'd had lung capacity tests and more x-rays. Thank God he'd never smoked. Then the surgeon had appeared early one evening, flipping through Ralph's notes to pronounce him an excellent candidate before rattling through his survival rates.

After the op and that visit from Simon and Stella, he'd been alone in the ward. Not alone in fact, but alone in some profound sense with his hurt. He'd remembered Raleigh's words to the executioner as he examined the axe: *Let me see it. Do you think I'm afraid of it? This is a sharp medicine, but it is a physician for all diseases.* And he'd realised that he wasn't really viable, after all. That sharp medicine had done its worst. He was stranded with his wound, his constant need of care. He was dependent. The hours had passed in a slow ache of realisation. Morphine had reduced the tangible to phantasmagorical shadows. The pain was coming closer; something stalking him, something he already knew. He asked the sister for some painkillers and he saw her approaching the consultant who was making a ward round. He'd stopped to fuss with Ralph's drip and reassure him about the operation. He'd done a quadruple bypass in the end, *the Greek*. When the ache began he felt as he'd been sawn in half, which he had. He saw the surgeon turn away from the nurse before she even asked her question. It was three hours later when the pain was rasping along his sternum that the ward sister came by with some tablets.

The first signs had first come on five years ago when he'd been playing cricket for the university. The senior team, that is. He'd bowled twelve consecutive overs: five maidens, twenty-seven for none because he'd been dropped five times. It was probably his best ever spell, the ball swinging away late, pitching just short of a length outside off stump and then seaming towards first slip. He'd crafted each over, swinging the odd ball in, getting some to lift from a length, even making some cut into the stumps. The batsman was an old adversary, a Professor of Music, and they'd been able to share a joke between overs. Then he'd stood under the trees on the boundary with an ache spreading from chest to shoulder. It came back when he was playing tennis, then cycling. He'd gone to his GP and been referred to cardiology and had the treadmill test. He didn't believe that there was anything seriously wrong with him. Re-reading *Lolita* he found that Nabakov's Humbert Humbert had suffered from intercostal neuralgia and he'd Googled it out of curiosity. It was a condition of the intercostal muscles that mimicked angina. Perfect. When the young cardiologist had told him – categorically – that there was nothing wrong with his heart he'd tried that bit of theory out on her. She'd smiled. No, she hadn't read Nabakov. Yes, it was possible.

Before the op they put him in a ward with men who'd already had it, coughing with rolled-up towels pressed to their chests. After the op, he was kept awake by old men who'd had heart or lung operations, breathing into oxygen masks and nebulisers, struggling for their lives or what was left of them. They'd brought a guy in, younger than him, who'd lain deliriously calling for his mother, shouting at ghosts. *Oh you fucking bastards!* His eyes were magnified behind smeared glasses and his hair was tangled with sweat. *Oh you cunts!* He pulled off his monitor so that the beeper sounded all night, ripped out his cannula so that blood sprayed the bed sheets. *Let me not be mad,* Ralph had prayed, let me not be, please.

He never imagined any of that when he walked away from the cardiologist with his Nabokov story and nothing wrong with his heart. When there was everything wrong with it. When something was working away inside him. He never found out why it hadn't been spotted, but five years later when the shoulder pain came back he had an MRI scan to check for a compressed vertebra. It was like being trapped in a toothpaste tube with a pod of whales calling. Nothing. Apart from the usual wear and tear. Then a humourless Slovakian neurologist had advised him to revisit cardiology. Hobbling back to the car, he realised that she was right. That he might be running out of time. The heart attack came two days before he was due to take a treadmill test again. Not a pain in the chest, but an intense ache in his jaw and shoulder. Simon had driven him to the hospital as he held a pack of ice to his clavicle. Friday night and the town had been full of young people out on the lash, boys in tight jeans and tee shirts, girls in short skirts and plunging halter tops. All that life, that vibrancy, that need, that sexual drive. He'd never been afraid to die, but he'd been afraid of losing Simon through dying. That had happened anyway. It was a fucking joke, really. Though he should have seen it coming, Paul Kretzinski and all.

The path was so steep now that Ralph could only walk in moderate spurts. Thirty or forty paces or so, then a rest, then forty more and a rest. The sun had swung higher in the sky and he could feel it burning behind his knees. He paused to rest his hat on a rock, smear on more sun cream, wipe the sweat from his neck. The sun glinted on a windscreen down in the village. There was a very faint breeze up this high, but the air was heated from its passage overland. The sea was crimped into wave crests and the wind surfers were almost invisible from this height. He could just make out one of the trawlers putting to sea. Yesterday he'd wandered down to the harbour with his camera in the early evening. They'd let him into the fish auction with a few other tourists as the crates of fish came by on the conveyor and the traders made hoarse bids in Catalan. A tall African sailor was shoveling ice into crates, muscular, high shouldered and narrow hipped. His skin gleamed in the dim interior light. He was a kind of perfection. But Ralph felt no desire, not even in the abstract.

He passed crates of squid, hake, cod. Some pink fish he didn't even recognise. Then a swordfish. It gleamed like beaten silver, its eyes huge and inky and indelibly sad. It had made him melancholy, as if what had happened to him had suddenly coalesced, had melded with all the other sadness of creation. He'd felt like an intruder, hadn't taken a photograph, an image that would sit uselessly on his hard-drive. Another *memento mori*. The camera was his way of putting a membrane between him and the world. Simon had told him that once, cruelly accurate.

Back at the flat he'd written in his notebook, covering the pages with fine script. He was supposed to be working on a new academic book this summer, but he'd started writing poems instead – actually writing poems instead of writing *about* them. It was nearly twenty years since he'd published some 'promising' work in *Poetry Review* and the

TLS, so it had all come as a bit of a surprise. He was due a term of research leave next year and he hardly knew what to do with it now. Maybe he'd go for a book of his own poems now that creative writing was all the rage. You had to laugh. The University was filling up with writers who needed to make a living on the side and what lazy, self-serving bastards most of them were.

The last hundred or so yards up the path were a slog though dust and sifting gravel. The breeze stiffened, bringing some relief from the heat. He saw a green wheelie bin, then a steel barrier. Incongruously the path ended at the car park for the monastery where a road zigzagged up the north side of the mountain in a series of stacked hairpin bends. The car park was about five hundred yards from the restored buildings, the path sagging into a dip then rising up to the squat towers and crenellated walls where the monks had looked down on everything and everyone below. It was said that the locals had sacked the place in the sixteenth century. It wasn't hard to imagine, living in the village under their gaze. The monks with all that wealth and self-sufficiency, their olives and vines and bakeries and tanneries, creaming it as the villagers flogged up and down the path with half-starved mules to trade with them. Ralph took another swig of water, stooping to pick dried grass and broken stems from his socks where they were scratching his ankle. The blood had dried on his right leg, congealing in a rivulet that matched the scar on the other. He was knackered but exultant. He'd done it. So fuck the lot of them, whoever they were. It was meant nothing: slog, slog, slog to the top. But it felt good. It felt like meaning. And he was looking forward to coffee and *agua mineral* in one of the cafés on the seafront when he got back. He'd feel good then, feel that he'd achieved something he'd set out to do. That was advance retrospection: another theory, but one that worked. One that existed, like experience did.

Ralph rested on the barrier for a few minutes. Three workmen arrived in a white Seat van and began to put on gauntlets and facemasks. They unloaded strimmers and started them up in a fug of white smoke, cutting back the grass and thistles at the edge of the steel barrier. When Simon walked on they snarled behind him like a three-headed dog.

He'd decided not to enter the monastery. Not this time. Sometimes he liked that holy feeling, that sense of connection with the past and a necessary God. But not today. He glanced at his watch. There was moisture clinging to the inside of the glass. His own sweat. It was only ten forty-five. He'd made it in good time, getting up before the main heat of the day set in. He followed the path to the side of the perimeter wall where there was a shady garden with a drinking tap set into a stone recess where he splashed his face.

The view to the northwest showed the Pyrenees still dusky in the morning heat. On the road below a posse of cyclists went past in yellow jerseys, toes pointed, legs pumping almost in unison. Ralph filled his water bottle from the brass tap, lingering in the shade. His route home lay down a gentler valley that would take him round the bay on the coastal path and back into the town. He'd have time for a shower and a change of clothes before taking the hire-car to meet Stella at Gerona. He placed his bag and hat and water bottle on the wall and took a photograph of them with the mountains in the distance. The last time he'd done this Simon had been with him and he had a shot of him leaning forwards and laughing, halfway through saying something. That'd been two years ago. One thing a scholar of the sonnet should know is that things change suddenly and then end.

Ralph sat on the wall and felt the breeze feather over his face. He imagined Stella clumping towards him, with her wheeled suitcase and ridiculous shoes and tattoo, to hug him and ask him how he was. Tomorrow, they'd settle into the flat together, reading, bitching about their colleagues, walking, swimming, touring bars in the early evening before settling down to eat somewhere. He'd choose the balconied restaurant where they'd have tuna salad with olives or *gazpacho*. Then freshly caught *merluza* and white wine. Then coffee and *crema catalana* and sweet Spanish brandy. She'd skip out between courses for a smoke and he'd warn her about cancer and she'd flick her finger against her nose, laughing, glad he was alive to goad her. Tomorrow, he'd watch her freckled body spread out on the stones of the beach, without desire but with a kind of amazement. He'd realise that his heart was good, that he was healed of all but the deepest pain and unworthiness. He'd realise that in their own unachievable way that they loved each other – without passion, without longing, but with a kind of recognition.

The future was uncertain again and in a good way. It was a premonition, like poetry coming on, its aura. The way things had to begin again, had to exist before they could mean anything. Ralph stood up and turned to leave.

He took up the bag and put on his damp hat, flexing his leg where the scar was tight again, reminding him. Then he set off, filling his lungs with dry air, crossing the metalled road, following the dusty track down through rock and scrub. It would take him through the valley to the sea. *La Vall de Santa Creu.* There were stands of broom in flower and the scent of jasmine. He found some ripe blackberries and picked them. They were tart and sweet at the same time, their seeds sticking in his teeth. Ralph took a swig of water and swallowed. It had the brackish taste of soil and rock. He never thought he would die.

PIANOFORTE

You get used to words. You have to. But they have meanings you don't always think about. Like *pianoforte*, meaning *soft* and *loud*. It's obvious, really, when you look. Then, *photography*, meaning *drawing* with *light*. Light, of all things. The reason we see, or don't. People find what they're looking for, what they *expect* to see. That's obvious when you develop their films.

That's how I started out after the war above our chemist's shop in Deansgate. People brought in roll film from their box cameras and I printed out what they'd seen – not what they thought they'd seen, but all the out of focus stuff, all the nonsense and clutter, the unflattering inbetween expressions, the mess that gets in the way of the essence. Photographs have to be composed to be any good. So do people for that matter. I've still got all my old cameras and light meters lined up in a glass case in the living room: that first Kodak, the Rolleiflex, the Leica I never stopped using, the big Mamiya twin-lens I kept for studio work.

Most of the bombing in Manchester was in 1940, two days before Christmas. People talk about 1939, *the phoney war*, that long summer. I remember all that, but it's not what sticks somehow. What I remember is the artificial Christmas tree we'd put up in the front parlour, strands of tinsel trembling in the draught from the front door and the little heap of presents tied up with string and blobs of sealing wax. Then hearing the sirens, pulling the blackout curtains and huddling under the kitchen table with our mother, waiting for the sound of aero engines. When the first bombs fell close by she grabbed my arm. *Jesus, sweet Jesus, they're killing us!* And they were. Killing us, killing the city I'd grown up in. It was all I knew and now it was shaking under us as the bombs fell. I could feel it under my hands as if an earth tremor was pulling Manchester apart.

I can't remember the weather, and there's no snow on the pictures. Judging by people's clothing – overcoats, gloves, hats, scarves – it was pretty cold. We heard they'd gone for the Avro factory in Chadderton and missed it, but they flattened Piccadilly, Corporation Street and the market. The cathedral took a hit and they brought in West Indian troops to clear the mess. That was the first time I'd seen black people, apart from in films.

I'd got my first decent camera – a folding Kodak Junior 6 – and was out photographing it all. You got some funny looks, but most people thought I worked for the *Evening News*. I was learning to use depth of field, to get what I wanted into focus – reading off the distance scale and f-stops – and blurring the rest. Or stopping down the lens and putting everything in the clear, with maybe just the foreground hazy. People got killed, I know, and it was a tragedy to see the old building and marketplace in ruins, but it looked amazing. It looked spectacular. Rubble, hosepipes, burst water mains, people staring upwards at the broken buildings or the sky, shock all over their faces.

There was a smell of plaster and the stink from a broken sewer, the strange feeling of looking into shattered houses with torn wallpaper and unmade beds in their upstairs rooms. It was all horribly intimate, as if the secrets of the city – all the things that should happen behind closed doors, under slate roofs and scarves of chimney smoke – were being exposed by the enemy. *Our* enemy. I remember a Yorkshire terrier stranded in a shattered gable-end and a fireman going up for it and the crowd cheering. That made the news. It was *extraordinary*. Another one of those words. It was even more extraordinary to make contact prints in my little curtained-off darkroom in the kitchen, working under a red lamp to see images rising through the chemicals in the developing tray. The blackout made that easy, of course. Ghostly outlines, at first, then real, sharp images. It was just chemistry, I know, but the nearest thing to magic, the way I watched Noel appear in black and white then lie down.

I'd set up a little studio in the front room at home with my camera and a tripod. I had some business cards printed: *Lewis Bannerman, Photographer.* Then I hiked around all the pubs and guesthouses. A lot of the negro troops came by to have their photographs taken to send home. They were just like everyone else, though the exposures were more difficult. Polite, softly spoken, so that I couldn't always tell what they were saying. Sometimes their English was beautiful, like something being read out of a book. Then posing for the camera, tucking in their stomachs, putting on a goofy smile. That's when I realised that it wasn't just me and Noel who were alike. We were all alike. More alike than we could ever be different. That's when I learned to hate the only thing I've ever hated. Narrow-mindedness. Contempt for skin colour, language or customs different from our own. Mother loved having the West Indians and Canadians and Americans in the house, especially if they were in uniform, and she'd be running around making cups of tea, making a fuss of them. She was animated and girlish then, her frizzy hair flying out of control, her cheeks flushed with embarrassment and excitement. She had no idea that I was trying to run a business, though that kind of thing can be good for business. The personal touch. You never see that now with the big companies and corporations. Not unless you're filthy rich.

In those days we lived in Crumpsall – me, my mother and my twin brother, Noel. We were identical twins, though I was the eldest by eight minutes. We were so hard to tell apart that we could fool the teachers at school most of the time. We did it for a laugh, swapping lessons. Sometimes, if one of us got into bother, they wouldn't know which one. Often, we got away scot-free. Other times we both copped for the cane or the plimsoll across the back of our legs. Our father had gone off with a sales assistant from Whitlow's shortly after we were born and was never seen again. Or at least,that was one story: that facing twins had been too much for him. The other story was that my mother and father had never actually married. Some fly-by-night had got her into trouble. There were no pictures of him. But we had a copper plate daguerreotype of a man with a winged collar and a waxed moustache that she kept wrapped in a silk scarf in a drawer. I think that was her father.

Only our mother could tell us apart. She worked in the Co-op on the bacon and cold meats counter – they'd call it the deli now. Somehow, she managed to raise two kids who never really went hungry. We started school together on the same day at six years old and left on the same day aged fourteen. He supported Man City and I supported United. Noel went to train as a gentleman's tailor with Henry Goldstein and I was apprenticed to Hardcastle the chemist and went to night school to pass my exams in pharmacology. But photography was my first love.

My mother was from the town of Shaw, beyond Oldham, and had come to the city after the first war. She'd been a doffer in a cotton mill and hated the work. It was fast and repetitive and the overseers gave no quarter. Mother was fair, with that pale freckled complexion some northerners have. But we were brown-haired and dark-eyed with light olive skin, though I never saw an olive until I flew to Majorca with Marcie in '64. They called us *jewboys* and *yids* at school, even though we didn't know who our father was, even though we'd never been to a synagogue. They didn't mean much by it. It was never really vicious. Mancunians had opposed slavery, they'd died at Peterloo fighting the Corn Laws and – most of them – had no time for fascism. It was too pompous for them by far. But they had quick, ironic, tongues, always at work, the way the looms and spinning frames ran on. Like a lot of things, an insult depends on how you say it and why. None of that really sank in until we were teenagers. Mosley's lot had come to Manchester with the BUF in '34 when we were too young to get involved. But it was in the papers and we were old enough to know what was happening in Italy and Germany by then. In '39 they came to Belle Vue. Noel had joined the Challenge Club (I'd joined Bury Camera

Club) and he dragged me along to the demonstration. I didn't take my camera. I'd have needed a Rolleiflex or even a Leica for that and they were way beyond my reach.

There were 500 of them and 3,000 of us. Mosley never got a word in. He looked like a demented little puppet with his nervous bodyguards. The crowd sang *Bye bye Blackshirt* and chanted *clear out the rats* at him. Amongst us was a group of hard cases in black berets who looked as if they might have fought in Spain. But you couldn't tell. A red-haired girl who stood next to us, and pressed up against Noel when the crowd surged, knew all the words to *The Internationale*. I could tell Noel was impressed. The police left Mosley and his crew to it in the end. He'd been given the KB, Manchester-style. If they'd started anything we'd have murdered them. It was a good day's work and we were proud to be Mancunians. It was the first time I'd been proud to be anything or felt I *was* anything.

I remember the smell of the crowd — a blend of sweat, beer, hair oil and tobacco. And something else. *Anger.* Anger at the last war, anger at years of poverty and hardship, anger at the way the future looked. A fat lad next to me had stood and roared, *Bastard! Fascist bastard!* over and over, until he was purple in the face. He turned to me at one point and grinned with gappy teeth. *I'm from Middleton.* As if that explained the language. As if that explained everything there was to know right then. The smell of the crowd was the smell of solidarity, of love and hatred mixed together. Even though we weren't really Jewish and had no idea then what happened to Jewish twins in Germany we thought we'd turned the fascists back for good.

We walked all the way home from Gorton and the crowd drained away around us into pubs and houses, trams and buses. We thought something new was beginning. But a few months later Hitler grabbed Czechoslovakia and the war came to bugger everything up. Later that year Noel was called up to the merchant navy. He didn't fancy the coal pits or the army. I was spared because of my weak chest. Some days you couldn't see to the end of the street in Crumpsall what with domestic fires and smoke from hundreds of mill chimneys, so it was no wonder I was bronchial. The smoke was yellow with sulphur, like a mangy tomcat slinking along the streets and alleyways. You couldn't hang washing out on cold days when everything was going full thrutch. Drying it indoors over a clothes maiden didn't help my respiration much. When the council came by to mend the roads, my mother stood me next to the boiler that heated up the tar and made me inhale the fumes. Maybe that started my interest in things medical. Coal tar. Respiration. Cause and effect. When the war started Noel and I were still living at home and we hardly knew what girls were.

The house we lived in was a two-up, two-down terrace with a tiny built-on kitchen rented from Ernie Hathaway, who my mother called *a twisted little crook*. He'd been buried by a Turkish shell at Gallipoli, so it wasn't his fault he walked like a lame frog. Our house had a front room with patterned glass and a parlour with a cast-iron range and a privy down the back yard where we learned to smoke. Noel and I shared a bedroom until we left home. Two single beds, side by side in the narrow room. Lino on the floor that gave you chilblains in a winter. A chamber pot under the bed. Net curtains at the windows because our mother couldn't abide nosiness.

In the front parlour was an old German piano with an iron frame and candlestick holders that she'd paid a few shillings for after a neighbour died. She took it and had it tuned because Noel had sat down at our uncle Ted's piano at the age of nine and picked out the theme of *Red Sails in the Sunset*. He had perfect pitch and by the age of sixteen could read music and play pretty much anything by ear. I was tone deaf, of course, and the sight of sheet music made me feel dizzy. But on winter evenings if there was nothing better on the wireless, we loved to sit in the parlour with the fire banked up and the coals hissing and hear him play. Our mother sometimes ventured to sing in her shaky contralto voice, the firelight making her look like a girl again.

The war made us short of everything, including temper. People talk about it now as if it was the best of times, but that's rubbish. What's good about being starved and bombed and anxious all the time? Everyone seemed expectant, on edge, especially our mother. We'd never been apart and when Noel went to the navy it was like losing a limb. I couldn't sleep for weeks and we waited for his letters every day. They came written in thick strokes of black ink with passages struck out by the censor's blue pencil. I used to hold them up to the kitchen window to see what had been crossed out, but it did no good. I wondered what he'd been trying to tell us that was so important to national security. It was OK when he was based in Portsmouth or Liverpool, but when he started on the Baltic convoys I thought our mother would die with worry. The German U-boats were dropping thousands of tons of shipping to the sea bottom every month. A lad two streets away had been torpedoed on an Atlantic convoy and spent three days on a life raft. When they sent him home on rest leave, he looked half drowned. He was so pale you felt you could see through him. Another unwilling warrior. I thought of Noel drowning in a steel box, his last breaths bubbling like Morse code through salt water and the ship's funnel tilting into grey waves as the boilers took in water and exploded. I'd seen enough newsreels of German ships going down to know it'd be no different.

It was just a year after the Manchester blitz, a few days before Christmas. They still hadn't cleared up the mess. That took years. The city was wounded, but we knew it would recover. That happened later, too, with the IRA bomb in '96. That would have been hard to imagine back then. I was off work sick again, lying on my bed all morning swotting up on the *British Pharmacopoeia*. Mother was out at the Co-op, checking ration cards and serving customers their meagre dues. I remember I was wearing a grey and maroon pullover she'd made for me the year before. She'd used wool unravelled from old jumpers we'd worn as kids and it was tight and itchy under the arms. It was quiet on the streets outside. Petrol rationing meant there was hardly any traffic now. I was angling the book into the wintry light when I heard a key click in the front door and assumed that mother must have forgotten something and nipped home for it. Then I heard footsteps coming up the stairs. Not the slow heavy steps of my mother, but something altogether more familiar. A sprung rhythm I'd always known. The hairs stood up on my arms and I half turned as the footsteps reached the landing.

– Noel?

He was framed in the doorway with his knapsack.

– Bloody hell! Noel!

We hugged and he was laughing, but there were shadows under his eyes, a vacant look of exhaustion.

– What're you doing here?

– We docked in Birkenhead and I got a three-day pass. Back the day after Boxing Day.

– Because?

– Because the next one's a big 'un. I'm not supposed to say where…

– Does Mum know?

– I nearly sent a telegram, but I thought the shock'd kill her!

He laughed again. We knew about telegrams from the first war. How after the Somme there were curtains drawn all across the city. Then later at Paschendaele. All those boys gone under all that mud. It was another thing Manchester never forgot or forgave. Noel patted my camera where I'd left it on the windowsill and slumped onto his bed.

– How's the photography business?

– Pretty good. I might be able to buy you a pint down at Ma Shiptons.

– You don't say.

That was an expression we used all the time.

– I do say.

He took out a brown paper package, then pushed his knapsack under the bed next to the chamber pot.

– I hope you've emptied that.

– Maybe.

He put the parcel on the little oak veneered cabinet beside the bed.

– What's that?

– Turkish delight.

– Blimey!

He slapped away my hand.

– For Mum, you greedy get. Got it in Chinatown in Liverpool. Rare as rocking horse shit, that.

That was an expression he'd got from the navy.

– Rare indeed. How's the sailor's life?

He rolled his eyes and unhooked the collar of his uniform.

– As per. The usual boring crap. You're well out of it, mate.

Noel laughed, unlacing his boots and tossing them on the floor. I went downstairs to put the kettle on the gas and made two mugs of tea. When I got back upstairs he'd slipped off his greatcoat and cap and lay full-length on the bed, fast asleep, his brown hair falling across his face and his neck just like a child's. We both had long eyelashes and dimpled chins. It was like looking at myself. Soon, he was softly snoring, each breath like tissue paper being torn and softly crumpled. Three days. It was Friday, so we'd be able to go out around Shude Hill and Stevenson Square, look for girls in the pubs and dance halls. Being a twin was always a good talking point. I suppose we thought we might meet twin girls one day. But we never did. I picked up my camera and took a photograph. There was a band of sunshine falling on the bed and the room was bright. I made the exposure: F5.6 at a 50th of a second. Then I drew the curtains and let him sleep.

I still have that photograph in a box of negatives and prints labelled with his name. He looks like a fallen knight, a sleeping warrior, one arm thrown across the bed, one across his chest. The light slanting into the room and onto his face. He's young there. Forever. I'm holding the image now, here in the future, my old hands bracketing his youth. I made an enlargement from the negative. It's soft-focus, but that gives it a tender quality, my brother sleeping, safe from all harm. His mouth curves into the dimpled shadow of a smile, as if he's glad to be home. One moment stopped from time's flow.

All that's a mystery, somehow. A paradox. An illusion. It'd take fifty of these images to capture even a whole second of the years we spent together, yet there are only seventeen images in the box labelled *Noel*. Seventeen fiftieths. A passage of time so small that it lies somewhere between the flicker of the second hand on my watch. It's a tremor, a measure of transition rather than time. The snap of the shutter. A serpent's eye blinking. The magician's sleight of hand. That man in the black suit we saw at Fred Karno's, closing his hand on a pigeon's egg, then opening it to show it had disappeared. When he took off his top hat to acknowledge our applause a pigeon flew up to the high wire and perched there. I never showed that picture of Noel to my mother.

When Noel woke up he drank the cold separated tea with a grimace, grinned and said *worse things happen at sea*. Then he took off his uniform and started opening drawers. For some reason he couldn't find his favourite shirt. Maybe our mother had washed it or was mending it. She loved to sit in the firelight with a piece of darning listening to the BBC.

– Where's she put my stuff?

– I don't know.

I tossed him a neatly ironed work shirt that mother had folded by my bed.

– Try this. It's clean.

– Ugh!

He pretended to smell it, but put it on anyway. He was wearing a vest and there were bruises down his arms. Later, over a drink, he told me about dragging cases of cannon shells into the magazine for the forward guns. *Bloody murder. Everyone bawling at you to go faster, as if you gave a monkey's.* He told me about trying to sleep in his bunk with the U-boats slinking beneath them, hiding in the darkest fathoms of the sea.

Then he couldn't find his trousers or shoes. I don't know where we got the idea, but Noel decided to dress up in my clothes for a prank. Mother was due back from work at five-thirty, so we had a couple of hours to practise. He dropped his voice slightly to mimic mine. The master-stroke was borrowing my reading spectacles. I'll swear to God he looked more like me than I did. I had three shots left in my camera and I'd just bought a flashgun. The plan was to follow Noel downstairs and catch the happy reunion when our mother realised what had happened.

The afternoon passed in chatting and lounging in the bedroom. We went out for a quick one at the local pub, where there'd be a decent fire. I seem to remember that the Christmas decorations were up. But we were careful to get back in good time. Noel was never much of a drinker anyway. Back at the house we piled upstairs and waited. Just after five-thirty, then voices in the street outside as mother said goodbye to a neighbour who'd walked with her. Then the key turned in the lock and she was hanging up her coat in the hall.

– Lewis?

I looked at Noel and he signalled at me to answer.

– Hiya.

– Are you OK? Feeling better?

– Yes, fine.

– Come down for tea in a few minutes OK?

– OK.

Noel was smiling delightedly. He put his finger on his lips. It couldn't have worked out better. We heard her clinking about the kitchen, cutting bread and heating up the soup she'd made from ham shank and dried peas the day before. It smelled good, drifting up the stairs. Noel waited a few minutes, then picked up my copy of *Picture Post* and went downstairs. I heard him grunt at Mother, a pretty good imitation of me on a grumpy day. She asked him if I was better and he coughed, a little too theatrically. I crept downstairs in my stockinged feet with the camera and flashgun and sat on the bottom step waiting for the moment.

When nothing happened I realised that they must be eating. I could hear the clink of soup spoons, odd distracted words from my mother, short replies from Noel. She hadn't been looking for him and so she hadn't noticed he wasn't me. I retreated back up the stairs. After about fifteen minutes I heard the table being cleared and knew my mother would be in the kitchen, so I slipped into the front parlour and hunkered down behind the settee where I couldn't be seen. It was a strange feeling. A cold, hungry feeling, as if I'd died. Noel was pretending to be me and she hadn't noticed. Yet I knew she was thinking about him all the time, beside herself with worry every day. Beside myself was how I felt now, that odd expression making sense at last.

It wasn't quite cold enough to set a fire. In the war, there'd have to be ice on the mantelpiece for that. Mother came in from the kitchen, wiping her hands on her apron, still wet from washing up. She picked up a bundle of knitting from the settee and began sorting through her needles. Noel came in and stood in the doorway for a moment. He was still wearing my striped pullover and reading glasses and the effect was uncanny. Even though we were used to being alike, had spent all our lives being mistaken for each other, we'd never taken it this far. It was like being out of my own body, like being a spirit and looking back at life from somewhere else. There was a look of bewilderment and pain on Noel's face. My mother was ignoring him and I realised that he didn't know what to do, didn't know how to break the spell.

I saw him move squeeze past the Christmas tree with its trembling tinsel streamers and sit down on the piano stool. He swung his legs under the keyboard and placed his hands above the keys. When I saw Noel's hands, they seemed to darken, like the severed hands King Leopold's men had taken to impose their rule on the Congo, stealing copper and mahogany, the iron, ivory and ebony that made an instrument. Noel nodded, as if swallowing something.

When his hands fell to the keys he played the first few bars of '*O Tannenbaum*', aka 'The Red Flag'. At first my mother seemed paralysed. Her head rose up by degrees like a periscope. The look on her face was indescribable, but one I'll never forget. It flickered between emotions: love, joy, pain, loss, discovery. I rose up from behind the settee with the camera and pressed the shutter, but I'd forgotten to switch on the flash, so the photograph was almost black when I developed it. Just shadows. Ghosts. I think the shock of light might have killed her anyway. She dropped the knitting and stood up. Then, quick as a whip, she cracked Noel around the face and cracked me one too. A full tilt smack of the hand that sent me reeling and nearly knocked Noel from the piano stool. My mother had never hit us before and now she stood with her chest heaving and tears streaming down her face. A huge sob bubbled up in her chest. It was only then we realised how cruel we'd been, how unending her love was, how inconsolable. After that evening, we never spoke about what had happened. Not that we got much chance.

We were eighteen when Mosley came to Belle Vue and we'd got quietly drunk on the way home, taking a half in each pub on the way. Our mother had been listening to it on the news and she'd hugged us on the doorstep, even though we were half cut. She'd heard it all on the wireless. She was proud of us then and she knew we'd look out for each other. Or that Noel would look out for me. He was lost in the Baring Sea when his ship was torpedoed in 1942, part of a Russian supply convoy. Some of the crew were saved and there were weeks of waiting. They turned into years, yet our mother would never agree to a headstone. I always knew he was drowned, because I'd seen that in my head, felt the seawater in my own chest. I took to wearing his clothes, took to *being* him. Neighbours stared at me in the street, a kind of hope darting into their faces. But they passed on with nothing said. He'd made some shirts with Goldstein when he was starting out. Cotton poplin. They lasted me for years. And I had that photograph of him where he looked as if he'd already passed away, though he was only asleep.

They say life goes on, and it's true, but life is never the same. Nor should it be. I remember going to the seaside near Aldeburgh on the Suffolk coast years later. The kids were playing with coal that had washed up on the beach, a long dark fan left by the tide with cuttlefish and bladderwrack and a woman's red shoe. I remember wondering if the coal had come from steamships sunk in the war. Everything is changed by such events. They reached out to hurt the quietest lives. To families all over Europe, then to Asia and Africa. And all because of hate.

After Noel left and never came home and for all the rest of the time I lived in Crumpsall, I hated that cold little front parlour. Whenever I was in there with my mother, especially just before Christmas when the days were short and we were supposed to be celebrating, she'd become cast down and watchful. Listening for the door, harkening to footsteps in the street. I had the feeling, even years afterwards when I had a wife and kids of my own, that she expected me at any moment to sit down at the piano and play.

ANGIE

He's walking over frost-stiffened grass, his shadow ahead of him, long-legged, stretched by the falling sun. The grass makes the sound of crunching gristle and Steve's shadow wears a brimmed hat. When he climbs a stile he sees his hands turning into his father's hands. Because things change like that, from one state to another, from one condition to the next. He's still weak from the flu, his legs heavy, his chest tight with infection. He has a three-week beard and it blows against his face, tickling him. Angie likes it. She says it makes him look nautical. It reminds him of days without shaving or washing, clothes salted with sweat. Watching a path zigzag though the bush. Hearing macaws shriek into a clearing where a bamboo hut is rotting under stray rays of light. Feeling the dust of a mountain trail sift through his fingers into a scorching breeze, shadows deepening in gullies, sky burnished to a blue dome. He rubs the long bristles with his fingers. Tomorrow he'll buy some clippers.

Angie always marvelled at his patience. However late she was, he'd be there, smoking a cigarette, chewing a stalk of grass, lying full length at the beach or their rendezvous under that giant Spanish chestnut by the river. She could never surprise him. Though he'd surprised her that time, outside McEnery's, where they'd arranged to meet under the canopy after work. Arriving so quietly, placing his hands over her eyes, then letting them slide to her hips, feeling her sag against him. *It's OK,* he said, *it's only the Grim Reaper.* And she'd laughed, her body warm against him, her eyes squinting as if he was still in the far distance of her life. *You're quiet,* she said, admiring him, *like a big cat, like a tiger or something.* He took his hands back. *A puma,* he said, they're really quiet, *I saw one in New Mexico.* They turned to see themselves reflected in plate glass, superimposed on streetlights and passing cars. The tailor's naked mannequins seemed to beckon them to their world of ghosts. *They look like dancers,* Angie said, *dancers who've forgotten how to dance.* Then she'd pulled him away, linking arms.

When he steps from the stile to the crusted grass, it's soft with mud. He feels the tendons tighten behind his knees. Once he could run 10k without slackening, drop his pack, crouch, then put five rounds into the red at sixty paces. Now two Suffolk tups stare at him, their black ears hanging, their fleeces tight as barristers' wigs. Ahead of him, the land rises to a copse of sycamores. An abandoned rookery is falling from the branches, plundered by magpies and carrion crows. The track is faint, hardly trodden now. The red cattle have been taken into the shippen for the winter. His looks at his hands again, their close-trimmed nails, the split skin on his thumb, brown freckles over blue veins, wrinkles, swollen knuckles, dark hairs. His father had collapsed and died at a bus stop in the Black Country town where he'd been born, a carrier bag holding the weekly shop at each side of him.

The town was a nothing place by then. Boarded-up shops and shuttered takeaways. Empty pubs where you'd be hard put to it to find a fight on Friday nights. Factories and engineering works and potteries turned into mail-order warehouses or gyms. Or left to rot with To Let notices peeling in the rain. Years later, he'd been called home to find his mother in the old city hospital, dehydrated, feverish and rambling. She had sores on her legs from lying in wet sheets. She hadn't recognised Steve, her eyes glazed by fever. *Don't worry,* she kept saying, *don't look so worried*. This wasn't his mother. Whatever else, she'd always known who was who and what was what. Steve was white with anger when the doctors came, though he never raised his voice, watching the nurses put up a saline drip. He sat by her bed for three days, hardly moving, living on coffee and sandwiches from a vending machine.

That first time with Angie, he was wound tight with anticipation. She'd promised to meet him on the beach at dusk, making her way from the town centre by bus after work. He got there early and waited, hearing faint hurdy-gurdy music from the merry-go-round, seeing its smudged carousel of lights. The air was still warm. Steve sat on a rock surrounded by a ribbon of water, not far from where waves hissed and retreated towards the sunset. It burned like a drowning foundry or evaporating wine, staining sea and clouds. To wait like that was to live inside another kind of time, because something good was about to happen. That was something he'd never thought until now. Then she was greeting him with a half wave of her hand, swaying as she walked, her hair tied up into a bunch that fell down over her collar.

It had been a four-way conversation: him, Angie, herring gulls and the sea. A faint scent of fish and chips came from the town, its curving row of shops and cafés, the statue of Prince Albert stranded in a lost century. A bottle of Chardonnay was lodged against the rock in the pool. He pushed in the cork and the wine spurted over his fingers. He washed them in the sea and she'd laughed, gulping the wine so it ran down her chin onto her blouse. He kissed her, very gently, and she'd felt extraordinary. The scent and taste of her, the softness of skin and silk as scarf and hair got tangled in the kiss. He thought afterwards about what it was like. It was as if a new room had been built in his life and he'd entered it at last.

When Steve turns onto the farm track, workmen are busy at the converted barn that sits on a small mound across the way. With its long views it's like a small fort. When he was at school, they'd visited an iron-age stockade, standing on the ramparts, looking at lines of solifluction, imagining the minds of another people for whom war was total: women taken for breeding stock, men and boys put to the sword. The archaeologists had excavated burned fencing stakes, a midden full of the bones of children. For a while that's what he wanted to, be: an archaeologist, uncovering the past. Something had knocked that out of him. Steve looks to the hilltop again: at the new build there's a haze of arc lights, bright as a spray of powdered ice. The builders' vans are parked at an angle to each other, the concrete mixer churning a slurry of lime and stone, the same question and answer going round and round. A line of breezeblocks flushes pink as the low light of the sun finds it.

There is something about the lie of the land here that reminds him. The way the hills fold into each other. That stray phrase, with a fist at its heart: *hand in glove.* They'd been waiting for a courier, a *foreigner*, whatever that meant. What made sense then sounded like bullshit now. But that's all they knew or wanted to, kicking their heels for three days on a wedge of deserted farmland. It'd been a bit like this place. The empty farmhouse on a slight rise, its windows dusty and webbed with winter light. The outbuildings straggling away from the farm. Just him and Len, their second job together.

They'd walked in from the drop by night, hunkering down in one of the old milking sheds that looked out on the path. At dawn, light grew from behind a copse of bare trees. Moles had been busy and the fields were thistled over, bringing gangs of goldfinches for the seeds. They had a converted L42 with a scope and ten rounds in the magazine. *Untraceable*, the armourer said with a laugh, *a real bastard's bastard*, tearing up the chitty they'd signed. They carried it in a canvas case like a shotgun, as if they were after partridge or pheasants. They wore civvies. Their wallets held creased family photographs that could have been anybody, that must have been somebody. The families they'd probably never have. No radio. They spent that first day not talking, watching magpies come and go. Pissing in the corner, staying away from the windows, keeping all movement to a minimum. When the job was done they'd walk out to a pick-up point that was checked by a patrol every three hours. It was cold, bone-piercingly cold, even with gloves and caps and tweed jackets.

Steve crosses the path, stopping to wipe mud and sheep shit from his boots against the grass verge. He feels a little crunch in his knee. That's never going to get any better now. The air is fine and cold and he tries to draw it into his lungs, but they are still solid with infection. He coughs hard and deep, hawks phlegm over the fence. The sheep stare at him stoically. Texels with stupid faces and yellow eyes. A tractor starts in the farmyard behind him. There's a slurry pit with aluminium sides gleaming in the half-light. The tractor rolls forward, spikes a round bale of hay and reverses towards the track. The parents will move out from the farmhouse to the converted barn they don't need for hay or beasts anymore, leaving their son behind in the old house to find a wife.

That time in the swamplands, in the south, they'd waited in reed beds. It'd been a long day with mosquitos torturing them, black beetles scurrying at their boots. Their bodies and elytra had a green sheen, like home-cured bacon. They smelled cigarette smoke before they saw them: a father and two sons, pushing bicycles with packages strapped to the back, chatting as if they were bringing figs to the market. That'd been a mess. Automatic fire, the rounds chinging and sparking off the bicycle frames. When they turned over the bodies, one of them was a girl and still alive.

The moon is on the rise now, huge and yellow as it floats above the line of hills that still carry traces of snow. That's an illusion. His mind is making the moon bigger than it really is. It's simply the way a round object appears when close to a horizontal line. But when he stares at it, the hair on his nape tingles with something like fear. A primordial apprehension tugging at his guts.

That last tour he'd worked in the mountains near the Kurdish border. They'd found a cleft in ancient rock, a vantage point above a narrow track that the sun crept above early in the morning. There were almond groves below, walled fields with scattered goats and women bending over a green crop. The dust was like fine rust sifting through his hands, staining them. That had been a long wait and nothing to think about but a name. *Hassan*. No name was better. He'd thought about nothing else. Hassan the child, following his father around the smallholding. Hassan taking out vegetable scraps to the donkey. Hassan courting a dark-eyed woman who wore a blue hijab and lived in the next village, a cousin's cousin. Hassan asking her father to marry her, then the wedding, then making love together in the cool white-walled room of their house. Hassan teaching school children from the Koran, writing the lesson on a blackboard in Arabic script.

Steve had been dozing, dreaming of Angie, thinking of the girls, thinking this would be his last tour. Then, late in the afternoon, after three o'clock prayers had drifted up from the village, the mobile phone had vibrated in his pocket. Then a figure in white robes had appeared. A man kicking up a low veil of dust. Older than he'd looked in the photograph, walking with a slight limp, using a walking stick – the kind made from aluminium sections that screw together. Through the scope he'd looked kindly, a patriarch with deep eyes that seemed to rest upon things then move with care to the next. He was walking through Steve's breath, thick and slow in his chest.

They'd use a drone now. That was a different kind of watching, staying awake in front of a plasma screen, its pixels drifting like sand. He'd made his way out thinking of Angie in the draper's shop, her neat hands tying a ribbon or cashing up the till at the end of the day. He thought of the brown mole near her belly button that showed when she tied up her blouse on the beach. He was counting the days, trying not to. He'd flown home three weeks later and the girls had raced each other to meet him at the station. This time, he was coming back for good. When they got home, he burned his kit and dropped his service medals in the bin.

In the beginning, that first week, they met every night at the same place. He'd jump off the rock when he saw her coming down the beach, shoes in one hand, his feet splashing in rings of water. Angie seemed to hover or sway across the sand, footprints stretching behind her. She'd put her hand on his arm and say something. He'd lean in to kiss her cheek, the dimple on her chin, her hair always in the way. Then, on day three, she caught his face in her hands and given him a real kiss; a deep kiss that melted him, her tongue slow and hot. He felt the way her hips curved into her waist and it made him lose his breath. She was wearing lipstick, faint cologne, a silk scarf above a green cardigan, a thin skirt that blew against her legs. She took off her sandals and laughed and ran to the sea shouting for him to follow. Every night they'd planned so see a film, but they never made it to the cinema.

Steve takes the incline slowly, feeling his breath crinkle. There is a line of tree stumps where the farmer has taken down some rotten ash trees. He runs his finger over their growth rings. His father had a woodturning workshop in the garden where he made fruit bowls and candlestick holders from spelted elm and oak. He ended up giving most of them away. It wasn't about making money, but making things, making them as well as you could. Making them beautiful. His father loved to take them and pour in linseed oil, working it into the grain with his hands. You had to wear a mask as you turned the wood or you breathed in the fungus that caused the patterns in the wood. It could grow in your lungs, there in your own warmth and darkness and moisture. White bristles stood out on his father's face as he lay covered with a sheet in the morgue. He'd looked tiny then.

A flock of fieldfare thrums from the field to his left. They whirl in the sky, parting then joining as a single flock. When his mother had finally slipped away, the staff had fussed round him. Guilty, because he'd complained about her care a few days before. The Patient Charter was hooked over the bottom of the bed. More bullshit. Steve was used to crap like that. Saying one thing and doing another had been the way of things. His mother looked like a husk, her forehead shiny, her hands folded, the plain gold wedding ring embedded in her finger. He'd whispered to her, a reproach because she'd died. Then kissed her on the forehead where the skin was tight and cold.

Now he's walking to the house where Angie is waiting for him, watching the TV, wrapping Christmas presents. Lights are coming on in the village, in the scattered farms that resist the dark. He thinks of Christ, the mess of birth, of red cattle treading their own muck in the barns. He's walking home to her, the past turning in his head, drawing close then retreating like a tide. He always imagines it as dark blue, the past.

After two days of waiting, Len's jaw was dark with stubble. His grey eyes seemed to change colour as dawn light peeled from the windows and they sat up in their sleeping bags. Steve had a .38 tucked into his boot. If anyone came upon them, a bolt-action rifle wouldn't be much good. No light, no soap, no toothpaste. Nothing that could give them away. They shat at the back of the barn at night where the farmhouse hid them and buried it. And there was little to say in case their voices carried. Just the glances they exchanged, staring at farmland, imagining a man stepping into view. A man they almost knew because he was all they had to think about. They were *acting on information*, and that went round in their minds, too. But they never spoke ill of the dead; the *about-to-be-deceased*. The Enfield stood against the wall in its canvas case, its metal parts cold, smelling faintly of oil. They had no idea who the courier was or what he was carrying or how. *Two shots, ideally*, the lieutenant had said. He'd tapped his lapel and Len had almost smiled.

Steve was on leave the first time he met Angie, avoiding going home. He'd drifted to a B&B on the Devon coast,

144

wasting a few days. He wanted to get something for his mother and was staring at silk scarves. He must have looked conspicuous. Angie asked him if she could help, pushing back a strand of hair, turning her face up to him. Those grey eyes with wide pupils that seemed to lock onto his. He got confused and dropped the scarf and she laughed, showing little creases around the mouth. Neat teeth. Everything about her was neat, from her shoulder-length hair to her tight calves, to the straps on her black leather shoes. Except there was something unruly about her smile, as if it was escaping from somewhere else, as if things delighted her. He tried to check her fingers for a ring, but didn't want to stare as she wrapped the parcel in deft little movements, adding a ribbon, which she teased into a bow. She had a tiny black mole on one ear. *There, your girlfriend will love it,* she said. *Mother,* he said, *it's for my mother.* And he asked her for a date right there and then because she might have been fishing for that, because one thing you mightn't have was time.

Fuck this now, Steve. It was dawn on the fourth day and they began to pack the gear. They could be at the pick-up in an hour, making their way through the fields before anyone was about. It was a no show. Another dud. They crushed their sleeping bags into the rucksack. It was cold. Cobwebs whitened the windows and there was the old smell of cattle and dried dung. They hadn't left a trace except for piss stains and drag marks in the dust and faint hollows in the hay they'd bunked down on. They scuffed it up with their boots and stepped through the door.

They were tired and stiff, maybe a little careless. Len slung the rifle over his shoulder and was checking his watch. Almost 7.15. It was light outside. There were clumps of snowdrops and crocus beside the path. The days were lengthening again. Every morning they'd been woken by jackdaws squabbling. They hadn't seen a soul in three days. The first snowflakes were beginning to blow. Steve was blinking them away, stooping into his own smoking breath to pick up the rucksack when there was a flash of light from the copse three hundred yards away – that rotten pelt clinging to the horizon. He saw it from the corner of his eye, a stray flicker. Like someone lighting a cigarette. Like those stars that appear then disappear when you look at them. Then a wet thwack and the side of Len's neck spurted into red mist, the crack of the shot bouncing from the outbuildings, colliding with its own echo.

He'd asked her out, the way soldiers do, the way they take advantage of circumstance, because you never know. And she said, *Yes, OK, I'd like that.* She said, *Alright, but it's just a date, don't get any ideas.* And he'd laughed, *Me? Ideas?* But he'd known something in the shop, something he felt again when he jumped from the rock that night, feeling the seawater cold against his feet. When he'd put his arm around her and felt her hips, her waist, kissing her lightly on the cheek. *That's forward!* she said, but with a smile, laying her hand on his arm. Whatever has to happen between people had already happened. Maybe had happened back there in the shop as she wrapped the parcel for him and handed him his change in small coins.

They met every night for five nights and on the fifth night she took him home to the crooked little terraced house she rented and they made love. He'd woken with her snoring against the pillow and slipped his arms around her to feel her skin, almost unbearably soft, the roughness of his hands against its smooth flow. He got up and made coffee and scrambled eggs and called up the stairs and she came down in her nightie and cardigan. She held her coffee cup in both hands and smiled across to him through the steam, her eyes amazing him again. Then it was just a question of detail. He'd already decided to leave the army as soon as he could. That had taken longer than he'd hoped, like jumping from a moving train.

It's darker now and Steve loops back towards their house along a bridleway laced with frozen puddles that goes over the flank of another hill. The land fades into dusk, a legend of the failing light. Angie had lost half of the sight in one eye in a freak accident in the shop, walking into a dress hanger as she locked up with the lights turned off. There'd been some compensation and they'd bought this place, nearer to his work, further out from the town. He loved her with her scarred eye, just as he had before, maybe more. He'd got through his army service without a wound and then that. It just goes to show.

Except that it didn't. The round that had killed Len had been meant for Len, he knew that. Someone had been waiting for them all the time they were waiting for someone else. Maybe it was a set-up. It didn't matter. He'd had a choice when they appeared from the barn. Luck had nothing to do with it, good or bad. He'd seen two men and made a decision, aiming and squeezing off the round. A good shot. A professional. Steve caught Len as he lurched sideways and lowered him to the ground. Not a sound except breath bubbling through his windpipe. The round had blown out a big hole that welled with blood. It ran onto the faded grass, bright as life.

Two fields to go and he'll be home. Whenever he goes uphill his chest feels tight again. That's the flu. It doesn't want to let go of him. He's got a couple more years to go at work and then he can sack it all. He'd retire as district manager. He never saw anyone from the old firm. Some of them ended up in gaol, others turned to Jesus. He'd heard that. But what they'd done couldn't be revoked. They'd known the deepest, most secret thing. To have someone in your sights, in the caught moment of your breath and heartbeat, then to squeeze the trigger. That was a feeling you couldn't describe and it never left you. He could remember every kill. Len's throat spouting as the impact spun him to the ground. He'd walked calmly to the drop with the rifle slung, the pistol in his pocket, ready for anyone who got in his way. A cock pheasant had been calling as he watched for the patrol. Ops like that, you were never more alive, never more alone. Until the guys were pulling you into the APC. *Man down*, he'd said, jerking his thumb back to where Len lay with darkness filling him. *Man down*.

He could see the roof of the house now, the black tips of the birch trees he'd planted to shield their view but not block it. The kitchen light was on. Once, when Angie was pregnant with Tricia, their first child, she was sick into the kitchen sink. It was before the accident. She got up from

148

the breakfast table and he saw her trying to hold it back, then vomit was glistening on the back of her hand. *I'm sorry, I'm sorry*, she kept saying, but *he* wasn't sorry. He knew then, of all their moments together, that he couldn't stop loving her. He'd stuck it out at his office job for the security firm, went on courses, got promoted. They'd brought up the girls who'd left home now. They were like Angie, not him, thank God. Both had gone into language teaching – EFL and Spanish – and Alison was not long married. Tricia had a girlfriend, though she hadn't said as much. But none of that was a problem. There was plenty of time for all that. When you loved somebody it came out of the blue, out of the instant, and you just knew. He'd known it again that morning, watching sick spill from her mouth without embarrassment or shame. If he felt shame it was for something else. He'd wondered about tracing Len's family, but what was the point? What would he have told them? That they were waiting for someone? *How do you know you've got the right guy?* he asked the firearms instructor when he was training. *Because he's dead and you aren't.*

Once, two years ago, he'd slipped and knocked himself unconscious on their garden path, salting the ice. He'd been out cold for a couple of minutes until Angie got to him. *You silly sod, Steve,* she said when he came-to and told her he was OK, *you silly sod. Tell me you love me*, he said, and she had right then, kneeling on the snow. What had bothered him was the fact he could have died – could have been dead – and not known it. *Why would you want to know?* Angie said, as he sat in a chair, trying to join it all together. She was holding a cloth soaked in witch hazel to his head, one eye milky now, as if a snowflake had landed on it.

Steve clicks open the last gate and sees the house with its bright windows. Beyond it, the orange lights from the town cast an aura, closing off the stars. The huge moon has pulled clear of the hills to the east. In the west a planet is rising, its winking opal slung above the horizon. He takes off his hat and lets cool air to his scalp. Then he walks again until he's in the field above their back gate. There's a fallen log where a thorn tree has come down, cut into sections by the farmer but not taken away. He sits on one of those, where the land falls away to their house. Angie would be wrapping Christmas presents in the living room where he's put up the tree, or maybe talking to one of the girls on the phone. As he watches, she comes into the kitchen in her brown cardigan, backlit, filling the kettle and pulling the teapot from the shelf. He'd said he'd be half an hour, so she's making tea for them both. She stands with her back to the window. Eighty metres. No wind.

He wonders if all that waiting had been a kind of love. He'd told her that he worked in signals. He'd told her that there was a lot he couldn't tell her. And one morning, lying with his hand on her belly as their first child was filling her, he'd cried. For his parents, he said, all they never had. For the past that was lost, for the unspoken love he'd learned to speak with her. A love that should have been lost to him because he should have died unburied for what he was. He'd thought about nothing else for three days but that stranger coming through the fields. He'd have taken the rifle and wasted him, snow drifting down over his cooling body and draining thoughts. But Len was dead instead. All that was dark blue now.

Steve skirts the frozen puddle inside the garden gate. Jock, their new Jack Russell, pads across the lawn to greet him. Steve thinks of spores growing in the rich sponge of a man's lung, spreading upwards though the alveoli to the throat. The dog loses interest and pees in the laurel bush, one leg trembling. Steve coughs and the cough goes on, wrenching at his chest. When he pushes open the kitchen door the light is harsh, making him blink. Angie's been baking shortbread and its spicy, sweet smell fills the rooms. When he slings the heavy overcoat and takes off his hat, she's holding a cup of tea in one hand, the telephone in the other. *It's Alison,* she says, with that smile she still sometimes has, *she's got some news.*

BULRUSHES

There was a sycamore tree near the village with a rope swing hanging from a branch. Down the lane and over the burn, past fields overgrown with thistle and sorrel. You could climb into a fork of the tree where a little puddle of water gathered and then catch the noose with your foot to swing out. The bark was flaking away from the trunk and if you prised a bit off with your fingers there were tiny insects that ran for cover. Everything turned then as you swooped and span. The sky and its streaky clouds, fields with ponies grazing, the dark smudges of towns and villages blurring far out. The cooling towers tilted with the horizon and as the swing slowed down everything came back into focus and the fizzing and the fear stopped in your head. In autumn, sycamore seeds spiralled down, covering bare earth beaten by the feet of the village children. When you looked upwards into the canopy they swirled and fell like specks of snow. In deep winter the sycamore stood in the landscape, a tree made of iron, stark against the light bulb glow of the sky.

The earth had washed away from the roots and if you lay down and peered inside it was a secret place. You could imagine living there, sheltered from rain and snow, the tree roots making a room, only a chink of light from the outside world. Cosy and safe, a world where the scale of everything was changed and you could live under the earth, under the tree's protection. Annie had imagined that with Jodie, lying full length on the ground to peer into the roots, then turning to lean against the tree to watch men and tractors in the fields, far away like figures in a painting. Jodie got bored quickly and wanted to move on or find where the boys were playing.

Annie was an only child and her father was a butcher. His cutting bench was made of sycamore. Her mother couldn't work in the shop. The smell made her feel sick. But she did the accounts on the computer from the big oak desk at home. It had been her grandfather's desk and built to last. They'd started to supply mail-order venison and rare breed pork and prize-winning sausages. Annie's mother handled all that from the website. The meat was sent out vacuum packed in special polystyrene boxes. It had all been her idea, to diversify when the high street started to die and Oxfam and Age Concern crept in to recycle cast-offs and the clothes of dead people. Everything in those shops smelt faintly of old age. *There's a wee smell of wee,* Jodie would whisper and they'd laugh hysterically, taking to the street under the scowls of the lady volunteers who ran the shops. Annie's father worked with the meat suppliers and the customers who came to the shop. He stayed late to make up the orders, scrubbing the sycamore chopping block clean of blood and fat each night. The old black bicycle he'd made deliveries on as a boy had rusted in the backyard until he had it repainted and mounted above the window to show the family tradition. He gave Annie spending money when she helped him make sausage at the weekend, adding herbs and pepper into the mixing machine, watching the clear sausage skin stiffen with pink meat from the mincer.

The three white cooling towers on the horizon were fed by a conveyor belt from the pit. Annie's uncle Ned worked there as a foreman. Three clouds of steam turned to orange and apricot at sunset. The sun seemed to gurgle and drown at the edges of the world as the lights of the village came on. Her grandfather had told her that when the houses first got electricity, light bulbs were precious. His own mother had travelled thirty miles to the town to buy them. They'd been wrapped in newspaper and had been broken somehow in the bus on the way home. Some old gentleman pushing past, afraid to miss his stop. Or one of those broad-beamed country women anxious to relieve their aching feet had smashed them with her arse. That had meant waiting another week for market day. The next time she'd brought them home in egg boxes, specially cut with kitchen scissors to hold them safe. Annie's grandfather had told her that when the lights came on in the church on Sunday all the lights in the houses went down and glowed as sullen cherry-red filaments. She thought of that as God alighting.

Her grandfather had been a butcher, too. Their shop stood in the main street of the town with a low slate roof and a hand-painted sign showing a jolly fat man in a white apron, festooned in sausages. *McClavertys'*. That apostrophe bothered her for years, all the way through secondary school. Then she came to like it. It seemed right for it to be there in the wrong place, like so many things. Her grandfather had been a hard man her mother said, hard on her father and his brothers who'd all gone away as soon as they could.

At the top of their three-storey house was the attic. In the long room – all bare bulbs and floorboards and peeling wallpaper – was a cupboard with folding doors that took up the narrowest wall. The doors got stuck if you wrenched them too hard because the runners were shot. There was a thick grey skylight, the glass covered in pigeon lime. If you peeled the wallpaper away crystals of white appeared behind where the salt was leaching from the plaster. In the cupboard was an old trunk full of scraps of animal fur. The fur was red like fox fur, or dark brown with pale stripes. There was dried skin on the back, real skin from when the animal had been alive. Annie didn't know where they'd come from, though perhaps her grandmother or great grandmother had used them to trim clothing. If you climbed into the cupboard and slid the doors shut, you could hear big birds pattering on the roof. The fur was soft against your cheek. It smelt faintly of perfume, of the forest where a woman was being drawn through the snow on a sledge, cracking her whip over a team of dogs that strained in their harnesses. Behind her in the forest the eyes of wolves glared yellow between tree trunks. Their tongues glowed like molten lava as darkness fell and stars sprinkled the sky. If you clenched your fingers hard, you could feel the woman's heart there, afraid, beating like a fisted bird.

After school Annie's mum used to picked her up from the playground, waiting with the other mothers with their prams and pushchairs, sharing the latest gossip or inventing it. Sometimes Annie was the last to leave the school, lingering over her painting, which had not quite dried, volunteering to tidy away the toys in the nursery classroom. Once she worked for Miss Sanderson, using a blob of Blu-Tack to get all the stray bits of Blu-Tack from the wall where things had been stuck. You had to press hard with your fingers and roll a fresh ball over the old stuff until it gradually came away. Copydex smelt like hot rubber and you could wipe that away with a damp cloth until everything was clean. She liked the smell of paper glue too, though someone had told her it was made from old horses, rendered down. Her mother had been cross that time, because she'd waited ages and Annie hadn't appeared until Mr Carstairs was locking up the school. Couldn't Annie understand how worried she was? Annie thought about that, about the kind of worry it might be. After all, she was safe in school, helping the teacher.

In summer you could hide in the long grass in the field, or in the patch of fennel that had been slung out of the gardens and gone wild. The stems had a minty smell and the dry seeds tasted wild and hot. In winter, Annie and Jodie roamed the lanes with torches, pressing themselves into the hawthorn hedges and signalling to each other by flashing the beam. When there was a fog or heavy mist it was like a horror story. The streetlamps shone with yellow haloes and vampires could emerge from alleyways and from around street corners to pierce your neck with their fangs and suck your blood and carry you off to be undead. Sometime they played at being zombies, stumbling forward with their eyes half closed and their hands held out, sleepwalking. Fear made your laughter spurt and bubble out.

In winter, flights of geese went over the low hills to the estuary where water gleamed and froze. They flew in a wide vee, sometimes in double formation, finding their way behind their leader. She'd seen in a nature programme on television about how the geese took turns at being leader, then dropped back. Her father had a special metal cabinet in the house where he kept a gun locked away. It had a long black barrel and a polished walnut stock and there were boxes of red cartridges with brass ends. Annie wasn't allowed to touch the gun and the key to the cabinet was on the bunch of keys chained to his belt. Sometimes he went with other men from the village in his waxed jacket and Wellingtons and cap to shoot rabbits that infested the meadows leading down to the river. She'd seen him pulling the skin from a dead one, the pink flesh appearing like melted pink plastic. Like when they'd burnt her old dolls because she was getting to be a big girl. Sometimes a policeman came to look at the cabinet and make sure it was safe and he and Annie's father stood chatting in the front room. They'd done that one time when the Christmas decorations were up and the tinsel had almost touched the policeman's hat with its silver badge and chequered band. Annie had giggled at that, covering her mouth up with her hand. At Christmas time, her father sold turkeys and geese and the shop window was filled with their pale plump breasts and thighs. There was a row of coloured lights that blinked on and off and her father moved in tangled reflections and shadows in his blue striped apron.

The railway ran close to the village. There was a crossing with a white signal box and an iron bridge where the railway lines went over the canal. On each side of the bridge a rampart of stone swept up to the metalwork in a long curve that held the banking on either side. You could walk up the slabs. At the top was a ledge that led into a space between the ironwork and the stone uprights. When you squeezed through you were in an iron box, hidden from view, the black ribbon of the canal spooling below. If you stayed there long enough a train would come by and the noise of iron wheels on iron tracks in an iron box was amazing. It shut out everything else until the surface of the water shuddered and the sound grated through to the roots of your teeth. The stones was cold against your bottom and legs and you had to be careful not to get tar on your clothes from the little stones that had dropped there. They called the bridge *the iron clanger* and it had a little chamber at each of its four corners. Annie had her favourite one just above the words *Ken loves Pat?* that someone had sprayed onto the stone with silver paint. She wondered about the question mark.

When her father got home from work he was careful to wash his hands at the kitchen sink. They were cold looking, red-skinned with blond hairs that grew up his arms and ticked your face and legs. He'd take off his wristwatch and soap them first, locking his fingers into each other, massaging his thumbs, wringing soap into his skin. Then he'd rinse them and dry them on the towel that hung over a radiator. It reminded Annie of the surgeons she'd seen on TV. He was washing away a good day's work, he said, but she saw threads and clots of blood flushing into the drain then down to the backyard grid where moss grew between the stones. Sometimes he brought home liver or slices of belly pork for their tea. At weekends it might be a joint of brisket or a corner of ham. A butcher could afford to eat well, if nothing else. Whenever she opened the fridge to get some orange juice or find the

eggs for her mother's baking, there was usually a piece of
meat lying on a special willow pattern plate. It was weird
to think that the red muscle lying there had once been
warm and alive. Cattle had wet, slobbery black noses and
pigs had white eyelashes. Lambs were really cute and clean
until they reached a certain age when they became just as
stupid and shitty and forgetful as their mothers.

Annie liked the bathroom where you could shoot the
long bolt on the door and run a deep soak in the cast-iron
tub. God knows how much water it used, but her Mum
and Dad never minded that. She loved to lie there, feeling
herself buoyant, floating away in the steam that rose to the
ceiling and formed little droplets. She remembered the
shouts in the swimming pool in the town, the sting of
chlorine, the way voices were shut out when you dived
and felt the pressure in your nose and ears, everything
bleary as the tiles wavered. The bath water was heated by
a big gas boiler that grumbled away in the basement. It
was like having an imp down there, making things work,
knowing everything. There was a blue glow from the pilot
light, deep shadows you could steal away to and the smell
of old cardboard. In the bath her knees were rough from
playing out and the skin on her thighs was mottled red
from standing too close to the coal fire in the lounge. She
loved the roughness of the big bath towel before her mum
started nagging at the door to use the toilet, telling her to
get on with it in the voice that came down her nose when
she was cross. Then it was pyjamas, toothbrush and
toothpaste; then her mum putting her hair into pigtails,
her dad reading her a bedtime story, his feet coming up
the creaking stairs like falling weights. Annie imagined him

as dense matter, a collapsing star, a black hole treading the timbers towards her, sucking in all the shadows of the house.

Down below the village in the river meadows they were building new bungalows. *A terrible eyesore* her mother called them, with that tight little sniff. *Bloody numpties*, her father said for building where the river would flood them, *not got God's sense they were born with*. Down there the diggers were parked at night when the workmen went home, carrying their hard hats. There was a stack of pipes that would line the new drains. They were so big that Jodie and Annie could crawl into them and sit sideways so their spines curled against the circle of cement, their knees almost touching their noses. Once Annie went down there on her own and crawled into one of the pipes and lay there in her duffle coat hearing her mother shouting her to come in for her tea. She waited a long time, then went home in the failing light, just so no one would worry. What she'd really wanted to do was go to sleep there inside that tight circle, inside the sycamore roots, shrinking herself down to something tiny and invisible. Once she caught a frog in the composter in the garden and held it in her hand so that its flat head and its bulging eyes stuck out. She wondered if it felt safe or felt frightened. When she put it down under the laurel bush it was too stunned to move, its legs hunched under itself, its throat panting. The frog was cold and her hand had been warm. It was strange to imagine its chilled blood, its cold heart pumping, its reptilian soul of ice.

At the end of that summer, in September, she'd be starting at the High School in town. That meant getting the bus each morning with Jodie and the older village kids. It meant braving the bullies who climbed on from the farms and villages on the way. Her mother was small with an upturned nose and springy brown hair that was going grey. *Stay away frae them and they'll leave ye be,* her mother said, as if she didn't believe Annie about the name-calling and sly punches. *Gie as good as ye get,* her father said, *gie 'em a smart crack.* But somehow Annie didn't think *he* ever could. Even her mother said he was soft-hearted and weak when it came down to it. *Talking the talk but nae walking the walk.*

That year they went on holiday near Anstruther, eating fish and chips on the beach, paddling in freezing seawater, watching the sun go down behind the harbour, her father's arm around her, her mother's eyes a bright slate blue in the falling light. They'd rented a fisherman's cottage in Cellardyke with crooked sash windows. Annie had imagined that lost way of life: fishing boats putting to sea or riding out the storms, the fishermen mending creels and nets on the cobblestones, their wives gutting the dead-eyed fish. In the evenings her father went for a pint in The Haven and she watched television with her mum or sat on the harbour wall watching the gulls rake over the sea until it went dark. At the night the floorboards creaked in a deep rhythm, like the movement of the sea, and she thought she could hear voices whispering through the hiss of waves.

Jodie's dad had come to the door once, the day after her dad had taken them to the pictures for Annie's tenth birthday and her mother had stayed at home to decorate the cake. They'd watched the film in the dark cinema that smelled of bubble gum. She couldn't remember what it was, the film, something weird. Something unsuitable. And something had happened though she never found out what it was. Jodie had started crying, then gone quiet on the way home in the van. *Naw, naw,* her father had said and his voice sounded like he was pleading with Jodie's dad who was a wiry wee bastard. *No like that Jamie, ye ken full well it wasnae like that.* After that, he sent Annie round with some meat for Jodie's mum – *That mingin' wee bitch.* Something *ay special,* a piece of topside with blood staining the paper, making it sticky. She'd stopped to smell the meat and it'd smelt like her dad's hands smelled after work.

Jodie's family were left-footers and there always seemed to be a new baby to look after and the house smelled of milk. Jodie's mum had a nose ring and worked part-time at the newsagent selling *The Scotsman* and lottery tickets and cans of lager. Her dad didn't do much. *Nae work,* Jodie said, shrugging. She became a mother at seventeen, like her own mother. *Nae bother.* Annie saw her once after leaving school, but she'd already gone her own way.

Once Annie was at the High School, she did her own pigtails and started her periods and there were no more stories and the stairs were silent as she lay in bed reading or listening to her radio, or finishing homework. Strange, how that silence seemed louder than the creak of timber under shoe leather and her father's bulk. She began to think of life after school, of life beyond the village, of a life that was her own and not everyone else's.

Down in the little bit of swampland beyond the sycamore there was a pathway you could find if you were careful. It was made of barrel lids laid on the marsh. James

Gowan had showed her. You had to step carefully, feeling for the timber with your feet, balancing as the marsh gave up an eggy smell of decay. The pathway led to a little island overgrown with willow trees. A wild place where no one went, where you couldn't be seen. In spring the hazels and willows were covered in yellow catkins and pussy willow. In late summer, there were bulrushes. You could brush your face against their brown velvet cylinders. They seemed a kind of perfection, symmetrically formed, perfect in their way, unspoilt. They reminded her of the story of Moses, the abandoned baby rescued by the pharaoh's daughter and restored to his mother.

That was a story about destiny. Destiny was a thing to dream about. Sometimes Annie went to the marsh and sat for hours, watching dragonflies and damsel flies flicker over orange water that let out bubbles of gas. There were sticklebacks and newts and tadpoles in spring. Mr Nidrie, their biology teacher, told them about the damsel flies, how they mated on the wing. He'd give a small smile at his own daring, pulling at his tie, blushing a little. He had short dark hair and dimples and some of the girls had a crush on him. *Damsels in distress.* She'd seen the gas-flame-blue insects stuck together, still hovering, coordinating their wing beats in a blur of passion. He told them about the mayfly, how it lived for one short summer's day; how in that day it had to find all the happiness and freedom that life could offer it as light faded and air turned cold and dusk came and the end of everything came.

Mr Monroli lived in the top end of the village, up the long hill where the houses were detached and looked down to the church and along to the open countryside.

He had dark eyebrows that joined in the middle and a huge St Bernard dog with white fur and a crooked brown stripe on its head. Mr Monroli's dog was called Mortimer and he'd let them ride on its back when they were children. He drove the fruit and veg van that called in at all the villages and towns that lay at the foot of that line of hills. Somehow he'd come into money. *Not by graftin' for it like the rest of us*, her father said. Her dad wanted a bigger house with a wide garden and gravel drive to park a car on and that's why he worked so hard in the butcher's shop.

Once she'd seen the dog chained outside her father's shop and her father and Mr Monroli chatting inside, behind rain clouds caught in the window glass. Mortimer peed up against the drainpipe and then his thing came out like a red dagger and he'd walked towards her until the leash dragged him back. Her father had seen all that and said something to Mr Monroli and they laughed, her father jerking his head in a certain way. She'd carried on walking to Jodie's, but she wished he hadn't laughed. She wished she hadn't seen the dog, its dark blank eyes under the dense bone of its brow. It made her flush for all the times she'd stroked it and climbed onto its back, feeling its fur silky and hot. She thought of her father feeding it scraps of liver and laughing.

Sometimes, when she helped her father on Saturdays, she climbed inside the big fridge in the back room of the shop and almost – but never quite – closed the door so that the electric light went out and there was just a crack of daylight. The chill began to enter her as she stood with the gutted carcases of pigs and lambs hanging next to her.

You could see where their spinal cords had been, where their skulls had been split, their eyes and brains taken out. Once her father had caught her in there and he'd been upset and explained to her very quietly how dangerous it was. He'd hugged her and told her how if the door ever clicked shut on her and he didn't know where she was, she'd never be able to get out. That eventually she'd suffocate from lack of air or freeze to death. Annie knew that, had always known it. And so she did do it again, feeling the big rubber seal of the door almost touch, the heavy chrome catch click against its sneck, the light extinguishing, the cold from dead animals chilling her.

Years later, following a memory to its source, she did it after her father had a stroke and couldn't work any more and the shop was being emptied to be converted into an estate agent's office. She'd been called home from university because he'd started to mix up his words, and then collapsed. *Went down like an ox,* her mother said. By the time he left hospital, he couldn't walk or talk, but sat in a special chair with furious blue eyes and curled fingers. He lost two stone in weight and his hands felt like the dried skin on the back of the fur she'd played with as a child. Annie found the scraps as she wandered the house, still stuffed into the metal trunk in the attic, asking her mother the old questions and getting the same vague, impatient answers. She stepped into the fridge in the tiled back room of the shop, one last time. The electricity was disconnected and warm instead of cold, smelling of old blood from the sheep and pigs and cattle that had hung there on steel hooks. Annie felt that lovely touch of darkness as the chink of light narrowed and the metal catch touched and clicked and swung ajar again. She pushed it open with both hands, walking free. She'd taken a year off from her studies to help her mum get things straight. It should have been her study abroad year, teaching at a primary school in Barcelona. But it could wait. She wondered what had happened to Jodie in the years that had swirled between them.

The day after they buried her father, Annie went on a walk that passed through all her childhood places, a stream of moment and memory. She thought of her father, his tread on the stairs, the dark mass of him touching her as he settled on the bed to read to her. Thank God he hadn't lasted. She thought of the boiler there in the basement, its light like the thwarted blue in her father's eyes.

On that thin November day she found the shrunken fragments of childhood that had stayed in her dreams. The frayed noose of rope; the tangled roots of the sycamore; the built bungalows, their red brick still livid; the iron bridge with its fading graffiti; the water of the canal shivering under the heft of a train, brightly lit and heading away to the cities that burned up the night to horizons where hours would harden into years. She thought about what had happened, what hadn't, about what she'd imagined and hoped. The hazel bushes and alders and willow trees were bare in the little swamp and a cold wind was starting from the east. A few flakes of snow had come down onto the turned earth of the kirkyard, but had ceased upon the final prayer. There was a thin skim of ice between the reeds and a stand of bulrushes still erect, their cylinders of brown velvet firm and smooth and exact.

She thought of a child in Egypt hidden in a fisherman's creel. She thought about destiny. When she breathed, moisture puffed and faded, her body heat dissipating. She was seeing a boy who was studying medicine, in his third year now. *Gavin*. He had cold hands so that she laughed and flinched and squirmed away when they made love. Annie said she pitied his patients, remembering her father's hands under the kitchen tap. Sometimes she had to shut that out, feeling him yelp and come in a little splutter of breath, then withdrawing gently, bending his head to kiss her belly button.

Annie wondered where he was now. Maybe thinking about her. Maybe not. She'd think about him on the train tomorrow, all the way to the city. He'd be a doctor one day, saving lives; she'd teach children to speak in foreign tongues, reshaping the world through the mouth's small sounds. She let go of the velvety heads. They rustled against dried reeds, swayed to a standstill. In the summer there'd be maiden flies and dragonflies and damsel flies; the rusty water would teem with sticklebacks and tadpoles and newts. Even if the rest of the world was annihilated, life could start again here, evolving over a million, million years. Maybe human beings or something close to them would emerge again to touch each other, to make love and language, to name everything again. Ice splintered underfoot as she shivered and turned to leave, brushing dried willow leaves from the branches. A stiff easterly deadened her cheeks as she walked towards tomorrow, towards home where her mother was sorting through her father's things. Three white cooling towers stood at the horizon, extinct.

JENNY BROWN'S POINT

Col settled his hands on the wheel. They were red from hot water. One wing mirror was broken and the black electrical tape he'd used to mend it fluttered from the shattered glass. The windscreen wipers were smearing spray from a lorry. He switched on the radio. There was a local station up here now. *96.9 FM.* A woman's voice sang it to a corny tune. Jason was strapped into the child seat behind. Col had access every other weekend, but this morning Janine had been a real cow about it. *You've got to make your mind up, Col. We can't plan anything like this.*

Like what? He'd missed a couple of weekends because of work, so things had got a bit out of sync. She'd had another kid – Kaylie – after he left, after shacking up with Simon who'd moved into the house. Simon who still had acne and did fuck-all in the scheme of things. They were supposed to be going to a kids' party together, Jason and Kaylie who was three now. Janine said it wasn't fair, expecting Jason to give that up. Col almost told her to fuck off but he bit his tongue because she'd be on the phone to her solicitor slagging him off if he didn't behave.

So he'd spoken to her quietly and she'd asked Jason and, yes, he wanted to go with his dad. Simon kept out of the way. Just as well. He needed chinning, the soft twat. They'd painted the front door dark blue since last time. You could see the brush marks, like a kid had done it. The kitchen was just as he'd left it when he moved out. Everything fitted tight as a glove, scribed, mitred and joined to perfection, the beech wood surfaces oiled to a deep sheen. He didn't begrudge Janine that; it was a bit of himself, a reminder.

They set off with rain hitting the windscreen. Kaylie cried on the doorstep as Col pulled away. All well and good, except it was November and grim as hell. Saturday, so the traffic in town wasn't bad. Twenty minutes to the motorway. He had the radio on and kept turning round on the M6 to see if Jason was OK. Thumbs up. The music was cool, old soul hits. He'd played bass in a band for a bit when he was a teenager, but they'd never done anything. A few village hall gigs with silly haircuts. But that's why Janine had looked across at him in English. She had shiny brown hair that she hadn't dyed blonde. Her eyes were grey, green, brown. He'd never figured it out. She wasn't tarty like the other girls. She wore flat-heeled shoes. Sensible. There was something calm and sure about her. Even his mum liked her.

They'd done this trip when he was a kid in their old Fiesta. Col, his mum and dad, his sister Becky. Following behind, his dad's brother Pete and auntie Edith. They had no kids themselves. They had a blue Datsun estate with loads of room in it, so Col and Becky got to ride in the back. Sometimes it was Southport or Blackpool, but they'd settled on Morecambe as he and Becky got older. They'd tried the east coast once, but that had been a nightmare. *Bloody Siberia in swimming trunks*. His dad and Pete worked together at the Post Office. They spent most of that week in the pub, coming back half-pissed for their tea at the self-catering place they'd hired, farting and laughing like teenagers. His granddad had been a postman, too.

Back then they never had much money, but they had jobs and people stayed together. Stayed together and fought. There in the tight terraced streets, shouting over the noise of the TV, over the screams of the baby, and no way out. For Col's parents marriage meant just trying to out-manoeuvre each other. Like that game: paper, stone, scissors. A form of attrition. A woman in Col's street had drowned herself in the reservoir one New Year's Eve. He remembered her husband's blotchy eyes, the hearse coming down the street, stretching their faces in its shiny coachwork. He thought of the dark hole they'd bury her in. Col wanted more than that. He wanted life, he wanted whatever love was, whatever it meant.

Col pulled in at Forton services to get a bottle of water and some ciggies. He'd just about got enough petrol. He bought a bottle of pop for Jason, a comic and some crisps. Jason looked as pleased as punch. He was good like that. A great kid. It didn't take much. He looked cute in his blue puffer jacket and trainers that lit up with red LEDs when he stamped his feet. Col was working shifts in a hotel restaurant as a kitchen porter, which wasn't ideal. He'd trained as a joiner. What he loved was building things. Fitting roofing timbers, architraves, skirting boards so they mitred snugly. He'd been taught to write on wood and gave a poem to Janine written on a length of tongue and groove. She thought it was cute. He'd fitted out the bathroom and kitchen when he and Janine moved into the end terrace.

All that had gone tits-up in the recession. The building trade fell on its arse and he'd been laid off. He'd got a shit job now and most of the wages went into rent and heating. He got housing benefit, but he wasn't going on the social. He'd still got his carpentry tools. His chisels and power drills and handsaws, the router and folding bench. He knew other blokes who trained with him who'd sold theirs. You were fucked once you did that. You went under and stayed there. He'd seen older guys sitting in the pub over halves of lager staring at the racing on TV. Not him. Fuck that. He got the odd carpentry job, moonlighting between shifts with a cash advance for materials. The rest of the money went on Jason.

He'd got Janine pregnant when she was seventeen and she was still at school. He was an apprentice and she was in the sixth form, thinking about Uni. He thought he'd loved her. Told her he loved her when they'd bunked off school and college to sneak back into her house, taking off her clothes, breathless in her bedroom with her Pop Idol posters and CDs everywhere. The teddy-bear pyjamas he found so sexy, making her put them on so he could take them off again, putting his tongue against her small breasts, wetting them, feeling her through the thin cotton of her pants. His mum had gone mad when she found out. They got married and never stopped arguing after that. All through her pregnancy, then when Jason was waking them up all night to feed. Things had got better for a bit, when he settled down, but then they'd slipped back into it again, struggling to make ends meet, blaming each other for things. Scissors and paper. Paper and stone. Whatever. Then the firm let him go and that was the beginning of the end.

Col changed down and pulled out into a pall of spray to overtake a lorry. He jinked in again, spotting the university

171

campus on the left. That meant he'd missed the first turning, hadn't been concentrating. The old mental hospital with its blackened stone came into view. Col had a map on the front seat beside him. Jason was spilling the crisps all over the car. It'd hoover. Sod it. Never mind Morecambe, he'd go a bit further, head for Carnforth, then Arnside. He hadn't been there for years. Not since he was eleven when the family had decided to go somewhere a bit quieter. His mum was bad with her nerves by then. Even Morecambe's West End had been too much for her. *You'd think it was friggin' Beirut.* His dad put on a long-suffering face, winking at him, shrugging on his jacket for a pint.

They were in Arnside by lunchtime and parked up at the seafront. It wasn't seaside exactly, but a wide sandy estuary with the River Kent running through it, widening towards the sea. The wooded hills came right down to the shore and there were big old houses hidden in the trees, a long railway bridge crossing the estuary on brick columns. The sky was prolapsed, sagging onto the horizon. Col reached back to unclip Jason's safety harness. He picked up his mobile phone and slipped it into his pocket. A light drizzle spattered their faces and streaked the baker's window. A row of gulls sat hunched on iron railings. A goods train went over the viaduct and Col held Jason up to see.

– See the train, Jason?

Jason didn't answer but burrowed into Col's shoulder.

– Raining, Daddy.

He seemed to find that funny, putting his thumb into his mouth and making a mock sour face. Col laughed. He loved it when he did that.

– Come on then, lunchtime!

Col put Jason down and reached into the car for his jacket.

– Are you hungry?

Jason nodded. He needed a pee first, so they walked to the conveniences, then wandered about a little until they found a café that sold postcards and souvenirs.

The café was called *The Posh Pilchard*. They had sandwiches with bits of salad that Jason pushed to the edge of the plate. The woman running the café had dangly earrings and a plaster cast on her wrist and moved carefully between the tables, making a smiley face at Jason whenever she passed. She must have been a looker when she was younger. Her husband – white slacks and a hand-knitted pullover – hovered in the background, helping out. It didn't look as if he'd ever cut bread before or sliced a tomato. It was expensive, but it was nice. They could have gone to the chip shop and sat in the car with the windows steaming up, but this was better and Janine couldn't say he'd stuffed Jason's face with rubbish. You'd think she was a fucking dietician sometimes.

Col poured out the last of the tea and finished Jason's crusts. The tide tables were posted on a chalkboard. There was a tidal bore at 4.17, when the incoming sea met the river. Col checked his watch, but the face had misted up. It was stuck at 11.45. He'd had it for years. It was probably knackered or maybe the battery had died.

The rain had eased off when they left the café. Gulls were stooping over the beach, quarrelling, calling out raucously. You could smell the chip shop. Last time they'd been here the whole family had walked along the beach towards the sea. His uncle Pete had taken his shoes off and gone into the water. He'd stepped on a flounder and pulled it out of the river casually, as if he did that every day. It was a miracle, the flat fish flopping about in his hands like a fumbled catch in the outfield. Now the water flowed brown and steady. There were a couple of fishermen huddled under umbrellas, a tall woman calling to two red setters that were running free, scuffing the sand beside the waterline. She had a blue plastic bag pulled over one hand. There was a line of cars with people inside, eating fish and chips, unwrapping sandwiches, balancing thermos flasks, listening to their radios. *96.9 FM.*

It was half-past two according to the clock on the old town hall. Col decided to drive round the headland and find a quiet spot near the nature reserve. Jenny Brown's Point. They'd camped out there once on one of those family holidays. There'd been an old barn with tractors and a cowshed where a herd of Jersey cattle trooped in each evening, their udders swaying. Col remembered the way milk and shit had mixed together on the concrete floor and he and Becky had got a massive telling off from their mum for flicking it at each other with sticks. She'd made them take a cold shower at the campsite and smacked their legs. It was bad enough washing clothes at home she said, without them making work on holiday. She wasn't a bloody skivvy. But she was. She had to be. His dad grinned at them, on his way out for a walk to the village, which meant a pint at the local.

Col drove to Silverdale and then got lost on a wooded lane that wound out of the village. Then there was an old-fashioned sign pointing to the right. *Jenny Brown's Point.* Soft rain tapped against the windscreen. The wipers were on intermittent, which Jason always found funny. The way they suddenly set off across the glass to smear it. He was giggling in the back and pointing. The road dipped and turned under overhanging trees until they were entering the village. A studio and café on the right, an old tower with windows that looked Elizabethan or something, then a left turn down a road through a farmyard with a blue plastic feed tub turned over as a kennel for the chained collie. *No Through Road*. It ended at the sea, or above it. The collie barked at them in the wing mirrors, tugging at its leash. They drove for almost a mile then Col found a layby and pulled in. The rain had stopped. Through the trees they could see the sands gleaming, seamed by gullies. There were seagulls feeding at the shore and some darker birds far out. The sky was huge. To the south were the square blocks of Heysham power station. They looked like a Lego house. Then skeins of mist blew in to blank them out.

Now they were squeezing past a stone stile onto a path that went through bracken until it reached a broken outcrop of limestone above the beach. A long groin made up of rocks and smaller stones tapered out over the sand. The green timbers of a jetty were rotting away. Black seaweed wrapped over white stones. A gulley ran parallel to the shore, almost empty of water. A thorn tree had been bent back towards the land by the sea wind. Col picked Jason up and splashed through the gully, feeling the sand firm underfoot. Mud and sand glinted, bright and flat and level. It reminded him of sharpening a hand-plane and looking down the blade.

Usually you could see the hills of the Lake District. Not today. A grey pall hung over Grange-over-Sands. He'd been there too. There'd been an arcade with charity shops and a line of mannequins dressed in tartan kilts and berets. His dad turned to them and laughed. *Bloody hell, the gathering of the clans. That's posh. You won't find that in Preston.* Then he got told off for swearing by Col's mum and winked at them when she wasn't looking. Col reached a stream and had to step over swinging Jason across.

– Where's the sea, Daddy?

He hadn't been paying attention. Jason was pulling at his hand.

– It's there, look!

Col pointed to where the sand and sky seemed to meet. Jason giggled. He had a front tooth missing and covered his mouth to hide it.

– Not there!

He looked suddenly stricken.

– It's not anywhere!

– Don't fret. We'll find it.

Col stooped to ruffle his hair.

– Was it a nice lunch with Daddy?

Jason nodded.

– Posh Pilchard!

He liked pilchards mashed up in tomato sauce.

– Will you tell Mummy?

Jason nodded again, suddenly looking serious, as if he was remembering the tension, the words that arced and sparked between them.

– Good lad!

This would be a good memory. They deserved that. Memories meant a lot. They meant everything in the end. Col hugged him and held him tight for a moment.

– Where's the sea?

Jason seemed doubtful that such a thing had ever existed.

– It's there, look!

The sea. It was a long way out, flat at the horizon. Behind them was Warton Crag with its limestone face. Somewhere behind that was Arnside Knott. They saw a deer there once, on that holiday. A small red deer with short antlers, running stiffly from the trees. Col took Jason's hand and they headed onto the sands ahead of them: ribbed river mud, brown water, the claw prints of scavengers.

When they were kids the sea here had always been a disappointment. Other kids had gone to Majorca or Tenerife where you could swim and lounge about in beachwear. Col hadn't stayed in a resort hotel before he went on honeymoon with Janine. They'd flown to the Costa Brava and Janine had got so badly burnt that she had to stay in her room for two days rubbing cream on her shoulders. She'd done some Spanish at school but was too frightened to use it. The waiters all spoke English, though they weren't used to being waited on. There was a tall one called José who'd worked in Bristol and leered at Janine when he thought Col wasn't watching. Back home he'd have fucking decked him. Janine had morning sickness, too, regular as clockwork. So it hadn't been much fun, holding her head over the toilet bowl, worrying what it was all costing.

They paused as Jason investigated a mussel shell then a dead crab with the toe of his trainer. Then set off again, hand in hand. There was no one else in sight. No fishermen. No dog walkers. Col looked back to where the trees were turning silvery leaves. An elderly couple in blue waterproofs were watching them. The man was waving at something. Silly twat. There was a steady breeze coming off the sea, the sting of salt in it. The silt was damp and firm underfoot. Jason bent down to pick up a handful. He examined it then smeared his hand on his jacket. Col wiped it clean.

– Your mum'll be cross.

Jason went solemn again.

– No she won't, it's OK, only kidding. Come on!

Rain began to darken the sand and Jason looked up, afraid that he'd miss the sea, that they'd have to turn back. He pulled away from Col's hand, ran ahead then screamed. He was sunk in up to his waist, his face gap-toothed, white with terror. For a few seconds he looked almost comical. Col's stomach lurched. He ran forward, his own feet suddenly dragged by suction. He grabbed the collar of Jason's puffer jacket and pulled him free with one jerk, then ran backwards onto firmer sand, almost stumbling. Jason was blubbering now and Col bent to wipe snot and tears from his face, his heart hammering. It had all been so quick. One minute he was laughing like any other kid, the next he could have drowned. Jesus. Jenny Brown's Point. It was lethal. How could he have forgotten that? People drowning trying to save their dogs. Others just losing their way in the mist. Those obituaries in the *Gazette*.

When Col stood up again he couldn't see Warton Crag or the limestone at the shoreline. The houses and trees on the far side of the estuary had disappeared into a wad of mist. He backed away slowly from the quicksand, picking Jason up and holding him tight.

– Want to go home!

– I know sweetheart, I know.

Col kissed him and pinched him on the cheek. Janine was going to have a field day with all this. He put Jason down and pushed his jacket cuff back out of habit. Jason was stamping his feet but his trainers were caked in sand and mud and they weren't lighting up any more. Fuck! He'd forgotten his watch was broken. He reached into his jacket pocket for his mobile phone. It wasn't there. He checked all his pockets. Lighter, cigarettes, keys, a damp tissue. You couldn't lose it, it was like a fucking brick. He retraced his steps, walking in a wide semi circle. Nothing. He'd put it on the table at The Posh Pilchard and then got up to pay the woman with the broken arm. She'd said something to Jason and given him a sweet from a screw-top jar. They'd thanked her and walked out. Bollocks. It was only a cheap Nokia, but now there was no way of knowing the time. The sky was a uniform grey and mist had settled in around them, nudging away the whispers of rain.

Col kissed Jason again and swung him up onto his shoulders. He watched the sand for darker patches that might be soft. If he could get a view of that shallow river as it ran though, he could get his bearings. They'd walked between the stone groin and the slime-covered timbers. All he had to do was cross the gully, then walk at right angles to it. But all that was easier said than done. There was no river now, just a flat plain of water that bled out into mist. He made a dozen strides, taking control. When he looked down a small depth of water was streaming around his shoes. He turned and went back over his own steps, except they weren't there any more. He remembered the way the tide turned here. A brown bore surging into the river mouth, choking it with seawater. He bent down and put his finger in to taste it. It was salty alright, but that didn't necessarily mean anything.

– What you doing, Daddy?

– Nothing, it's OK. Just checking something.

– Are we going home?

No answer.

– Are we?

– For fuck's sake Jason, just can it.

The child went quiet, stark with fear. He shouldn't have sworn. If that got back to Janine she'd go nuts. Col tried to think of anything that might lead them back, but the sand was flat, featureless. It had lost even that vague seam of sky.

Col was sure he'd walked at ninety degrees to the channel they'd crossed. His jacket was covered in seeds of drizzle, his shoes soaked to the ankle. Visibility was about twenty yards. Fuck-all. They began to jog towards the shore, shouting as he went. Jason was laughing with tears on his face. This was all a game. Silly Daddy. They went for five minutes before turning back. Something in Col's head was jabbering, telling him not to panic. He walked to the left and thought he saw the distant line of the groin. The sea would have covered the tip, shortening it. He steered to the right, rubbing Jason's legs to put some blood into them. There was a wide section of water and he thought he could see limestone beyond. His feet plunged into a hidden gully and he almost fell forwards. In moments, Col was knee deep in the channel, then thigh deep. He strode through it, dragging his legs against the force of water, hoping to Christ he was going in the right direction.

Jason had gone quiet again. There was a spike of ice in Col's chest. He was a fucking idiot. Janine was right. He'd put everything he loved at risk because he didn't sort things out. He hadn't had his watch mended, hadn't checked his pockets in the café. He thought of the drive home. How sweet that would be, him and Jason in the car with the heater on and music playing, the windows misting up. *96.9 FM*. That stupid tune. They'd be laughing all the way because they were alive. Somewhere, at the back of his mind, he was rehearsing a story for Janine. He stood with Jason on his shoulders, holding onto his legs, the water streaming past them and deepening. He tried shouting for help, but Jason panicked and started jigging up and down, throwing Col's balance. The current was coming from his right, which must mean that he was facing the sea, that the shore was behind him. It was walk or drown, right now before it was too late. Right or left? Front, behind? He had to decide, he had to go for it. What a cunt he'd been. He turned 180 degrees until the current was pushing against his left thigh, almost waist deep.

Col set off into a brown flood. It was seaming past him, into him with its cold weight. He stepped deeper, then deeper again. Fuck! There was a scream building in his chest. He beat it down like a snarling dog. He took a lungful of pure rage, then three shallower steps, almost off balance, then upright again.

– Daddy, Daddy!

– It's OK sweetheart, it's OK, we're almost there.

He felt a slight breeze on his face. Two more shallow steps onto firm sand, the drag of water falling below his waist.

– Nearly there, Jason, nearly there!

There was a tear in the mist. Suddenly, the groin was on their right, a long spear of stone. They were a long way from where he'd thought they were. He could see the shore now: white rock, a line of trees. He took another step and sank deeper. If he got swept away they'd be fucked. The current had reversed, that's what had thrown him. The tide was dragging at his waist again. It was only a few yards. He was a shite swimmer. Jason was screaming now, punching at his head. He took another step and another, almost lost his footing and then was across, scrabbling the last yards to the sharp rocks on his hands and knees. Col put Jason down and he was lunging at him, hysterical, punching him, aiming for his balls, screaming.

– You, you!

Col stepped back, feeling his trainers pump out water.

– Horrible! Horrible!

– Hey, hey, it's OK. We're safe darling.

His heart was thumping like a fist on a church door. He wiped Jason's face with his hand then scrambled over the rocks, lifting him and scrambling up behind until they reached the path and then a green metal gate that led onto the road. A magpie flew off as they went through and found the car. His chest was tight again.

They were both soaked, covered in stinking mud and sand. Col fastened Jason into the child seat and found him a half a bar of chocolate, kissing his face. He brushed the crisps from the back seat with his hand and sat with the door open. Then he took off his trousers and socks and wrung them out. A middle-aged couple with rucksacks and walking sticks passed and gave him a funny look. He didn't give a fuck. The couple stopped and glanced back. The woman said something, touching the man's arm and they went on again. They looked well-off. Fuck them.

Col was sobbing quietly, feeling a great bubble of relief break from his chest. They could have been dead by now, face down in the water. There would have been an inquest, a few lines in the newspaper. His fingers were numb as he dressed himself, fumbled with his shoelaces. He pulled off his watch and flung it over the wall towards the sea. Fucking thing. He thought of his phone, tucked behind the salt grinder in the café, of the woman with the broken arm fumbling with the sweet jar, Jason's big eyes following her.

He'd explain it all to Janine, somehow. He'd unbuttoned her pyjamas and kissed her, sliding his hand over her belly. She smelled of shampoo, her hair shiny and soft, her mouth wet and yielding. She'd made him feel he existed. There in that hot little bedroom in a nowhere town in the northwest of England, somewhere in the Universe. He'd say he was sorry. What else? It'd all got messed up.

Col checked that Jason was alright. He was asleep in the back seat, his head lolling. There was sand in his hair. Col fished out his lighter and an unopened cigarette packet from his jacket pocket, picking off the cellophane. They were still dry. Janine hated him smoking near Jason. His lighter wouldn't work so he lit the cigarette from the gadget in the car. He remembered when uncle Pete had got one of those. He thought it was the dog's bollocks back then. Col leaned against the hatchback, blowing out smoke, picking specks of tobacco from his lip.

There was a gap in the clouds over the bay and light bore down through it, glittering on the sea. It looked like the scales of a huge serpent. It'd turned on them, but they'd survived. What was he going to say to Janine? What would Jason say when she gave him the third degree? It was a mess alright. But they were alive and that was all that mattered now. Other things would matter later, the usual crap. But this was life, for fuck's sake, life. He flicked the cigarette stub away, watching it hiss and extinguish in a puddle, staining with water, sucking up darkness. He should give up.

When he got in the car and switched on the engine, Bay Radio was playing. *96.9 FM*. Col glimpsed a white house though overgrown trees. There was a man in a blue jumper putting the lead on an English sheepdog. Then black and white calves glimpsed in the fields. Jason was still asleep in his harness. Col drove slowly, his hands still gritty with sand. He looked in the wing mirror and the black ribbon of tape flickered from the cracked glass. He changed gear, glancing at Jason as they reached the dead end where he'd turn the car around to head for home.

SOLOMON

'Whereas my father laid upon you a heavy yoke, so shall I add tenfold thereto. Whereas my father chastised you with whips, so shall I scourge you with scorpions.' **Kings 1, 12:11**

A wave hit the pier and exploded, hurling a plume of foam against the sky and chasing it down the stonework to collapse into the sea. They came in succession, sideways to the pier and the lighthouse at its tip, huge columns of spume that hit with a deep, dull thud that was part sound, part vibration. There was a rusted tramway set into the stone. The old iron was flaking away under salt water and salt air. Opposite this arm of the harbour was another pier with an identical lighthouse. There would be identical tram tracks, the same decay of iron and stone. What had once been becoming what is.

A series of archways cemented into the cliff on the harbour's north side had been colonised by seagulls and rock doves. A small hawk with barred plumage and one tail feather missing hunted over the scrubland above, its wings quivering against the sea-wind, its head swivelling from side to side. Slim-winged gulls with forked tails and black caps sidled into the wind then dropped to the waves as if entering slits. A pied duck bobbed with its head tucked between its shoulders, seemingly asleep. In the village there had been hammerkop birds that built big unruly nests in trees near the river. The village kids sometimes put a piece of red cloth on a nest and the parent birds would exhaust themselves scooping water from the river to put out the fire. That was cruel. There had been crested cranes, even shoebills, treading the marshland where the river widened.

A team of women wearing yellow life vests was launching a rowing boat in the harbour, laughing as they struggled against the swell that wrenched them off balance. On the horizon, almost lost in bands of grey where sea and sky merged, a car ferry was heading for Norway. Behind them was the town with its blackened church spire and pubs and charity shops and ex-servicemen's club and empty days where people carried on somehow.

Solomon bent down to his mother, touching her shoulder. As he stooped, he noticed that one of his shoelaces had frayed.

– Enough?

She didn't speak.

– Enough, now, eh?

Then, almost whispering, her lips dried by the wind.

–Yes.

Then, half rising and sinking again to find some comfort.

– Enough. Let us go back.

Solomon lifted his mother's twisted feet back onto the wheelchair's swivelling supports. Her legs were like wood. He checked her hands for warmth and felt her veins ebbing there. He tucked the blanket around her legs and tightened the strings of her anorak hood.

They'd beaten her feet with rifle butts, flames pouring

from the thatch, sparks spiralling upwards in a stink of kerosene as the circle of huts collapsed. Doves panicked from the schoolhouse roof as smoke coiled and flames *crack-cracked* like pounded grain.

She nodded. Her eyes were dark. Their pupils merged into the irises, the colour of old passion fruit. Her face still had the light skin and fine bones that had made her beautiful. She nodded again. *Enough.* Solomon helped turn the wheelchair around as she pushed at the wheels, tilting it backwards to steer. They set off along the sea front, past the old swimming pool with its rusted railings that were painted white, where it was safe to swim in seawater. Past the ruined abbey that Norse raiders had sacked. Past the beach with its café and cuticle of pale sand. There were surfers in dark wetsuits bobbing chest-deep in the breakers like seals, waiting for a wave they could ride to shore. The clouds on the northern horizon boiled, gaseous and volatile behind the white spire of another lighthouse. It had been a treacherous coast, a coast where wreckers and raiders had used the sea against the men of God, against the poor in spirit who succumbed, defenceless.

Solomon reached to check his mother's body heat again. Her hands were folded on the chequered blanket, the knuckles swollen. He should find her some gloves. As a child she'd shown him how to split jackfruit with a machete, laughing at his efforts. She'd taught him how to throw a mango against the wall of the barracks so that it softened and the flesh could be cut from the stone at its centre. How to thresh grain from wheat stalks in the little granary in their compound. She was a foreigner in the village but she didn't care, laughing at the local people when they ignored her or made remarks about her accent. The soldiers paraded in their uniforms and maroon berets and black calf-length boots and the boy, Solomon, watched them with sweet mango juiced dribbling onto his shirt. At the weekends they'd used her as their whore, throwing thousand shilling notes onto the bed or paying her in beer which she could sell afterwards. He'd learned to be quiet, to become invisible. That's how she'd paid his school fees. Selling vegetables at the market, cleaning or cooking for the soldiers. She'd thank them as he watched through the dusty curtain that divided the house. Then she washed in the bucket of water drawn from the standpipe. Then she prayed, always mentioning his father's name before she finished, pressing her hands to her face like the open leaves of a book. His father had gone to Congo to find gold, back to his own father's land.

Solomon wrapped his fingers around the wheelchair's handles, pressing his palms to their butts to push, trying not to lose his grip. The gush of shame that memory brought drenched him. Even here, where the wind was hurling off the North Sea. Even here, near those ruins of an ancient war that told him what history was and what it would be. For evermore.

He'd led them to the other boys, to where they were hiding in a crook of the river. Where the bank was licked away by its brown water and they could crouch underneath. Where they'd played hide and seek when they were kids. They'd seen a young crocodile there once, lying out in the sun. It fled into the water at their approach, its eyes just broaching the surface as it drifted downstream with the current. It became a legend of their own daring,

how they drove it away. *A crocodile!* Back then all they had
to hide from was each other.

After Solomon betrayed them, that August day, they
were rounded up and marched to the village and stood in
a circle with their hands on their heads like kids in school.
Then the rebel commander hacked Solomon's thumbs off
on the chopping block where his mother killed chickens.
It was a warning. Two soldiers held his mother back with
their rifles, fencing her in. He was fifteen. He didn't feel
anything at first. Just the thud and shock of the blade. Then
sheared bone and flesh and thick, oozing blood. He
remembered a day when his mother took a white hen and
struck off its head with one blow, letting its blood spurt
into dust. Flies darkened the severed head with its scarlet
comb, the beak gaping, the eye shuttered by a white
membrane. If you pulled the tendons that trailed from its
neck, a dead hen's beak opened and closed in a silent cry.

The rebel soldiers left, driving the village children into
exile. His mother bathed his hands, weeping, tearing an
old *gomesi* to bind them. There was nothing to stay for.
Even the soldiers at the barracks daren't return. Solomon
and his mother set off for the trading centre where there
was a dispensary, following the river to stay hidden, then
finding the road. That's where he went to school, staying
over, returning only at Christmas and Easter and for the
long summer holiday. His mother hobbled with a stick for
a crutch, a machete hanging from her waist. For two days
they walked down the dirt road, eating cold cassava,
sleeping under a coffee sack with nothing to keep the
mosquitos away. They got to the school at dawn on the
third day, watching it drift on the early mist like a mirage.

The market stalls were deserted and the people had left. A starved white dog wandered in and out of the empty compounds. The head teacher, an Irish priest, cleaned up Solomon's wounds as his mother watched. Father Brian. His English was soft, liquid, like first rain when it patters against earth and darkens it. *Here is Solomon in all his glory.* That was his joke if he was late for Biology lessons. The other teachers had escaped, taking their pupils into the bush, making their way to the town.

They stayed with the priest for one night. He showed them the deserted schoolrooms, the empty dormitory where Solomon had slept with five other boys. There was a fish tank, green with algae, in which five dead goldfish floated belly up, stinking of slime and death. It had been Solomon's job to feed them from a special packet of food. It lay burst open on the floor and a line of ants was carrying it away, grain by grain.

In the dispensary, Father Brian soaked off the bloody bandages and dusted Solomon's wounds with antibiotic powder. They were black and swollen where his thumbs had been. He swabbed his thigh with alcohol and gave him an injection of ampicillin, patting his shoulder. *Good boy, good boy, now.* Solomon had never seen a white man cry before. He'd wanted to talk, the priest, telling them about the north of Ireland, where he'd grown up in a small village, before the seminary, before Africa. There were woods that he played in as a child, with trees that shed their leaves in winter then grew them again at another time. There was a flower called the bluebell that came in April or May, like faint mist covering everything, he said. Like morning mist, when roosters woke the village. He scratched at the grey stubble on his cheeks, leaving white track marks.

Father Brian shuttered the windows to hide the light of the paraffin lamp and then made them a meal. They sat at a table with a tablecloth and cutlery. They were served rice and beans and Solomon's mother fed him like a child with a metal fork. His hands throbbed with pain that was so constant he had to shut down his mind to close it out. He remembered those days as dull and grey and heavy with an underwater slowness, even though they were bright with sunlight.

The dog yelped in the night where Solomon lay awake on a mattress in an empty dormitory. His mother stayed at the priest's house, sleeping in the only bed. In the morning they were woken by pied crows calling. No voices or engines. The rebel soldiers had swept through days before, driving away goats, tying the legs of chickens and slinging them from their truck. If they caught you, they cut off your ears and lips. Children were forced to kill children. That way they could never leave.

His mother brought him black tea, holding the cup for him. They breakfasted on cold chapatti and leftover beans. Then Father Brian drove them south, the Toyota with its dusty windows rocking and creaking until they reached a metaled road. Then he paid a lorry driver to take them into the next town, away from the border. Father Brian gave Solomon's mother a tight roll of money, a packet of white tablets, a bible with a maroon cover. In the town they found every language. Solomon spoke in English to find a lorry that was going south. Then two days of driving, one night sleeping sitting upright in the cab like a row of dolls. The lorry driver was a tall Tanzanian who wore jeans and a torn vest. He spoke Swahili and was carrying sugar cane to the refinery built by the Chinese at the edge of the great lake.

Solomon had blanked out the pain in his memory. What he remembered was the traffic in the city, swirling in all directions. *Matatu*, *boda boda*, bicycles, cars, buses and trucks; the myriad blue windows of a tall concrete building winking in the sun; traffic lights that changed colour as a *matatu* driver took them to the University hospital. A small man with missing eyeteeth, he'd refused the money they offered, calling his mother *Sister*, showing them the kindness of strangers. At the hospital Solomon had two operations on his hands to cut away the damaged flesh and bone. Gradually they healed, leaving uneven stumps. His hands were like those of some human prototype. Unevolved. Primitive.

He remembered the smell of the hospital, the self-important voices of the doctors, the bright white tiles in the operating theatre. He remembered the surgeon who operated on him ruffling his hair and telling him how lucky he was. His mother was given ankle splints and a walking frame to heal her broken feet. She'd thrown the bible from the truck window on the first day, her face cut from stone. She never complained about what they had done to her. Whenever he woke at night, she seemed to be watching him, her eyes dissolving in the dimmed lights.

By the time Solomon had wheeled his mother down the high street and around to their flat on the brick built estate, a fierce little wind was whipping the litter down the pavements, shaking the neon sign above the off-licence that flickered at night like gunfire in a silent film. They shared a ground floor flat, part of a pebble-dashed terrace stuck with satellite dishes. Solomon helped his mother from the wheelchair in the hall, folding it under the stairs and unzipping her waterproof coat, making pliers with his first and second fingers. The heating had switched on and the flat was warm. He gave her his arm and supported her as she took tiny steps towards the living room. She lowered herself into an armchair and nodded at him.

– Thank you, son.

They spoke only English now. When he asked her to sing to him, to sing the old songs of their tribe, she refused.

– They would be bitter on my tongue.

When they had named him Solomon, they were hoping for great things. The way parents did, naming their children after kings or political leaders. The way all people hoped for better things for their children. But in the bible Solomon had been denied by God. Then his son Jeroboam took the throne, bringing slaughter, taxing his own people. Names were just foolishness. History itself was the scourge, curling around them like a whip – a scorpion's tail – to remind them of how little had changed or could.

Now Solomon's mother fumbled with the TV remote control to watch a gardening programme. A talkative woman with red hair and breasts half exposed was laying out a vegetable garden. Solomon watched from the doorway. He'd carried water for his mother from the river to the village, struggling to lift the weight of the cooking oil tin she'd threaded with rope to make a bucket. She'd shown him how to pour it at the base of each plant, how to water when the heat of the day was ebbing and the sun's fury was passing. He watched her now, yearning for a piece of land where she could grow tomatoes, beans, a little spinach. Back home she'd considered growing coffee as a cash crop now that the government was encouraging it. She wasn't too old, even if her feet were useless. Now their food came from the little supermarket down the road that had a green pine tree in a green circle as its symbol. It was special place, a shrine, with its neatly packaged food lying under white light in the fridges and freezers. It was clean, without the red dust that covered everything back home. Dust that his mother swept from the house every morning. Dust that had soaked up their blood and language and history and erased them.

Solomon set about making tea in the little kitchen. He'd been surprised at how difficult it was to do things without thumbs – dressing oneself, washing with soap, wiping himself after defecation, even urinating without splashing everywhere. In England, he had reconstructive surgery, the surgeons working with the remaining muscle and bone. They told him there would be some movement, but little sensitivity. He would have to use his eyes to gauge how and where to grip. He'd been helped by a physiotherapist who taught him to do these things. For a while he'd worn prosthetic thumbs that strapped to each hand with Velcro fasteners and helped him to hold things. They were the colour of white skin, as if that didn't matter. The rebel commander had been a man of imagination.

Solomon took teabags from the caddy, holding it against his stomach with one hand and pulling off the lid with the fingers of the other, then making the tea in the pot with milk already added. He had to hold the milk bottle with both hands. He could see his mother nodding in her chair in the adjoining room. The woman on the television was flicking out a length of hosepipe and watering a row of plants. Every now and then she looked up and forced a smile for the camera and said something he couldn't hear above the noise of the kettle. Solomon lifted the teapot and poured the tea, then placed the cups on a tin tray and carried it into the living room. His mother's eyes were hooded, as if she was almost asleep. Rain was dashing softly against the windows. He could hear music from upstairs where the Polish electrician lived. Sometimes they passed in the hallway, the electrician carrying his bag of tools and humming under his breath in a language where all the words seemed melodious, already joined together as song.

That night, Solomon lay in bed listening to his mother's breath in the next room. He thought of the sea ravaging the coastline, of Norse raiders in their longboats sculling to shore under the cliffs. As a child, the sea had been hard to imagine, though he'd been told about it, had read about it in books. When they left Africa, they'd flown over Lake Victoria, which had seemed endless, but even that didn't prepared him. On the lake there were small fishing boats and islands covered in palm trees, but the Mediterranean was truly huge, with an endless depth. Then this grey North Sea confronting them after they flew into Manchester and travelled by train to Newcastle. In the last world war, each nation had a navy and their sailors fought in steel ships. In Africa, they killed each other out in the open, under the sun. Here, there were even ships that sailed below the surface in the cold darkness. All that energy, all that human ingenuity gone into killing each other, the sea blazing with burning oil. Now submarines carried nuclear weapons, patrolling under the ice caps, watching and waiting. A Russian submarine, The Kursk, had become trapped on the seabed and all the sailors died. But not before they had time to write to their wives and sweethearts, feeling the oxygen become exhausted, holding each other's hands in the dark, dying for the Fatherland. Such thoughts carried him into sleep. He dreamed of the village where they'd played football, marking out goalposts on the barracks wall. He saw the river flowing like liquid metal, the crocodile lurch into its broken light.

When he woke, Solomon experienced a little spasm of surprise as he tried to close his hands around the sheets to throw them back. It was easier to think about the sea than to think about the future. The future should have run ahead of him like a road or a track clearing tangled bush. It was hard to walk that road when there seemed to be nothing there. The future, he'd realised, waking in the hospital with bandaged hands, his mother watching him from her chair beside the bed, was more than events that happened and days that dawned. The future was something you imagined in order to live. A promise you made to yourself against the curse the past had pronounced.

When the rebel soldiers came, he was with a group of younger boys in the centre of the village, playing under the jacaranda tree. Its purple flowers spilled onto the dirt. It was where the village elders held their meetings, where the government soldiers paraded to show the villagers how safe they were. It was where they had their primary school lessons – when the teacher wasn't drunk on *waragi*, or sleeping it off. *Education is light*. That's what he'd told them on his better days, smiling foolishly with perfect teeth, struggling to muster pencils and notebooks, propping up the blackboard in the decayed schoolhouse where termites ate the desks and floorboards and roof beams, where the rotted thatch let in snakes and rain.

Education? Light? That had been about the future. Solomon knew that now. Education was about acquiring wisdom. To know about the world was to know how the world had been and might be. History made the future. *Suffer the little children, to come unto me*. The rebel leader had quoted Jesus, gripping Solomon's arm, his eyes jumping like sparks, his uniform smelling of smoke, sweat and *ganja*. His fingers were hard and the vein on his forearm stood out, darkening the skin.

They'd been playing soccer with a ball made from banana fibre tied with string and Solomon was been in goal, laughing as he caught shot after shot. He'd been placing the ball to kick it out when he heard the silence and looked up to see a line of solders in rag-tag uniforms. They wore necklaces to feed a heavy machine gun and carried AK47s. The brass cartridge cases glittered in the sun as they closed in. The younger kids had already fled, but Solomon was trapped against the wall between the goalposts. And he couldn't leave his mother. So he'd been captured. There were reasons. The garrison at the base had gone out on patrol that morning, and those left – the fat quartermaster and cook – were shot down as they tried to escape. Two bursts on an automatic weapon, the crack of single shots, a chemical smell of spent cartridges dispersing. The rebels dragged their bodies into the village and laid them up against the jacaranda tree like a couple of drunks who'd fallen asleep against each other. The rebel commander wore a pair of women's boots with a leopard fur trim. He'd put his arm around Solomon as he led him to the chopping block, the way his father might have done.

Father Brian had given them the address and name of a contact in the city and they were taken in and cared for by a European charity. A journalist visited, scribbling in his notebook, setting off a flash camera. They'd been featured in the newspaper as an example of what the rebels did to innocent citizens. A *cause célèbre*. When it was clear that Solomon needed treatment that couldn't be given at the local hospital, they were asked if they wanted to go to Sweden or the UK. Solomon remembered Manchester United. He'd seen them play on the television set that ran from a stinking generator at the local bar. He knew nothing about Sweden, except that the people there had white hair, like albinos or ghosts.

Visas were arranged, the airfare donated from a UK charity, and they were taken to the airport. It was at the tip of a finger of land that jutted into the lake. From the porthole of the plane, between wing and fuselage, the lake passed under them like varnished copper. They were heading northwest, over deserts and mountains into Europe. It was strange how the desert seemed to have been shaped by water, with valleys and gullies wrinkling it. Solomon watched the outsized plane on the electronic map, nudging over Libya, Italy, Germany and France towards the small island of Britain. When their meals arrived in little plastic containers with foil covers, the airhostess helped him to open them. He'd grasped the fork as if it was a trowel. She was a beautiful girl in a cream suit with red lipstick and caramel skin and she was trying not to look at his hands. His mother told him how she had once been on an aeroplane to Nairobi, when she'd worked for a Muslim businessman before she'd met Solomon's father. They'd gone there to buy fabric for his clothing business. *Aigh!* she said in English, shrugging into the thin blanket the airline issued, *We will survive.* Solomon asked what happened to the businessman. His mother shrugged. He had disappeared in the civil war. What had happened to his father would have to wait. He wanted to know, but he daren't ask in case his mother knew, had really known all this time.

The cabin lights dimmed and the aeroplane droned on, hardly seeming to move, yet its airspeed was hundreds of miles an hour. His other life felt like the memory of something now, the way we remember a dream that has never happened, the way the mind can think anything, but can't unthink it.

When his mother was safely in bed, Solomon took the laptop computer into the living room and switched it on. He was taking online courses in English, Accounting and Computing and he'd been lent a machine to practise on. When they returned home he would be able to earn his living. They'd build a house with a veranda where his mother could sit out of the sun. They'd have a little ornamental garden and a *shamba* to grow food and a fishpond, all in a compound with iron gates.

The screen lit up slowly and he typed in his password.

He had a Facebook account and was gradually collecting friends. Some in the UK, some in Africa – even America and Canada. It was exciting to check his email and find a request to confirm someone as a friend. Someone he'd never meet, but who smiled out at him from their photograph. Then there were friends who knew friends and so the network grew. Sometimes he chatted to them about football, the premier league; usually he had little to say. He followed Manchester United; he lived with his mother; he was studying to be an accountant. He tried to type with all his fingers as he'd been taught, but it was hard. It was hard to do things in the correct way when *he* was no longer correct.

He had a bank account into which a monthly allowance came from the charity. He spent very little, even saved a little money, so sometimes he shopped online for small things. A tee shirt. A pair of jeans. Music for the Ipod he'd been given. There was no room for a garden in the little flat, not even a window box like those he'd seen in the town, so Solomon sent away for a fish tank. It arrived in a great cardboard box packed with polystyrene. *Aigh!* his mother had said, frowning, *What have you bought now?* But Solomon had shaken his head and said nothing, smiling and placing one finger flat against his forehead, the way she'd shown him to keep secrets as a child.

Tonight, as she was sleeping, he went shopping for goldfish. Amazingly, they could be sent through the post. *Quality English-bred pond fish delivered to your door.* The tank came with a packet of gravel and water conditioner and a special bag of plastic pondweed to plant it out with. There was a little filter that you plugged into the electricity to freshen the water. You added a fish food and let it decompose to make bacteria, then after a week or so, you could add fish. He remembered that from Father Brian's lessons.

Solomon chose three goldfish – Comet Tails, three to four inches long – entering his credit card details carefully with the delivery address. They would arrive the day after tomorrow. Not long. He thought of the fish being chosen for him from hundreds of possibilities, one almost indistinguishable from another. The way they wouldn't know anything about it, because they had such a short memory span. Three seconds, they said, then everything was lost to them and began again. That was a myth of course, but they'd laughed about it with Father Brian when he teased someone for not paying attention. The next day was Thursday. Then Friday, when his English language assignment was due.

On Thursday afternoon he asked the woman in the supermarket about bluebells. The one who smiled at him and placed the coins so carefully into his hands. In her strange accent she told him that they grew in late April, that there was a famous bluebell wood just a few miles from town. In the spring he would take a taxi and drive his mother there to see them. They hadn't promised Father Brian anything, but they owed him that, at least. When they returned home to Uganda, they'd take some of those blue flowers in a box, their bulbs nested in damp cotton wool in a plastic bag in the darkness of the aeroplane's hold. One day, in the little house with its veranda and garden, he'd dig them into a shady place. Transplanted, they would have a new life, a new home.

On Friday morning he was downloading some free software in his bedroom when the doorbell rang. He went to the window before he went to the door. There was a white van parked crookedly on the pavement. On the doorstep a small man with tattooed arms checking a hand-held electronic terminal. He pronounced Solomon's name awkwardly, apologetically. Scottish. *Cattle raiders.* Another of Father Brian's jokes. The man fetched a small cardboard box from the van and jammed it under one arm, scanning a barcode on the label, holding the terminal steady for Solomon as he scratched his name on the screen, making a fist to grip the pen. The driver handed over the box, it had a shifting weight in it, slipping weirdly from side to side.

His mother called from the living room as he took the box into the kitchen, but he ignored her. It was to be a surprise, after all. His father told him how they had netted river fish in the Congo as a boy. He remembered that. A line of boys waded out barefoot, drawing the net tight between them and feeling the fish strike it, becoming lodged by their gills. His father ended the story like that, on a dramatic flourish: *What should have helped them breathe killed them!* Afterward they pulled the leeches from their legs and skewered the fish over a campfire, taking the rest home to share out in the village. He left when Solomon was eight years old. And, yes, he was called David. David Patrice Kubamba. The night before the box was delivered Solomon heard his mother talking in her sleep in a language he didn't understand. Perhaps she was talking to his father in his own tongue. She never spoke of him now.

Solomon took the box to the kitchen sink and found a kitchen knife. He had to grip the knife with both hands, carefully cutting though the tape that fastened the box. Inside was a plastic bag full of water and when the light entered the three goldfish in the bag exploded, making it jump and thrum. Solomon closed the lid quickly, pulling the delivery note from inside the box that told him to open it only in dim light to avoid shocking the fish. His heart had jumped and it was pounding now. There was a word for such situations, when you tried to do something good and something bad resulted. The fish had travelled in a complete absence of light, feeling the box lift and sway, then drop and lift again. Then the van's engine throbbing through water. All the time, seeing nothing. That was how the Russian sailor must have felt as power on The Kursk failed and they faced death, writing letters to their mothers and wives under dimming torches. Dying one by one with their memories in the face of the only certainty. The goldfish had travelled towards him in their own element, their gills kneading oxygen from water, touching against each other in liquid darkness. Solomon let the box stand with the lid half closed. Then, when they were used to the light, he took the knife and the box and carried them to the front room where his mother dozed and the fish tank stood on a low table.

Solomon cut the bag and poured the fish awkwardly into the tank where they darted and swirled, golden ricochets flashing with fire and life. His eyes could hardly follow them or know which was which. Then they were still, breathing calmly, their fins and tails swaying, nosing at the gravel or the strands of artificial weed. Solomon hoped they had already forgotten everything that had happened to them: their own surprise and terror, that sudden blast of light. They would be satisfied with the passing moment. What *had* been meant nothing to them. They were what *was*, pure and simple. They feared nothing except what the present turned into. Their eyes were wide, watchful and indifferent. They swam to unknown territories, nudging gravel or air bubbles that rose to the water's surface, moving on to what was endlessly new. Solomon pressed his hands against the glass of the tank, feeling it cold and smooth. The fish watched him with open mouths, their gills working. They flickered away, a shower of golden meteorites. Then he called his mother to wake her.

WHERE STORIES GO

Night-time shadows touching me. Big yellow moon at the window, low on the hill. Little Puck's there, staring, bleating. A lost lamb in a striped shirt, face turned up under his trilby hat. Hands atremble like leaves in a windy wood. Like trees at home behind the house. Me and Rufus in bed with dirty knees taking turns to listen to the crystal set. Wind in the trees like voices. Moon lemon cut with a knife. Voices from the BBC telling us news in whispers. Voices in the next room and Rufus holding my hand. Before bedtime on Friday, Mum stoking the fire to make the boiler work, a bucket of coal wet from rain. Me and Rufus in the zinc bath with Mum scrubbing us, dragging the nit comb through our hair. Rufus crying because it hurts, because his hair curls. Dad coming home from the pub with bottles in his pockets, his boots banging on the yard stones. Then Mum getting into the bath with her blue veins sticking out and Dad pulling off a Guinness cap with his teeth and laughing. Now here, awake, all these years later. Awake now and Puck looking up through the window. Those ghosts tumbling at the glass.

That night we went to Easter Fair, me and Dad, his arm around me on the ghost ride, smelling of armpits and beer and oil from the mill. His face all bristly when he kissed me. Laughing. Aiming for ducks on the rifle range. *Phat! Phat!* He held my arms and let me shoot for a goldfish that went fluffy white and died belly up in a pickle jar in the backyard. We had candy floss on a stick and toffee apples and a twist of paper with hot peas and vinegar and a wooden fork we licked and kept in our pockets just in case. Coloured light bulbs and the smell of everything mixed up and my mouth burnt. Mum not there. But another woman with red lips and black hair and a glittery headscarf and a gold tooth laughing, holding onto Dad's arm. I didn't know her. Dad shushing me with a wink, the woman laughing on the rides, her blue skirt flapping in the wind, showing her legs. *Mavis from work.*

There was a hurdy-gurdy man and a big nigger man in a white vest boxing in a ring for shillings. Watching him knock the skinny lads down, noses all snot and blood. *Silly bastards.* The fat man in a black suit counting backwards. *Too much ale and no sense.* A gypsy fortune-teller with a pack of cards and silver rings in her ears. She scared me. Dad laughing and the woman kissing goodbye and hugging me like Mum, but smelling of ciggies. I had to pee in the fields on the way home, wetting my legs, and Dad still laughing and saying don't tell Mum he'd given me a taste of beer. Don't tell Mum about Mavis. And I never did, dreaming of the gypsy woman, the ghost ride, dizzy all night, the carriage rocking and Dad close by, kissing my hair, wiping sick off my cardie with his fingers.

Bed sheet's wet now. Warm on my legs then cold. Bad smell. Back ache. Pissing blood when it's bad. I'm thirsty. Nothing to drink until breakfast. Try to tell them, sometimes, tell the nurses, but words won't. Stuck in my mouth, not my head. Words like dust or feather bits in my throat. *Dumby. Larry the dumby can't talk. But he can if he tries, can't you, Larry?* Little Puck can't talk, never could, bleating, humming. Moving foot to foot. Shivering at moon's big yellow face.

Night-shift Jack laughing with the others. In the office where the electric light is. Laughing with the Scotch one. Alice. Her tits against my face. Her soft bottom, her smoky breath like Dad's. Like Mavis from the mill. Slack Alice. *What's up Larry, can you smell her fanny?* No it's flower perfume like Mum had on. The ward full of breathing beds now. Full of sleepy-time dust and body smell. It's where we rest, where we wake, dream we wake. *I bet you'd like to give her one, eh, Larry? Up the shitter, eh?* Alice is too nice for them.

When I wake I'll know O'Donnell is dead. I had to wait a long time. All those years here. A nurse. Now dead and gone to hell. Gone before. O'Donnell whispering behind. *You're a goner, Larry. Going to the morgue. Going to the cooler like your bum-chum, Henry. The doctor cut him open to find what he died of. Put his fucking brain in a bucket. Larry, you're going too, you crippled cunt.* That was before. Long ago. Sometimes sleep makes me forget he's dead, makes it like now. Like today. Tonight. Past midnight. Moon at the window and Little Puck calling to it. Now every day it's good to wake up. To know O'Donnell's dead. Like something happy happened.

Night-Shift Jack putting Little Puck to bed. *Fucking stay there, or you'll catch it. Are you fucking listening?* Little Puck can't listen, can't talk more than lamb sounds. *Baa, baa, black sheep.* Loving the moon. When I sleep, O'Donnell comes: white coat, black shoes, black tooth, hairy face whispering bad-breath things. Bernard the porter said he was a twisted Irish cunt, wanted to hit him once when I fell on hot pipes and he left me to burn. *You're toasting there, Larry, aren't you? Is it nice? Is it, you fucking spastic?* O'Donnell laughs and laughs in my sleep with red eyes. Dead rabbit eyes. Dad shot them on Sundays. Would have shot O'Donnell too, hung him up in the shed, hooks through his feet. I don't like to sleep in those dreams.

Waking is good. Remembering he's gone away. Gone to his sin. Gone before. Like at Sunday school before the green car with fins hit me. A big car like a green fish. Trying to pick up a ciggy card. *Heroes of test cricket.* I needed Harold Larwood. Before fits and Mum crying because I was useless. My dad smelling of beer and oil, spitting out blood from pub fighting because someone called me a name. *Ellen, let them take the lad. It'll be better for him there. They'll tend to him. We can visit.* But only Mum did. Mum and Rufus. Then Rufus stopped and Mum kept coming in her black coat with the velvet collar, bringing comics, bringing stripy sweets in a paper bag. *I'm getting to be an old lady, Larry, what are we going to do?* Then stopped coming. Once a man came. A stranger. *Larry your brother's come to see you.* I didn't believe them. Rufus wouldn't leave me here. And it wasn't Rufus, it was a man with dark hair who looked like someone else. He told me Dad had passed away, not Mum. *Where is she?* Not understanding my voice. Kept wanting to see her again. Wouldn't look at the man, his voice remembering things not true.

Morning tastes of night. Sour medicine smells. Piss-wet bed. Night-shift Jack gone to let Sal in to change sheets and dry and dress me, put me into the wheelchair for another day with the clock and TV and sun rising at the window. I used to watch TV, but eyes are bad now. Kept breaking my specs. Sun's hot face at the window all day on the day ward. Sleeping with nothing to do but think on things. Round and round. Who that man was. How once upon a time we all die. Like stories that get told, then they're over. Now here's little Puck, standing over me in the moonshine waterfall, touching my face, smiling, touching me like flowers. Like Mum did when my story began.

Living in the railway cottage up a lane on the edge of town, Dad working as a mill spinner, trains going past all day with yellow smoke and coal in the tenders and the drivers waving at me where I watched from the end of the garden, holding little Rufus by the hand so he wouldn't run away. Little brother. All blond and sleepy and too small to look after himself. Mum in the kitchen, working in a blue dress, pushing her hair back, crying at the sink and I didn't know why. Her kissing when she put us to bed, me and Rufus in one big bed and the town all lit up below the window and the mill chimneys smoking and Dad coming home late and sitting on the bed smelling of work and beer, his face all bristles. Then Mum's voice hard and angry and Dad's voice low like a saw going though damp wood. Then silence and the wind in the wires like owls and rain at the window pattering and Rufus curling into me and dreaming, the way Terry our Jack Russell dreamed, twitching and kicking like he was going down a dark hole after rabbits. After O'Donnell. O'Donnell hiding in the dark from Dad who'd snap his neck and kill him easy as rabbits.

Dad up early filling the coal scuttles and whistling and Mum calling upstairs for us to go to school and struggling into cold shoes that had stood on the flags all night, soaking up cold. *They should've used headstones, it'd have been warmer.* Then he was gone to work singing and Mum tutting and washing us with cold water and a flannel then walking us down the lane for the school bus that bandy Jimmy Dodgson drove who Dad said couldn't stop a pig in a ginnel. *All hail the Mattinson boys!* We climb aboard, Rufus dropping his bag and Jimmy's wire-haired little dog staring at us from the seat where he lay out on a stinky towel. Then the drive to school into town over potholes and cobbles, past black iron railings and coal carts and the cemetery, the sound of the mills whirring and turning like big clocks and shadows moving at the windows, all lit up. All that time melts together now into pictures. Pictures still happening when I wake and the night's there, hunching at the window. A beast from the hills. *Being dead goes on a long while, live for today.*

Dad had an allotment, taking me along at weekend to help him dig the vegetables and tie up bean canes and hunt for rats. There was a wooden shed with a tarpaulin roof where you could light a rusty stove with newspapers and watch the rain and sit in saggy armchairs with a mushroom smell. Clay plant pots stacked together and magazines to look at. Spades and a fork and Dad's old clogs by the door and his gardening jacket that he'd worn in the war, somewhere far away, before I was born, and Rufus. Somewhere hot, where he'd been a prisoner. Not for doing something wrong, but because of the war. Prisoner of war. Like the war was a prison, but it was in Burma and he was in it. He was there in the army and the Japs caught him and marched him to prison to make a railway. Going quiet sometimes then, stamping on a wooden apple box to light the stove with curls of wood looking up when rain came at the window. *Snug as bugs in a rug, Larry, snug as bugs.* We'd watch the spiders in the corners and the flames starting up from a Swan Vesta and a feather of smoke from the chimney pipe where it leaked before we set to work pulling up cabbages and spuds and putting them in a sack for Mum.

Once Dad wasn't working because of short time at the mill and I went down to get him for dinner. There were pigeons in the next-door shed making that noise in their throats like a cat purring. The spade and fork were sticking in the ground and there was a robin on the fork twisting its head like it was laughing at me then shitting and flying off. The fairground lady from the mill was there. Not the fortune-teller, but her with the gold tooth. She was putting on stockings in Dad's shed. When I looked through cobwebby glass she smiled and put her finger to her lips. *Larry sweetheart, I was just smartening myself up*, and Dad looked at me his eyes very blue and shook his head meaning *Nothing to your mum, say nothing*. I knew it was a secret then, like things in the war. She was Mavis from the mill.

Dad took me into town, Whit Sunday. I was eight. Rufus at home with Mum because he was too frightened of the crowds. Too much a baby, when I was a big lad now and could reckon with it. We waited at the edge of the road. I could hear the big drum beating under my ribs like sick coming up and going down again. Excitement in all the faces. Then the church procession came down Mytholmroyd Street and the May Queen with spots on her face in a white frock with long ribbons and bridesmaids and a band marching with brass trumpets and trombones and a man banging the drum so that you could feel it in your heart. Feel it in the nights still, when the dark's quiet. Dad's hand on my shoulder, laughing with me. Then Mavis was there behind him and I saw her hand touching his hand. *Oh, hello, love, fancy seeing you here!* Mavis laughing with a gold tooth and another tooth missing at the side. *Oh, I know, I'm a bad penny, I am.*

The procession went past and Mavis leaning down and putting a kiss on my cheek with lipstick and Dad wiping it off with his hand. Lipstick and spit and I said *Uugh!* and they both were laughing. *Come on Larry, smartly does it!* And Dad taking me away to a long street where there was a pub with its doors open and a white lion on the sign and a seat outside and a beery smell wafting like breath that Dad had sometimes when he came home and sat on the bed to tell a story. Not about the war because that's all done with and gone and good riddance. Life has to go on. Dad and Mavis inside with their wet whistles and me sat on the bench with a shilling in my pocket and Dad bringing me lemonade and crisps in a packet with salt in a twist of blue paper. And I sat and waited and knew I couldn't tell anybody because Dad touched the side of his nose and Mavis' eyes had gone all wide. Big brown eyes like toffees. *Are you sure? Are you sure?* Dad laughing deep laughs, all stiff like a soldier with her. *Larry's a good lad, he knows what's what, he's …* then another man was pushing past in a black suit and I couldn't hear. Then I was waiting outside, hearing the big drum get fainter like a heart fading away as the Whit walks went across town.

Finishing the lemonade, bubbles all up my nose. Too hot for a jacket so I took it off and rolled up my shirtsleeves like Dad. *Cracking on with it.* Putting the glass on the bench, all sticky, careful not to break it, like Mum said. Then pouring the last crunchy bits into my mouth when I saw the man across the street. A long coat on like a Teddy Boy and a quiff combed back and big shoes that had soft soles and a rude name Dad told me, but not why it was rude. Mavis laughing then and a bit of pork pie coming from her mouth, wiping her eyes. *Oh excuse me love, I'm three sheets gone already.* The man taking a packet of ciggies from his pocket and opened it, throwing the silver bit and the picture card away into the road. Lighting one like a film star does at the flicks and walking off, looking back at me. Winking like he knew what I wanted all the time. Harold Larwood for a full set. Then standing up and pulling my socks straight. Right left and right again. There was a green car with big fins and lights like goggle eyes but I didn't see it moving when I bent down. Something banging hard, pushing me on the road into all the wet stuff that was coming out of me and Dad kneeling down crying, the pint still in his hand, all white froth. *Fucking hell! Fucking hell, Larry! I was only gone five minutes.*

Then I was on a bed with Dettol smells and Mum was white in the face and angry and a doctor was pushing a needle into my arse and I could hear Dad's voice, at the edge of the room and Rufus holding Mum's hand, swinging his legs. Mum was angry because I was run over. I was frightened and didn't want her to be cross, her mouth small and hard where the words had got stuck and couldn't come out. After the needle my left arm and leg never worked. I got a purple scar on my head and then fits. So I was put on a special bus to special school. *Spacker school with spacker kids.* The other alright kids on Jimmy's bus laughing and Rufus frightened again and Jimmy's wire-haired dog jumping down to sniff at me where I stood with Mum, then getting back onto the towel, licking itself between the legs and Jimmy letting off the brake and Rufus waving goodbye.

Wondering when I'd ever get better. Leg irons with leather straps so I could walk. A special brace on my arm. *Larry, you crippled cunt.* Then the fits getting worse like being struck by lightning. That smell of burning like walking through a wood with no shadows and every tree on fire and crackling out bright light and heat. Everything white and screaming and falling down and hurting myself. Things going blank so I could never remember. Just all spit and words mixed up when I was trying to talk. I had a leather helmet like a boxer and had to wear that in case. Sometimes I saw Dad looking at me. Then Mum. *Look what you did Ted, look what you did. Are you proud of yourself now? Are you? You and that painted tart.* On and on, until he lifted his hand to her and whipped her across the face and she sat, not crying, but *angry to her soul* she said, holding Rufus, holding me, red finger marks on her cheeks. After that, things got too hard for me to do any more.

They brought me here in winter in a blue van with seats that smelled of plastic and petrol. Dad came with me because Mum couldn't bear the betrayal, the shame, her own flesh and blood abandoned, and he sat next to me smoking and pointing at things outside the window as they went by. Dirty snow in all the side roads and the driver going slowly, taking the wide road out of town and into the countryside. Old stone houses, ice frozen to trees, a waterfall, red horses in a field, their breath like steam from the mill. Dad smiling and huddling into his big coat because it was an adventure to leave home, like going for a soldier when he went into the army to build a railway in Burma far from here, where snow was sliding away from the rooftops and the van went down a hill into a little town with smoke coming from all the chimneys and then here to the hospital with tall iron gates. To keep me safe Dad said. *To keep the world away.* All windows and black stone and O'Donnell waiting for us in his white jacket and grey moustache, shaking Dad's hand and winking at me like Jimmy in the school van, just waiting to be on his own with me to show me what was what. The right way and the wrong way. *That's all over now, you little twat. Welcome to paradise.* Dad kissing me and his face wet again like when he sat in the hospital watching me, breaking his heart to see me suffer because of that stupid bitch and not being able to keep his cock in his trousers.

Mum came to see me after that. Came on the long bus ride. Sundays usually. Rufus, too sometimes. Getting bigger and not knowing anything to say. *Dumby.* I couldn't look after him any more with fits and leg irons and days and years staring out of the windows, watching time go by in the clouds, in the sun and stars and moon rising and falling into the hills. Nurses coming and going home, then work, then home again. Day shift and night shift. Then Rufus stopped and Mum stopped and they told me she'd passed away. Then that man coming saying about Dad, looking like someone with a red mouth. All the time, O'Donnell tormenting us in the showers, in the dorm, in the toilet block where no one could see. Until the day the princess came. Lady Di who died in a crash on the news. She came to the village in a long car and walked to the hospital through a crowd, all painted and smelling now, and the staff meeting her on the lawn and giving her flowers. She came to help us in a long frock and flowers in her hair, smiling for everyone.

I got the wheelchair to the corridor, pulled myself out with my good arm, strong as anything and swung on my good leg to the door. When they looked up I was there at the top of the steps. *Larry! Larry!* Then me letting go, tumbling down in front of them all. To let them know that hurting pain didn't matter. That wasn't it. What mattered was our lives locked away. *You dense cunt, Larry, I'll fucking get you for that.* But he never did. He died before he got chance. A stroke in the pub, like a stroke of lightning or stroking Jimmy's dog or our Jack Russell or Rufus when he was little in bed and frightened. That's what Bernard said. He died being stroked, ordering a drink. No one else knew what I'd done on purpose even though it did no good, just O'Donnell dying like that afterwards. All that time ago and me still here, watching the days go round and never ending.

There's Puck at the window again like every bright night, moonlight dusting his face white. Moon low on the hill. Shadows trembling. His hands flickering in the light. There's a big star low down. A planet my dad said, Mars or Jupiter, taking me through the fields in the dark away

216

from the fairground lights and the hurdy-gurdy music. The smells of everything. Sweet candyfloss and sick down my jumper that Mum knitted from Dad's old one. Weeing in the field together and wetting my legs and looking at the sky all stuck with stars. *Like your mum's pin cushion* Dad said, laughing and rocking on his boot heels, pissing out the sweet beer smell, spraying my legs.

They're talking in the office now. Smoking outside the window, smelling of ciggies and flower perfume. That's Alice, nice Alice, her voice warm like her tits and bum and breath pressing my face as she tucks me in. O'Donnell is dead. And my mum and dad and the woman with the red mouth and black hair and gold tooth at the fair and the goldfish in the pickle jar.

All dead. The fortune-teller and nigger boxer and the drunken boys he knocked down. And the man who came one time, all that way to tell me something not true. All gone into a place where times go and get forgotten. Where stories go. O'Donnell is dead and always unforgiven. Forever. Never to be loved. Dead today, dead tomorrow. There's Puck, trying to catch the moon and pull it down, bleating small sounds from his mouth like bubbles. The moon bigger every night until it falls into a shadow like a voice into quietness. Then he'll sleep, Little Puck. A sleep with no words. *Blessed*, they said on Sundays. Blessed sleep. Deeper because of no words.

Come on now, Larry. You silly old bugger. That's Alice, whispering close by, taking Puck to bed again, stroking his hair, patting my face like pastry on a board. *We're watching over you. Sleep now.* Today becomes tomorrow becomes today, turning like a fairground wheel with hurdy-gurdy

217

light bulbs, stars, coloured planets spinning in the black. Today is now and angels do that watching, if only I could say it. *This is the life, eh? You're a long time dead*. A rusty old stove and the smell of newspapers and tar burning on wood. This is the life. Pigeons making that over and over noise with their throats, then their wings crackling like fire from the roof in the next plot. My leg all stiff and eyes blurry. Thinking I saw that woman's face at the window through the cobwebs and dust, come to say something. *Something important, Ted, please*. Tapping on the window like birds scratching the roof to get in. But Dad wouldn't let her. Then she was crying, her voice shaking, banging, the door locked. Then she was gone, the stove smoking in the room and Dad's face wet like afterwards at the hospital, his arm round me tight as a barrel hoop.

THE GLOVER

He was woken by the sound of water. The distant thrumming of a great river and the closer, lighter sound of rain against leaves and thatch. He lay still for a moment. His pillow was soaked in sweat and he turned it over to find a dry patch, plumping it in his fists. Reaching to his right, he found a small cane table laid out with his things: spectacles, a glass of water, a torch, the pistol in its holster, a blister pack of tablets he took to keep his cholesterol down, another for malaria, a novel with a cigar wrapper as a bookmark. He'd smoked one cigar before turning in. A small vice, perhaps. He'd watched bugs circling the hurricane lamp he'd brought to the veranda, organza wings stiffening as they fell. There was something beautiful in their quest for death, for light. He took up his spectacles and sat for a moment with them in his hands. He knew all his things by touch and was fastidious by nature. Each time he laid them out in exactly the same way so that he could find them in the dark.

When he was a small boy his nanny had been a French girl from Languedoc. She'd taught him to play chess blindfolded. He remembered their fingers touching, the faint blonde hair on her arms. She had blue eyes and small ears with jade studs, the first woman he'd loved after his mother. He swung his legs from the damp bed to face the window. He could see the outline faintly – no glazing, but steel bars and mosquito mesh. He'd been bitten on the arms yesterday as they brought him to the compound. He wore impregnated shirts that were supposed to prevent that. Now he was surrounded by the night sounds of the forest: the rubbery belching of bullfrogs, cicadas chafing, the piping of tree frogs.

He sighed and put on the spectacles. The room brightened a little and he stood up in his boxer shorts, slipping his feet into flip-flops that lay under the bed. He slung the pistol over his shoulder and felt his way to the bathroom. No lights. He found the toilet, wrinkling his nose; sat down to pass water, never turning his back, the pistol against his thigh. He was distracted and it took a long time. Sometimes he had a stricture and sat there unable to piss, thinking things more intense than that need. He wiped himself and rinsed his fingers at the sink, finding the foot pedal that pumped water. When he returned to bed he laid the gun down and lay listening to water running outside in the forest. The bullfrogs were a macho chorus, boasting, threatening, beguiling. He thought of their throats pulsing with all that spunk, all that sex. And water, yes. That was a good metaphor for what he did – it was reassuring, essential, even beautiful, but it flowed under constant pressure. And it wore things away, imperceptibly, until they were changed or gone.

He checked his watch. The luminous hands showed up in faint light that was gathered at the mosquito screen. Four-thirty. He was tired after the flight. The Cessna had followed the brown coils of a river into the jungle, dipping low over the trees, making him feel queasy. There were columns of blue smoke where illegal settlers were clearing the mahogany. They'd put down on an airstrip near a frontier town: corrugated iron shacks and makeshift bars. Whores by a dirt road. Trucks stacked with timber. An unmarked helicopter had taken him deeper, the pilot swearing in Greek, keeping low over the green canopy before dropping him into a clearing. Then a rutted track, the jeep jolting, wheels spurting mud, a driver who wouldn't stop talking and two soldiers in the back: helmeted, capes and combat fatigues soaked in rain. Their faces were impassive, their rifles laid across their knees. They were mixed race. Negroes with a lot of Indian blood in them. Dark eyes, without pupils or expression. They, at least, were silent, touching their helmets in a half salute. That always surprised him. Though he was a specialist, he had no rank.

One of the soldiers was a sergeant. Things must be changing in the army. They carried his bags to the boat for him: a canoe with an outboard motor that sputtered white smoke as it started out over the tea-coloured surface of the river. Two bright red and green parakeets hurled from the tree line, twin grenades startling him. The prow of the canoe cut a wide vee. The river was still more than a kilometre across here. Rain gathered on a leaf, dripped to another leaf then ran to the forest floor. A trickle became a rivulet, a stream a tributary, then the river was formed from many small rivers, like a language made of water. The compound lay close to the jetty, invisible from the shore. He'd been here twice before. There were other camps like it scattered across the country.

So he was awake again in the jungle, its dark interior like past time that was gradually being eroded, revealed, civilized by the future. It was primeval. It had its own rules and outcomes. In the city, he lived in a four-bedroomed apartment with his wife, a Filipino maid, two sons. He was anxious because one of his sons was having trouble at school with a new teacher. Anxious because Justina, his wife, had been bleeding again and had to have some medical tests. Ultrasound and MRI scans. His own mother had a hysterectomy at the same age. She'd been a cream-skinned beauty, brought out into society in the 1950s. She'd even danced with the President before he came to power. Maybe more than danced. But she'd aged quickly after the operation, becoming grey-skinned and gaunt, spending her days ordering the cook about, staving off boredom, visiting her friends to play cribbage or bridge, drinking brandy, Crème de Menthe.

His father had taken a mistress. That was normal at the bank. It was what they did in those days. If he even thought about that, Justina would take him to the cleaners. In any case, he still loved her and their two boys. Men of his age made themselves ridiculous with younger women. All that false masculinity. Like the bullfrogs out there, squaring up to each other with their machismo, their bullshit. He rolled over on to his side, listening to the pulsing layers of sound. They seemed to come in waves, from all sides though the humid air. It was unbearably hot, of course. It was always so. His lot was to endure the heat and humidity of places that didn't exist. If he couldn't settle his thoughts it was going to be a long night. And he had work tomorrow.

He placed his spectacles back on the cane table, touching the pistol butt. It wasn't that he fancied himself in a firefight. All logic was against that. And he was a man of imagination, not fantasy. The pistol was for himself, for his own use, as it were. On one operation, three years ago, he'd been woken by incoming fire. They'd used anti-tank rockets and mortars. The compound had boomed and flashed with exploding ordnance. Then flares going up and tracer rounds fired off into the forest, a white-hot chain falling into space. Some shell fragments had come into his room and he'd sat watching a disk of red-hot iron spin and hiss on the floorboards. He'd had to consider that. To think it through to the final consequence. As far as he knew, he was untraceable. But in that operation security had been breached and two of his patients had been liberated. The others, beyond help, had been finished by their own comrades as they crouched, praying. That was the mercy of the jungle.

So, if they had made it out of there alive, he'd be on a list. Whether he had a name or not, he would be known. Most likely he was just a rumour. *The Glover.* He'd asked for the pistol the next day, after the attack. Keeping his arm steady as he squeezed the trigger, he watched each shot rip the pith out of a capirona tree. It was shocking, the kick of the gun in his hand – action here, reaction there – the sudden remote violence as bullets struck. Whenever he had to work away up-country he collected it from a safe-deposit box at the city bank, where his father had worked, where he'd been known since he was a child. There were no other traces. Not on his cellphone, not on his laptop or desktop computer. Just a pistol lying in the darkness of a steel box in a granite building with cool marble corridors and softly spoken staff to care for him. When he was needed, they sent someone in person to the Institute with a message. Then he'd meet another contact with train or air tickets, a false ID card that he destroyed as he completed the final stage of the assignment. By the time he got home he'd shed another identity to become himself again. Reborn. Born again. What was the difference?

He lifted the glass in the dark and sipped at the tepid water. Jesus! He spat something out in disgust. A moth? He could feel it fluttering and tingling against his lips. It must have dropped into the glass when he was relieving himself. Christ, how he hated the jungle! Hated being this deep in its canopy of trees. He loathed its steaming damp, its greenness, its secrecy. Everything preying upon everything else: jaguars on monkeys, crocodiles on fish, mongoose on snakes, snakes on frogs and beetles, leeches and ticks on everything. Then there was the river, alive with unimaginable horror: a tiny translucent fish, the candiru, that could enter the body through an orifice and eat away at a man's insides, gorging itself on shit and flesh in the dark. Pirhana could strip a horse to a skeleton in minutes. Swarming and tearing, frenzied, the water boiling with blood. He'd seen that on a film. Mindless appetite. Then crocodiles and black caiman, anaconda and coral snakes. Primitive killers that had never evolved. Above all, there was the colossal surge of insect life waiting to invade skin and clothing. He'd read his English novel under the sheets like a child for a just few minutes with the help of a torch and heard the thud of moths against the mosquito netting. He wiped the back of his hand against his mouth and a shudder passed through him, a dark current of apprehension. He needed to retire. Then none of this would not be necessary. He shifted the pillow again, feeling it damp against his nape hair. The inside of his body felt turgid, as if his bowels had filled with clay.

Tomorrow he'd look at the prisoners through the shuttered windows of their cell doors. He'd study reports, photographs if there were any. Sometimes they were in poor condition, the prisoners. After all, army intelligence officers usually lacked intelligence. They made up for it in brutality, though: breaking teeth, collar bones, cheekbones, gouging eyes, ramming in cattle probes, burning skin with lighter fluid. When he met the prisoners, one by one, the first thing he did was offer them medical attention. He spoke to them softly, touched them solicitously. He wasn't a doctor himself. Well, not a doctor of medicine. He had a PhD from an American University in corpus linguistics. He'd made a study of the untruths people told to maintain relationships with their partners. What was said and wasn't said. What interested him was information and communication. Even statistics had their aesthetic. In these situations of enquiry – he'd never liked the word *interrogation* – information and its communication worked both ways. All that started with the body, with eye contact, with the position of the head or hands, with an unspoken dress code. Sometimes he wore casual clothes: slacks and a polo shirt. Sometimes a smart suit with a crisp shirt and cuff links. Sometimes – in the later stages – a white coat or the short jacket a dentist wears.

And he had no name, never gave a name, never allowed a prisoner to address him in that way. They were usually stubborn. They'd had silence instilled, beaten into them, whereas it's the natural inclination of a human being to give utterance, to speak, to communicate, to share their humanity. He could tell very quickly if the prisoners knew anything, if they were hiding anything worth knowing. That often went with rank, education, where they sat in the hierarchy. Generally speaking, he was sent for when someone important turned up. The rest could be tamed with rifle butts, bare wires and a generator. The outcome was always the same, whatever the interim situation or the nature of the enquiry. Once he had done with them, once his records were complete and his report written, they were taken away and given final treatment. That, at least, was merciful. And it was cheap. It cost the country next to nothing.

People didn't understand interrogation. They thought it was merely about getting prisoners to speak, asking them questions, dragging out answers at any cost, even if they were lies. For him – and he was a specialist – it began with solicitude. The medical kind came first – a plaster cast, a sterile dressing, sutures, even pain relief. Because pain drove things from a person's head, it gave them a focus, something to fight. What he liked to work with was an open mind. Once they were more comfortable they could be more amenable. He took fingerprints, DNA samples, mug shots. It made the prisoners feel that they'd left the realm of random brutality, of arbitrary violence – things they'd shared and perpetrated, after all – and entered a rational world of lawful procedure. They didn't know where they were, though they could guess if they lay awake listening to the night in their pitch-black cells. The trick was maintaining that darkness, never giving them quite enough to drink, keeping them on the edge of thirst and fever where their thoughts could multiply. It was he who brought them into the light, who'd order a jug of iced water and let them drink from it, though never too much at one time. That increased expectation, the thought that they *might* drink. Sometimes they'd ask him for water and he'd smile, solicitous again. *Soon, soon,* he would say, soothing them, offering them a future.

He spoke Portuguese of course, Spanish, was fluent in English, which he used for the educated cadres, but he also had a smattering of the hill and river dialects. It was amazing how the sound of a few words in their own language could melt a man's tongue. Or a woman's for that matter. He'd seen prisoners who'd been beaten almost beyond recognition and endured, cry at the sound of their own language. The language of their childhood, the language their mothers had first spoken to them. *The procedure is called de-gloving,* he'd say unexpectedly, softly, turning as he was leaving the room.

He lay in the dark now, listening to the forest seethe around him. His lip was swelling. Maybe it wasn't a moth he'd spat out. There were species in the jungle that had never even been identified. Even a venomous moth wasn't beyond imagination. Nothing was beyond that.

Because tomorrow was a working day, he remembered all the childhoods he'd had. A miner's son marching with his father from the pithead to a strike meeting. A peasant farmer's son staking out a clearing in the jungle, burning and chopping the bush to grow maize, sweet potatoes. Or his father was dead and his mother was a teacher in the village school, keeping things together, observing decency, feeding her large family of which he was the youngest. Or he'd been raised in the city in a steady family, his father working at the fuel plant, his mother a maid. Maybe he'd been rescued from the streets where an uncle had dumped him, where he'd sold himself to businessmen cruising in cars to survive. There was a web of stories, of names, locations, family members. All of them were interchangeable, all of them familiar to him, as if they'd been real. He told them about his childhood so that they would remember theirs, that was all. It was all lies, of course. Though in the wider scheme of things it was all truth. The way fiction is the ultimate truth because it is reality processed and projected by the mind. It is experience – actuality – synthesized. What led them to him was their own imagination: that ultimate instrument of consciousness. The idea of *breaking* them was never part of his method. That was both stupid and barbaric. It was realisation that made them talk, encouraged them to share the burden they carried.

It was rarely necessary to tell the ones who knew something exactly what he wanted to know. Those ones who resisted and stayed silent had been well trained at those camps in the jungle or in the mountains. The ones they were still finding and strafing from helicopter gunships, burning them out like wasps' nests. He and his brother had done that in the story where they'd survived as orphans at a coffee plantation, living on scraps of charity, barefoot and dressed in rags until they were old enough to plant and weed and pick coffee. They'd saved up for paraffin and matches and destroyed the nests that lay below the surface of the ground for a few cents, saving up the money to buy shoes so they could walk to school. Every story was a story of redemption, how he'd gone from that condition to this.

Sometimes they asked him what had happened to his brother and he couldn't answer, his eyes wet with the sadness of memory. He'd touch the prisoner's arm then and smile, as if he'd caught himself in a moment of self-indulgence, had disclosed too much.

They knew what they knew; that he wanted to know all of it. He was merely interested in everything. The question was how they came to that moment. In many ways, he'd rather they spoke about anything other than that at first. Denials were tiresome and got in the way. They made him look needy, anxious for the truth. That was something to be approached gently, step-by-step. It was their redemption, their rendition from one state to another, from sin to a state of grace. Because all knowledge lay heavy, all secrets were burdensome. If they could be released from their secrets, they could be free. To stay silent was to betray themselves.

It was not necessary to use violence. He had photographs of the procedure. They were of high resolution and could have come from a lecture he might give to clinicians. The images showed the first incisions, the skin being peeled back, the final result. They showed the faces of the people being operated upon. Without anesthetic, of course. They showed the faces of others watching. And he was careful to match the photograph to the skin tone of the prisoner – no use showing a black man a white subject or vice versa. No use showing a coffee-skinned woman the exfoliated breast of a negress. What they had to imagine was themselves. He would bring the photographs in a portfolio and spread them on the table, as if they were choosing a new body shape with a helpful consultant. *This is the procedure that has been recommended,* he'd say, *we would like you to take a close look.* He'd let the prisoners gaze at the photographs so that they could be in no doubt. A man having his penis skinned back. A fat guy flayed to the spine. A woman with her breasts hanging by a thread of flesh. Someone with no face, just a mask of blood with bared teeth and lidless eyes. Then he'd take them away again, because images grow in the imagination. They grow especially at night with the appetites of the forest at work, the sound of rain and the river pouring through your head.

The next day he might not visit at all, breaking his routine. The day after he would appear, all solicitude, asking them if they'd had enough time to think things over, glancing at his watch occasionally, as if late for another appointment. *Shall I bring the tape recorder? Would you like a glass of water? Ice?* It was remarkable how few of them lied under such circumstances. When they spoke it was almost always the truth. *Where, when, who, how and why.* After all, those were the essential elements of a story, the essential components of a narrative. Those elements gave truth the *ring* of truth. He thought of that as a sacred ring, a contract they'd made together. He would stand between them and all hurt if only they would make him believe.

It was amazing how many of them were grateful afterwards, how many of them thanked him, tried to press his hands before they were taken to the forest. He wondered if the soldiers gloated before they killed them. Or if it was sudden: a shot to the head from behind, so their fading consciousness couldn't keep up with the realisation of what had become of them. He always hoped that it was sudden. For his own part, he had no political views. He was only interested in what they had to say, not why they had to say it. Then it was written down. Not in plain view, but there would be a record. Unsigned. Anonymous.

Himself? He'd fade into history, be remembered only for his linguistic work at the Institute, the recording and archiving of native dialects, the extensive fieldwork that had often taken him away for weeks on end. He'd die a natural death of cancer, stroke, or heart failure. After all, the work was stressful. Or he'd die by his own hand, his grip slackening on the pistol. He'd thought of that too, how his thoughts would explode like stars and then fade.

He was still awake when the dawn came up over the forest, tainting the room with light. There were bird calls piercing the jungle canopy, monkey calls like harsh reproaches mixed with laughter. Steam was rising from the river beyond the trees that spread like a green fire. They were holding two men and a woman who'd been swept up in a raid across the border. They believed at least one of them was of high importance. Which one, was the question.

As he dressed, putting on his watch, his spectacles, he thought of his wife seeing the consultant on her own, having to go through all that in the city hospital without him being with her. The taxi, the waiting room, the nurses who'd treat her as if she was stupid, as if she was meat. A nobody. He thought of his oldest son training for the basketball team, of his youngest who was struggling at his new school. He'd make an appointment with the teacher, make it clear he suspected bullying, that she should be vigilant. Moving from primary to secondary school had

231

been traumatic, but the boy wouldn't say why. The teacher's attitude was insensitive and hadn't helped. Not all children were the same. They had to be treated as individuals. He'd speak to her, and he'd be reasonable. He'd be persuasive in that gentle way he had. They were good boys, Raoul and Paul, and everything would be alright in the end. They'd go to university as he had, meet nice girls, have children he could walk to the park and play with in his old age.

Next week he'd return to the Institute from this period of research leave. He'd visit his mother in the home, enquiring after her, holding her hand as she sat in an armchair, puzzled at which son he was and why he was there to see her. Sometimes she knew him, sometimes she didn't. Always he took her gardenias from the same florist who had a roadside stall just near the home. The woman had a gold incisor and a low-cut top over tanned, flamboyant breasts. She'd pick and wrap the flowers carefully as the traffic went past. He'd choose a buttonhole as she tied them with a bow of glittering ribbon. He'd tell her to keep the change, even though she'd overcharged him in the first place. Routine was important. He was his mother's youngest son, the son who brought gardenias, the son who had made something of himself in Higher Education, not in politics or business. The son who wore an impeccable suit, a white handkerchief folded into his pocket, a cream carnation pinned to the lapel. He had a slightly swollen lip from his recent research trip, but that was healing now. *The specialist*, she would say, if ever a scrap of memory floated by for her to grasp and hold onto. *My son,* looking up, the skin of her face etched by her long lifetime, the skin of her arms hanging loose, *my son, the specialist.*

CHERRY TREE

Yesterday it was the ATM. Whispering to me outside the chemist's as I typed in my PIN and waited for the cash. I had to lean close in to catch the words. The sounds of the machine muttering, those tricky shifts of pitch trickling inside. The screen flashing up messages. Choices to make about what I wanted. Then my card appearing and the bank notes rustling through the flap seemed to drown them out. It's hard not to imagine someone behind there counting the notes and pushing them at the slit. But it's just a machine. It can't feel anything. After the voices it was like the sound of the sea or washing machines. Maybe a dozen washing machines in a launderette. I thought of that young woman with a baby in her arms staring at her washing going round and round. Watching the pink bedspread turn and turn, wondering where her life was taking her. When I came away from the ATM the man behind me was coughing as if I'd been making him wait too long. That baby was Alex, the one in the launderette.

This morning I woke early and put my hair into a plait. There was sunshine after days of rain. It fell against the bedroom blinds and spilled through like golden grain from a silo. The birds have been active for weeks now, as soon as the shortest day passed. They're wonderful mathematicians, waking at first light to patrol the roof. First jackdaws, then chaffinches, thrushes and blackbirds. Soon the collared doves will be back, making those throaty cries that make you want to run from your life. To run and start again. Jake's still away and I have the house to myself: the width of the bed all night and now the breadth of the day, like something you could put your arms round and squeeze. This morning I rinsed some dark bristles from the sink.

After breakfast and the smell of toast, I put the ladder up against the cherry tree and set to work with a bow saw and lops. Like Abe Lincoln, that old story from my school books, though I'm sure he used an axe. I wanted to prune it before the blackbird came back to sing in it, telling us all about love and conquest. I used the folding stepladders and had to climb into the tree with the saw. It's funny how the flesh of the tree is pink as if it has sucked up cherry juice from the soil. It's an intimate pink, like the secret flesh of a woman. There's been a lot in the news about FGM recently. Girls from the Middle East and Africa. The thought of it's hard to bear. A razor blade or a piece of broken glass. The women do it and the men look away. Then, if the girls are British and sent away for a holiday, the government looks away. That's the way a secret grows deeper. The secret's not the *thing*, the mutilation – those tender clitorises thrown to the crows – but the reason it's wrong and we don't say anything. One thing I never wanted was a daughter.

The neighbours were watching at the windows again. *Look, that woman's in the cherry tree. What is she thinking at her age?* I could hear them saying it. I could feel the pressure of water vibrating through the tree, all those capillaries sucking at the earth and singing when you put your ear to the bole. I had to drag the cut branches out of the tree, all tangled with the uncut ones, the ones that would live. Very awkward, balanced on a branch twelve feet up. I used to go rock climbing with my first boy friend. But he was more interested in finding new routes than being with me, unless I was belaying him. Love never happened between us, but I still like that feeling of being high up above the ground, the feeling that things are about to spin. There's a white and ginger cat watching me from the garden wall. Next door, their leylandii's dying off, all brown and stiff on the western side where the wind comes into it. Good. The other trees in that godforsaken garden are a sycamore with the crown cut out of it – *excised* – then an ash tree that's far too close to the house. Ash Dieback's crossing the country like a plague, so it's only a matter of time before it crashes through their roof. That would serve them right in the eyes of God. Well, in my eyes, too. They never said a word to us.

There's a ladybird clinging to one of the branches of the tree as I saw. The branch creaks against the blade as the cut tightens, but I manage it, making damp sawdust sift down to the grass. A pink snowdrift. The way snow is on the hills when the sunset touches it. My arms are aching by then. I take off a few smaller branches with the lops, still balancing. The ladybird's there an hour later when I'm trimming off the small branches to make a bonfire. I ease it onto my hand and put it on the trunk of the rowan. *Fly away home*, I whisper, but it doesn't. Its wing-casings are dark red so maybe it's very old. Maybe it's too old to have children or to rescue them. *Rucuse them.* A very different thing and complicated to explain when I checked up on what it meant. There are lots of fragments like that. Words and bits of words that join together when it suits them. Promiscuous words that breed or propagate themselves. I don't know whether they're animal or vegetable, really. A life form that evolves in-between everything else. In-between music and poetry and the sound of wind and the other little secret sounds that the world makes to itself. But words are sounds that mean things. And things are what we do.

I pile the cherry branches on top of our cast-off Christmas tree on the heap at the bottom of the garden where we make bonfires. It overlooks open fields with Holsteins grazing. They're huge cattle, bred for milk alone. Milk and procreation. Every summer they take the calves away one night in July and the cows moan for them, heavy with milk. You can understand why that Christmas carol says *the cattle are lowing,* as if their voices are rising out of the earth. In the early morning, when the light catches them on the field grazing under the thorn trees, they have this epic quality, like beasts from an ancient myth. The needles on the Christmas tree have turned brown. I reckon it'll go up like a torch and take the cherry tree with it. Once you've got a core of heat, a fire will burn green wood. It'll burn any young growth to ash. Then the wind takes the ash and scatters it. Last year I stood on the decking at the end of the garden with a candle and waved it so the cows could see. They came to me through the dark fields, dragging their bellies, pawing the ground with cloven hoofs, their eyes circling me, drooling, moaning in bovine sorrow for all their lost children.

Who knows what it is they know or feel? They feel the loss but have no words for it. They feel the dark music of

abandonment in their mouths, dripping from their jaws. I
was still there when Jake came to get me with a blanket.
A blanket and a cup of tea, his cheeks stubbly and wet. He
was trying to look upset for me. *Barbara, sweetheart, you
can't go on like this, come on in.* I took the blanket and draped
it like a priestess. *Let it lie, Barb, for God's sake let it lie.* He
calls me *Barb*, like the old days. I would like to be that
cursed dart. I can't cry any more and I can't love him now.
It was him who wanted Alex to go for a soldier. I poured
the cup of tea slowly into the field and it steamed like
entrails, a libation, watching Jake walk back to the house,
his shoulders stooped under the load of me, the burden of
me.

It's one o'clock before I even get near a sandwich. I've
got half a dozen decent sized boles to saw into logs for the
winter stove. I've got a pile of brushwood ready to feed
the bonfire. I start that by trimming off branches with the
lops and piling them to make a dense core. I've got petrol
in the shed for the mower. That'll start it. Dangerous, I
know. But I'm always really careful. You'd just got to
remember that vapour is invisible. Alex told me that when
he was at school, the way they come home full of
knowledge, full of things to say, the world amazing to them
with its chemistry and biology and physics. Suddenly they
want to know *how* things work. They want to know *why*.

After a quick lunch I tidy the tools away into the shed.
I decide to wait before trying to start the fire. Some of the
neighbours have washing out and I don't want them
complaining. I check the compost bins for rats, but they
look OK. Just recently they'd been getting into the plastic
containers. Leptospirosis can be serious, so I'm always

fastidious with the kitchen waste. This is a rural area and I came across a few cases when I was a practice nurse and the farmers came in. Some of them used to take the drugs the vet prescribed for their stock. That's not as daft as it sounds. They were stoic breed, taking illness as it came. Watching death with a steady eye. Yet the seasons turn in them when the peewits return and the curlews and oystercatchers and new lambs run under the hawthorns or play king of the castle on the river bluffs. They turn like something immense and slow and nothing is said or needs to be. That's a kind of joy, a kind of heaven on earth.

There are a couple of suspicious-looking holes in the base of the garden wall, so I take a lump hammer and tap some stones in there to block them up. Jake's hammer. Thor's hammer. The vengeance of God just to keep a few rats in PJ's garden. A nice feeling. Their house is a holiday cottage, so they're only there a few weekends of the year. He emailed me to say they had *unwelcome visitors* and could I check? He couldn't bring himself to use the word *rats* like the rest of us. That was a cheek. It's nice to think of them breaking into his house, shitting on the kitchen floor, pissing on the working tops, gnawing at the skirting boards and wiring. Finding tubs of humus or guacamole or stray bacon rind or scraps of leftover bread. PJ and his wife never hang any washing out, which is weird. She looks like butter wouldn't melt, all dimples and softly permed hair. But just try parking outside their house and she'll cut you to pieces in a few words with that sabre of a tongue.

I told Jake I'd put some poison down for the *rats rats rats rats rats*, which I did, but not enough to slaughter the entire population. RATS! We used to say that to our first Jack Russell, Maisie and she'd go crazy pawing at the back door. Just enough poison to keep Jake happy and PJ on the hook. Blue pellets in a plastic tray. I pushed them under the garden shed like some mad emperor poisoning the guests at a feast. *Keep your friends close and your enemies closer.* Once Alex set up a rat sniper post at the bedroom window with an air rifle. He had no shirt on and it was summer. He was doing his basic training and he'd lost weight. His hair was very short, like spikes of ice or glass. He looked like a little god up there with the airgun Jake had got him when he was sixteen. He never actually shot anything apart from a target pinned to the mountain ash. He hadn't the heart. When I put the ladybird down I tried not to look at the pellets that were still stuck in the bark.

We've got a little conservatory made of PVC that opens out onto a patio. In the afternoon I get into one of the cane armchairs and listen to the Archers, then the afternoon play. Shula's kicking off about something. The play's about some kids in London who steal a car and find a baby strapped into the back. It's a comedy. But it isn't funny for the baby or the baby's mum. That's the trouble with comedy, it's funny sometimes because it's being cruel or forgetting one side of the story, or pretending that people don't feel everything that happens to them. That's how we get by. I like the old-fashioned comedians who could twist words open like party crackers. That one about being on the Underground and missing the stop in the blackout: *I say, is this Cockfosters? I can't tell whose it is, it's dark in here.* Pure innuendo. That old joke with a straight face from the Blitz when my granddad was in London doing fire duty on St Pauls. Putting out incendiaries with a bucket of sand. All for the sake of the house of God. That's about three Gods already. Maybe it should be gods. With the old comedians it was all in the way they said things, just a little more weight from the tongue here rather than there. That's the beauty of radio, it makes them work harder to get things across. Pure sound, with all the pictures in your head. Where they can multiply if you're not careful.

I fall asleep in the middle of the play and when I wake up I'm hungry. I cut a slice from the loaves I made yesterday. I've still got my mother's old Moulinex with the dough hook, so making bread is easy, once you've got a method. I mix the yeast with the flour, add olive oil, dissolve the salt in hot water and then set the whole thing going. The trick is to add water slowly as the dough gathers around the hook. When it's formed a beehive shape and cleans the bowl, it's ready, whatever the flour. When I let it fall from the mixing bowl to the bread board it makes a sound like wax coming out of an ear. I did a lot of syringing when I was at the practice, though I think it's frowned on now. I toasted the bread and coated it with peanut butter and marmite. Alex's favourite. That's what he asked for when he was in Helmand. Marmite. He told me the Americans couldn't understand it. He sent me a picture from his mobile phone holding the jar and grinning with his mates in the background.

There's a message on the answerphone, which is probably Jake. *Blink, blink. You have one new message.* He travels a lot for his work. He's an advanced driving instructor and does those talks for drivers who get out of trouble by choosing a refresher course instead of a fine and points on their license. He always made me feel safe in a car, I'll say that. He taught Alex to drive and he passed first time. I hate driving at night now. Ever since I started wearing glasses for long-sightedness. The worst time is at dusk when the light's fading and everything seems to be in shades of grey. I'm terrified that I'll miss a child crossing the road or knock someone off their bike. And the dusk seems to whisper the way mist whispers or owls when they're really far away. I can hear them calling from telegraph poles across the valley when I'm out there in the dusk and Jake's watching TV. It's the sexiest sound, the sound of desire and distance.

Right now the brightest planet on the horizon is Jupiter. Alex got me one of those apps for my phone. You hold it up to the night sky and it tells you the names of the heavenly bodies. Jupiter's like an opal glowing on a silver chain of stars, as if the sky was a black velvet dress, or dark skin, the way some African people are dark. We had a Sudanese doctor for a time. Mohammed something. I mean *someone*. Blue-black skin. Black velvet, like the inside of my mother's jewel box in the bedside cabinet that smelt of cologne. I've got it somewhere in the attic, packed away with some of her wedding presents. The Sunday roast knives and a sharpener and the ivory serviette rings carved into curled elephant trunks.

At four o'clock I get the photographs out and search through them. I don't know what I'm looking for yet. Alex on his tricycle. Alex with Jake sailing a model yacht. Alex with that first girlfriend who never had anything to say. *Jenn.* Then I'm in his room pulling shirts from the hangers and smelling them. Smelling *him*. I get into his bed and sleep for an hour. When I wake up I could swear he'd just spoken to me, but I haven't quite caught the words. It's going dark outside and I should probably make some proper food, though Jake won't be home tonight. That's the message. It's why he ever leaves a message. I make the bed and tidy Alex's things and sweep a dead bluebottle into the bin. I'm drifting in the house now. It's really quiet like the sea, just those deep sounds of sea creatures bleeping far away below the foundations. Whales moving slowly through drifts of krill in fathoms of salt water. Shoals of jellyfish drifting by in their venomous veils. The house is old and that's what you get in an old house: the voices of the dead passing down through its layers of air or rising like faint prophecies. Once when Alex was ill, I put the vaporizer on and set tea lights all round the bed on the floor and we pretended it was a ship at night. Sailing to Africa in the scent of eucalyptus as he sat up against the pillows with big feverish eyes.

The first inkling that something was wrong was just before Alex was due to finish his first tour. Until then he'd been in touch every few days. Texting. Skyping. He'd trained as a radio operator. So when they were on patrol he was the crucial link with the base, coordinating things. I watched that series on TV and it showed the soldiers – just children, under the helmets and body armour – filing out, looking for insurgents. It's provocation, really. When they get fired at, they call down the air force to drop bombs or fire missiles. It looks like a video game on TV, like that X Box things Alex used to have. But there are real people behind the dust. Real bodies and bowels and blood. We shouldn't have been there, but Alex never wanted to talk about that. It was a job. He kept saying that, he had a job to do and his mates relied upon him. That's how they weave the web that holds them: duty, obligation, like funnel spiders making their traps.

Jake said no way, it was all bullshit when we finally heard what was going on. About the charges. There'd been an IED and one of Alex's company had been hurt. He'd lost a leg and he had a wife and baby. They'd caught the Afghan men who did it or thought they had. They were wounded in an air strike and couldn't get away. What happened then would have been the end of it except one of the soldiers had used his mobile phone to record everything. It was all a jumble of radio static, helmets, desert fatigues, and faces behind orange goggles. There's one glimpse of Alex under the radio pack. Their voices all hyped up with adrenaline. *Still alive, sergeant.* Rustling. The scuffle of boots, clink of equipment. *And this one. Fuck, this!* Then a Scottish accent. *Oh, shall we or shan't we?* It's like they're playing a game. Then you can hear a voice crackling through Alex's radio, but you can't tell what it's saying. Then Alex acknowledging: *Roger that.* Then … *ucking rag head bastards* where the f has floated away from the obscenity. That's close up. Then a heavy breathing sound that makes you feel the heat. Someone's humming in the background with almost-words. *Pat a cake pat a cake.* The video's all jumbled up then. Sand and green foliage and a strip of canal and sky whirling. *It's a waste, lads.* Those are the words, if you really listen.

There's a pause then and the video goes black because the soldier's put the phone away, though it's still recording. *Bake me a cake as fast as you can.* Then there are two shots.

Not very loud. Alex said they played the *digitally enhanced* loop over and over again at the court martial. I saw it on the news. It was all over the TV and then YouTube when they were acquitted because there was insufficient evidence of wrongdoing. It was all about *waste*. Whether that was a noun or a verb, whether it was a kind of code; an order or an observation. We used to sing that song whenever we made pastry together and there was a little bit left over. Whenever we made a pastry man Alex would bite the head off first. That's how I knew. Even though none of it was proven, even though he's still out there and a corporal now. I couldn't look at him when he walked free. Jake punched the air when he heard, like a footballer who'd hit the back of the net. *Oh yes,* he said, *oh yes!*

They didn't find any weapons and the men's families said they were just farmers working in the fields. Tending to the goats and a crop of melons. They had wives, children. They had mothers. That wrung my heart out so that I wished it was made of stone. A heart of pumice instead of a heart of flesh and hot blood. Stone that's spurted from a volcano and gone cool and hard. Instead, it wakes me at night like something running wild. A creature hurling itself at a fence again and again as light thrums against the windows. I think of the sun rising in the east then, warming the dust on their cold graves.

I've got the matches from the kitchen drawer and I put on one of Jake's old donkey jackets and a scarf. It's almost dark, so I need a head torch in the shed to find the petrol can. That smell of soil and damp. Woodlice running for cover. There's still half a sack of last year's potatoes. Jake's tools all haphazard. The lops where I left them, smelling of sap. There's a stiff wind now, blowing steadily towards the fields, which is good. It'll carry the smoke away. I splash a cupful of petrol onto the base of the heap I've made. Then I fasten up the can and take it back to the shed so the flames can't leap back and make it explode. The petrol smells sharp, like the garage where my dad worked. In those days the pumps had a little twisty thing at the top and you could watch the petrol flowing to the hose. A bit like a barber's pole turning.

Next comes the tricky bit: tossing a match onto the fire without getting too close. The first two go out straight away. I manage it third time and the whole thing goes up with a *whumpf*, a blast of heat against my face, a column of orange flame where the vapour is trying to escape. The Christmas tree catches at once and then the wind sends a stream of sparks out towards the fields where the cattle are standing, afraid in the dark. I think of their cloven hooves pressing into mud, treading their own dung. There's no moon and Jupiter is there in the east, a luminous orb above the invisible line of hills. It's the same planet the Romans sacrificed white oxen to when they made a conquest here in the North. Setting up their shrines, making their way across the Pennines, afraid of what was out there, the wild tribes watching them from marshes and hilltops. They were the invaders with their new language and weapons and shining armour and all-powerful gods. It's strange to think they ruled for five hundred years and then went home to have everything they built here torn down to make barns and shippens.

Flames swirl and flare up as the wind catches them, like a beacon, lighting up my face for the neighbours to see. There's a fierce core fanned by the wind. A red core, like war. Everything will burn now. I'll stay as long as it takes to feed the cherry tree to the flames. When I go to bed my hair will smell of smoke. I'll lie there alone and listen to the empty house trying to tell me what I know. Maybe Jake will come home late. I never did check his message. He'll ask me what I've been up to all day, slipping in beside me with cold hands and feet, hoping I'll warm him. Maybe Alex will text me to send his love, a picture of himself in uniform with some of the local kids.

THE DIG

A Thistlethwaite, red-haired like all her clan. Long-shanked, full-breasted, tall. Freckled, grey-eyed, jug-eared, a crooked smile creasing into dimples. Climber of rock faces for hawk's eggs. Horse breeder, dog hater. Broad-shouldered, a fighter who'll take on her brothers and anyone else. Fey, man-shy, loyal. Fierce to the lie, quick to offence. Footsore now, limping from a bruised knee where the gelding took her into a dry stone boundary. Homeward bound, the moor's peat squelching underfoot, the heather springy, bog cotton in the hollows. Hungry and used to it.

The Land Rover lurches on the bridleway, loaded with wire ladders and lamps, yellow waterproofs, digging gear. The man's helmet lies beside him on the front seat. His hair is spiky grey, his hands badly scarred from a fire. The flesh has grown back in purple patches. He's got a blue thumbnail where a hammer missed. He wears a diver's watch with a black plastic wristband. Sun shows up the scratches on the spattered windscreen, tyres jog over stones and ruts and into mud puddles. The exhaust stinks in low gear. He's arranged to meet the others at the dig. This one's been on the go for months and you never knew who'd turn up.

She's a long hour from home after trading her grey horse in the next dale. There are coins in her purse but she's packed it tight with grass to stop them chinking. She rode the gelding bareback to the Sykes place, now she has the walk home. It was a good sale. The bridle and harness are tight under her jerkin. She's taken a short cut over a flank of moorland, crossing a corner of Abel Rintner's land, past his new peat cuttings where turves are piled. She's black to the ankles and there's a foul gas from the moss. She could have played it safe and detoured by the valley head, then down past the inn where there were other folk. There'd be drunken, groping bastards too. Fenmen and Dutchlanders draining the land for the monks, gabbling, fetching up phlegm and laughter. She can't bear that. No need if the light holds. Her feet catch in rushes. She can hear the calling of fat lambs. Soon they'd be cutting their throats for Eric's wedding.

There's a dirty Peugeot estate parked where the bridleways meet. Dark blue with a roof rack. Two other cavers are already climbing into their gear. A woman in her late thirties with pulled-back hair and acute blue eyes; a fifty-year-old man, bow-legged, short and bearded. He's coiling a climbing rope clarted in dried clay and she's fastening her overalls over rubber boots. Their greeting is a stubbing of cigarette butts, a faint smile, nods to the stile, the causeway they've laid across the marsh that leads to the dig. Another path goes up over the limestone edge, past the killing pit – a swallow-hole with almost sheer sides, twenty yards across and twelve deep. They'd help excavate that for an archaeological dig, uncovering broken animal bones and Mesolithic flints. Hand axes, arrow tips, flensing blades. The ancient people had hunted with dogs, driving red deer, elk, auroch, and wild boar over the edge then stoning them to death. They'd been proud of that dig, the way it made sense of things, of the past. The man with the scarred hands slams the Land Rover door and takes two yellow plastic trugs from the back. They pick up their lamps, two folding spades, a short-handled pick. The bearded man carries the rolled-up ladder and the woman with blue eyes lifts a coil of rope.

Jogging across the moor to strike the track, Hannah's breath is harsh now. She's anxious to get to the commons below. Sun is dropping over the sea about thirty miles west. The air is cooling, smoke coiling from the farmstead she's too close to. A flight of geese follows the river to the estuary in a double vee. She stumbles, pauses, rights herself, touching a hand to her sore knee. There's the sudden hiss and flicker of plumage. A streaking bird is attacking her. Then the arrow strikes into her forearm, almost parallel to the bone, the point driving right through. She sucks her breath, freckles starring her suddenly white face. She glares round quickly and keeps moving. She should have covered her hair. That was stupid. The mistake will cost her. She's wearing an amber amulet that hangs from a leather thong. It tosses as she runs. The arrow stings, evilly. She needs to get out of view, jags to the left, drops into a gulley and lies listening for dogs. Nothing. She follows the gulley down, stumbling, nursing her arm, trying to let blood drip onto her and not bare rocks where they can track her. There's a little water in the beck bottom, not much.

They walk up the lane in single file, trudging a little after their day of work. Each to their own: wrought iron making, timberwork, the work of the body. There's a gate on the left leading to the wooden causeway laid over the moor. The timber smells of creosote. The man with the beard grimaces, but the woman half smiles, bends her head a little closer as she swings the gate back onto its catch, savouring a memory. They move across the peat bog, feeling the planks sink a little under their weight. There are black pools on either side. Petroleum from the peat has stained them with iridescent patterns. A stand of bog cotton stirs in a slight breeze coming off the Irish sea. The man in the lead flexes his fingers and switches hands on the trug. The woman's eyes are paler here, bluer, as if cut from underwater stones. She's thinking of a bright room, how she loves the touch and smell of babies though she's had none of her own. Their pure skin, their tiny hands reaching to their awed mothers' faces.

Voices, thick and faint, not far off. A hundred yards. Maybe more. Men's bass tones. She pauses, hunched over. Dark blood is oozing where the arrow tip has gone through. It's fletched with partridge feathers. There's a waterfall ahead where the beck drops twelve feet. Another stream trickles out beneath it from a tunnel behind. It starts half a mile away on the fell where a gill runs into a long shaft, down into its darkly dropping space. Dan, her elder brother, had shown her the place. They'd played a game once. He'd let a handful of duck down fall into the shaft and she'd waited. Sure enough, white tufts appeared in the stream below the waterfall, where overground water met underground. She's there now and needs to be careful. The cave entrance is awkward to scramble into. She grips wet rock slimed with moss and lowers herself, then swings on one hand and leg into the space behind falling water. She holds her arm under its chill so that the pain is dulled, then draws her knife. The arrow is new and smooth. A shaft of alder. She cuts into it below the fletching, snapping it close to her arm, pulling it through the wound. It hurts like fire, like devil's breath. She bites on a corner of her gansey so she won't call out. The she holds her arm under the water again, numbing it, watching the blood thin and run away. It's nasty. But it could have lodged in her guts with no way out. That way you bled to death, drained like a slaughtered sow. She throws the broken arrow deep into the tunnel behind her.

They've diverted the stream where it seeps from the bog and runs into the pothole. Digging and sandbagging. They've rigged iron loops next to the lip, set into an old railway sleeper pinned onto rock that underlies peat. These lugs will hold a ladder safely down the first pitch. The hole smells of under earth, of nether space, of what draws them. Something hidden or lost, something unknown, othered by upward space. They fasten the ladder and let it down and the bearded man puts on his helmet and begins to descend. When he calls up that he's safe, they lower the folding spades and the little pick in one of the trugs. It's almost luminous as it sinks below them, like spilled sulphur or a patch of primroses. The woman looks out to black-headed gulls and curlews and withered birch trees. Her eyes are those of an arctic fox. There is the sunset beyond the sea, a smudge of orange that darkness is gulping, bay and sky smeared into light's entropy.

Hannah pulls her arm from the water and flexes her wrist. Everything is working, but the wound will stiffen and there are ugly, ragged edges of flesh where the point of the arrow tore in. Lucky it had pierced right through. The head looked clean enough, but you could never tell. She spits on her arm and massages saliva gently into the wound, a trick her father had showed her when one of the longhorns had grazed her forehead, nearly catching her eye. She leans back against the cave wall, spreading her wet skirts. Hannah has a piece of black bread tucked into her purse. She takes it out and divides it with the knife. Half for now and half for whenever. When she peers through a gap in the falling water there's a heron standing at a small pool just below, its white breast-feathers puffed out. Its eye is yellow as flame, relentless as the spearing beak, the stillness it makes deeper around itself. It hears something and takes off, a ghost, jerky and awkward in the air, as if stillness is all it has really practised.

The first pitch – the only pitch as far as they know – is twenty feet down to a ledge then an easy drop to a sandy floor where a long chamber with three symmetrically formed flowstones runs away and narrows. A thin stream flows over gravel at the bottom, gathered elsewhere from the fell, seeping through moss and stone. They've dyed the water and know where it comes out. What they don't know is exactly how. That's what they're here to find out.

The bearded man pulls on a woollen hat and sorts through the tools. The woman thinks of the inside of a human body, how dark it is, how unrevealed, palpitating with life. It pleases her to risk her own life underground where a sudden flood can leave you perched beside tons of falling water. Courting oblivion, seducing the icy touch of eternity. And maybe for no better reason than a feral need, a wayward longing.

When Hannah turned fourteen she had fine breasts, freckled where they parted, stiff-nippled. *You'll never starve,* her mother said. She'd not liked the sound of that. *A fair handful alright,* Dan laughed, but with that watchful look all the same, as if her breasts might bring trouble, like her bright hair. Years later she'd remember it when they drove a score of cattle to market, sold them above price because beef was scarce, then had a night of tripe and ale in the tavern. A man with a damson birthmark over a half-closed eye tried to grope her in the back ginnel when she went to relieve herself from the weight of drink. He stank of sweat so rank it made her retch. He'd grinned with brown teeth, backing her against the wall, his breath meaty. *A twat like butter,* he'd wagered. Hannah hadn't contradicted or resisted, even managed a smile she knew would show her dimples. When he unfastened his britches she put her arm around him, drew her knife and ran it across him, low down into his bowel. He slumped away, gasping, surprised. Then lay in dung and straw and fear, white-faced, holding his belly. When he whispered *Help me,* she pulled his hands away and his guts had spilled like a butcher's parcel. *That'll hasten it,* she said, mocking his blank eyes, grown shallow of light. Then wiping the blade on his filthy jerkin. Then stepping out into the dim street.

The trug comes down, blocking faint light from the entrance, dislodging small stones and clods of mud. He pulls his helmet straight with the flat of his palm and reaches to help it down, unties it, calls for the others to follow. In the space underground his voice seems to trap him. The ladder tightens again and boots appear, gleaming wet from the moor. Her body is unrecognisable as a woman's in the yellow wetsuit. He tugs at his beard, hoiks up phlegm from the cigarette, shoots it into the stream, thinks of it travelling underground to the exit half a mile away. Then she's beside him, switching on her helmet lamp, stooping to direct the beam, letting it bob around the walls of the chamber, casting their shadows. He thinks of cave dwellers, of what they feared more than the dark. The ladder tightens again with the next man's weight on it. His hands are livid on the rungs as they look up to him, caught in the light.

She covered her hair with her shawl, went back into the lantern light of the tavern, opening her eyes wide and jerking her head back at her father and Daniel. They'd slipped away, one by one. When her father asked her what had passed she'd shaken her head. The less anyone knew about anything the better. Dan gave her a queer look as they tied their gear to the ponies. At least they'd known better than to get drunk with coin on them. There'd be half a dozen corpses in the town by morning. Those murdered for their money and those who'd gone at each other in drunken hate and lust, clawing, stabbing, cursing in the filth. They passed a woman in a doorway, her face bloodied, snoring in spasms. One hand lay on a heap of horse dung as if she'd been searching in it. A whore probably, but you couldn't tell which were whores and which were honest women. Then the whores were as honest as most. It was their men who ran them you had to watch. They were rich and sly as stoats.

They'd been digging for weeks. You could forget things underground where the world let your imperfections be, didn't find fault. Where time had a different motion or none at all. They'd made a spoil-heap in the broader chamber under the entrance, scattering the debris to the far corners. There was nowhere else to take it, except up to the moor. Which made no sense. If you balanced on the ledge, the pitch to the entrance started just below shoulder height. The exit was narrow, so a fit person who was tall enough could chimney out, jamming their knees against the far wall and squirming upwards. The tricky bit was at the top where the lip overhung on one side. An aluminium ladder was easier. That was a no-brainer, though the first blokes down in the twenties had done it with candles and carbide lamps, hemp ropes, bloody-mindedness and muscle. They were still around in the seventies. Legends who sat at bars in the local pubs with their pipes and pints, breaking open a pasty or a meat pie. They hardly spoke, hardly had to. They'd seen what they'd seen and done what they'd done, including two wars. A hole in the ground was nothing. Holes in the ground were second nature. They were a piece of piss. Pioneers of the underworld, they never said what it was they'd been looking for back then between the wars, the post-war letdown and dark.

The light is almost lost to the fell, sunk into grass and heather to soak away underground. She thinks of it flowing to the sea, surging, glinting against black rocks through the weed-green timber of jetties. She'd seen mercury once that a peddler had brought, breaking and flowing and reforming in the palm of his hand, like light itself. Her mother had scolded him and turned him away for hawking things they'd no use for. In the hollow behind the waterfall Hannah checks out her options. Not many and not good. They'd found Dan last Michaelmas on their own land with a broken back, choking on blood from a rib that'd been kicked into his lung. He'd not come home after going out for hares with his lurcher. That had been shot with an arrow, too. He was out all night but they knew it wasn't over a woman. Not this time. At first light they found him where he'd crawled from the path into ferns and rocks, making a trail like an animal. Hannah, her father and the two youngest boys had found him. *We'll get you home,* Hannah whispered, stroking his hair that was flat with dew. *You needn't bother,* he said. Then, before his eyes closed, *It were't Rintner boys.* Abel Rintner's sons. Eric and Sam. Those limping, stuttering bastards.

Speleology was one name for it. Call it want you want: *caving* or *crag ratting*, you either got it or you didn't. It wasn't like rock climbing, but it wasn't the opposite either. Sometimes they climbed underground in a capsule of light, never knowing what was beyond. Sometimes hearing the terrific roar and weight of falling water. No one had ever been there before, so they were back at the formation of the earth, the universe billowing through a choke in the rock, time roaring through the eye of a needle. They climbed down towards whatever lay beneath them, shaped by water from the melting Ice Age. They found things that had lain there under human history and since long before. No sun or moon or stars or wind. No radio signal. No time passing except the reminder of hunger, the need to pass water, tiredness itself. The woman crawls forward through the shallow spillage, pulling the trug behind her, feeling it drag at her elbow joint, where the humerus and the ulna join, her elbow swollen and tender. A paediatrician. A speleologist.

He'd taken a long time to die, Daniel, and he was right: they should have left him near the stand of birch trees where crows were gathering. Where his mother couldn't see him and rage and wail and swear revenge. Her father had set fire to the Rintner place the next night as they celebrated, drunk as hogs on windfalls. Sarah Rintner's new baby died that night, thrown from a window hole to safety, lying with a staved skull. The valley and its homesteads sank into flames and blood. Revenge and hate gave suck and the taste was sweet as ewe's cheese and honey to them. Then, after months of it, tit for tat, eye for eye, tooth for tooth, Abe Rintner had choked to death on a mutton steak at his own table, falling face forward into the trencher. So they'd stopped killing each other and their horses and black cattle and made a kind of peace. Then her father and brothers had wanted Hannah to marry a Rintner to put a long end to it. They chose Eric with the crooked leg, but she said she'd rather fuck a pig. So it was never settled, the hate between them. He got another lass pregnant; a pox-faced, wizen-dugged little bitch from town who'd hate every minute she spent wedded to rain and cow shit and drudgery on the steading. Then this. An ambush when she'd trespassed too close. Hannah decides to sit it out unless she hears their dogs. The wound hurts where her blood throbs over the bone.

He leads, the bearded man, down to the boulder choke, crawling on his hands and knees in the low passage to do a recce. He'll dig for now. The other man will drag the trug back and the woman will take it to tip it into the bigger chamber below the ladder. They have headlamps and batteries strapped to their waists. Limestone gleams and the tunnel curves inside the earth's gut, its infinitely slow peristalsis. They reach the choke through its old digestions. Sixty yards of standing water, crawling, head down. The woman takes a look, nods, then turns back. He starts to dig in the tight space, though the roof is higher here, so they can crouch. He uses the spade and his hands. The trug fills with rounded river pebbles and sand and water. He guesses that a larger boulder has dropped into the space and allowed debris to gather, gradually choking the tunnel's throat.

Think like the animal, her father said when they were chasing game. They'd wounded her and she'd been spotting blood over heather and moss like a bitch in season. They'd have followed her. They'd have an idea where she was – if she hadn't slipped away over the fell. They'd bring their dogs over and wait, enjoying the thought of her fear. They'd fuck her before they killed her, or they'd try. She'd paunch them before that happened, the rank bastards. She isn't afraid, not now they've drawn blood. She's in hate of them and always has been and always will be after Daniel. Hannah creeps back to the cave entrance, crouching behind the sheet of falling water. She thinks she smells a peat fire, hears the whimper of hounds, laughter. Their low voices are like smoke, absent and present at the same time, carrying and dissolving in the air. The noise of the water cloaks everything, makes her unsure. She needs to piss and lowers herself to the cave floor, balancing awkwardly.

After an hour the two men swap positions and all three of them take a breather. The bearded one has a smear of clay across his face.

– Will it go?

– What, tonight?

The woman is doing something with her lamp cable and the light flickers yellow then burns white again. She turns to listen, a faint smile on her face.

– Doubt it.

That's almost a night's conversation used up between them. The woman turns back to pick up the trugs.

– Come on. I need to be home before midnight. I've got a clinic first thing.

The bearded man moves aside so the other can get to the crawl. The woman upturns the trug and tips out water. He can't remember the name for what she is.

259

– Bugger it.

– Let's have another bash.

The digging, dragging, digging goes on. They've pulled out about nine metres of debris over the past weeks, maybe more. Pebbles, boulders, sheep bones, rabbit spines. The dead. History's mulch.

Hannah waits. She binds up her arm with a strip of cloth cut from her skirt. It's awkward and she pulls it tight with her teeth. It hurts now with a dull pain and the muscle is stiffening. She dozes for a while and then the barking of a dog close by jerks her awake. She must have slept for hours because darkness has fallen and light risen again as she lies against the cave wall. She's stiff and wet and cold, hungry now the nausea has passed. Her arm throbs and feels hot. It's maybe an hour from dawn. She's guessing that. They have mastiffs. If they let the dogs into the cave, she's done. She'll have to go inside and trust to darkness. If she makes it home there'll be blood let, though. The thought satisfies her, slakes her, gives her purpose. She sees it bubbling from Eric's throat into his beard. He'll die like a slaughtered tup if she gets her way. Hannah finishes the bread, scooping water to her mouth. Them she crawls in twenty feet or so. The tunnel curves slightly and it's absolutely dark ahead, only a faint glimmer behind, where they are waiting for her. A rivulet of water runs between her knees. She can feel the steady current guiding her. It's so dark that white stars dance in front of her like tiny maids at a maypole.

The shovel strikes against a bigger stone and the man with scarred hands prises and levers it to one side. There's a faint draught of air and the water under him begins to quicken, emptying the shallow lake behind. He calls back to the others but his voice bounces off the rock walls, distorted.

– What's happening?

– She's draining out. We're through. Or close.

– That'll do.

Their voices sound stifled in the hall of rock. The bearded man is panting when he reaches the others, the skin around his eyes pale in the electric light. He withdraws to the entrance and they take it in turns to crawl to the dig to watch the water level falling. Enough for one night. They pack away their gear and climb out to the moor. There are stars mixed with clouds, the faint gleam of limestone from the escarpment as their eyes adjust. They drag the timbers back over the entrance. Then the walk back to their vehicles, their helmet lights bobbing on the wooden causeway, its darkly oozing water. The stone path is rough underfoot. A dog barks from a nearby farm. There's the rasp of sheep close by, their teeth tearing at grass. An aircraft goes over with its wing lights blinking. Then they're fumbling for car keys and the fascias of their vehicles light up, showing their hollowed cheeks. The woman climbs into the passenger seat of the Peugeot. *Home James.* She laughs and they start engines, headlights nosing down the bridleway in convoy to where the faint lights of the village stain the sky.

Hannah crawls on through water that covers her knees and freezes them. The tunnel narrows and she feels ahead with her hands. She wonders if there is a God. They rent their farm from the monks and their agent is a fat-gutted

Italian friar. He comes twice a year with his black-grey beard and leather cap and halting accent to take their money. The tunnel widens slightly, letting her breathe, then narrows again almost at once. She has to pass though a pelvic girdle of rock. There in the dark she retreats and strips, lying full length, shuffling out of her clothes, loosening the bridle and harness. She ties her things together awkwardly with the leather straps, then loops them to her ankle so she can pull them behind. She rests, panting, ignoring the pain in her arm and knee. Nearly naked, she forces herself, her head and breasts and hips, through the squeeze and into the wider passage beyond. She's cold and bruised and blind and the rock has scraped her skin the way they scarify a scalded pig at Yuletide. She crawls on, thinking of Daniel, what they did to him; thinking of that man in the alleyway dying because of her. Because of his own foul-breathed presumption. Hannah sees the faintest gleam of light, as if Christ has stepped into darkness to bless her. She crawls towards it until it glows bright and clear as vengeance.

They return to the dig on a fine day with white clouds rising at the horizon, an unsteady breeze bending bog cotton, throwing crows from the moor like charred fragments of a burning. They drop the ladder and file down into the chamber. They are able to follow the passageway to the almost-cleared obstruction, its scattering of stone that they shovel free and cart back in the trugs. Then they crouch for the final push: the man with his scarred hands, the bearded man, the woman with pale blue eyes. They're through and they crawl for a long time, along a tight squeeze towards the entrance under the waterfall until they see light, hear the beck thrumming. The doctor with blue eyes finds a handful of dull beads, a rusted tang of iron, some scraps of leather in the diggings. She sifts through gravel and collects the beads in her pocket. She'll give them to her niece. The bearded man let the rusted metal fall back into the stream and shrugs. Somehow it doesn't feel archaeological; it doesn't feel as if anything has ever really happened here. He has a nose for these things. The other man, the one with scarred hands, is already coiling the rope. That way you know a job is done. He's forgotten his camera, but there is always tomorrow. They'll get their names into the club newsletter, maybe more. Thumbs up. They clamber out and sit happily on the moor in daylight, trailing their rubber boots in the stream. A heron flies off from the pool below them. A grey omen, a premonition taking to the air.

FIRE FOX

There it was, in Sophie's memory. The time her dad had told her how he'd seen a fox on his way home, how it had flickered like a flame from the larch woods to stare into his headlights. *Met a fox*, he said, not *seen* but *met*, as if it was meant to happen. There was snow on the road, but he had winter tyres on the van and put the brakes on before he hit it. The van had skidded to a halt, slewing in the road. Then it had stared at him, the fox, its retinas flaring.

– It was daring me! Bold as anything!

Sophie thought of the fox staring at her father.

– *How* was it daring you?

Her dad shrugged and laughed, pulling off his shoes.

– Oh, I dunno. Daring me to run away to the woods, mebbe!

– That's silly!

– Mebbe…

He rubbed his nose against hers and she giggled.

– Mebbe not.

Then her mother was calling up the stairs and he picked up his shoes and padded out. *Like a fox.* That's what went through her mind, round and round as she pressed her face into the feather pillow.

Her father told her that after arriving home. He'd been working late, fitting a kitchen in someone's house, all whiskery, smelling of adhesive, cigarillos and beer. Later she woke in the middle of the night because the fox was licking all the windows of the mill. She could hear its fur crackling. Her mother had been making yoghurt in the kitchen and a smell of sour milk rose up the green painted staircase. Then the smell of smoke, her mother wrapping her in a blanket so she could watch instead of going to sleep. Tomorrow she'd have a day off school.

The mill burned all night and they watched from the window, feeling the heat, seeing frost melt on the glass, white ferns running to water. The mill workers and the firemen in their yellow jackets teemed in the darkness under arc lights, their shadows thrown onto trodden snow. Her parents watched with her at the bedroom window, their arms around her. Her dad couldn't stop shaking his head.

– All that cotton, it'll burn like a wick!

Her mother tightened her arms around Sophie.

– My God! All that waste.

Want not. Cotton waste. Candlewick. The phrases banged against each other and Sophie piped up.

– Waste not, want not!

Her mother gave her a queer look and Sophie went quiet. Afterwards it became a family joke, what she'd said when the mill was burning. But they would want, all those people moving below. Water arced from the hoses into the windows and ran back out down the road towards them, glistening blackly as if the tar itself was melting, as if it would engulf the house.

The mill did burn like a wick. It burned for three days as if it was sucking up some reservoir of wax from below the surface of the earth. Thousands of rats had fled from the basements, invading the neighbourhood. People talked about them as a latter-day plague. Sophie thought of them panicking out from under spinning frames, pouring out from windows and under doors and down the winding staircases. A river of rats; a rat-river. For weeks afterwards their big grey limping cat, Janus, laid one on the back door mat with its head neatly bitten off. A gift.

The boy was still asleep. His head turned sideways on the pillow, his hurt mouth fallen open a little. She'd let him sleep a few more minutes and then wake him. She'd wake him with a kiss, watch his eyes flutter open, his wry smile. There was a smattering of freckles across his nose and his neck was translucently white. He looked as if he'd never been in the sun. His breath was soft and even and when he breathed in his nostrils pinched a little. *Stephen*.

The mill fire happened the winter Sophie was nine years old. It was their own apocalypse: things either happened before or after it. In the morning, she woke to see the walls of the mill still smouldering. It looked like one of those monochrome photographs from the war. Collapsed roofs and tilted beams and shattered windows blackened like broken lamp-glass. Snow was still falling sparsely, rising as steam from the ruins. Flames kept appearing as the wind stirred cotton bales that were still burning at their core. Hosepipes criss-crossed the ground and their little leaks turned to streams and deltas of ice. Firemen were picking through the rubble with axes fastened to their waists and the mill owners arrived in a long grey car to look on. A crane was delivered on a huge trailer. When it was assembled, it began to knock down the walls with a wrecking ball. The brickwork crumbled to dust and ash and sparks shot up from the debris. It took almost a year to rebuild it, a whole storey shorter in height and with a modern steel roof instead of slate. The old chimney came down too, and the little red hawk that had nested there moved on.

The memory had nudged her this morning, heading to work. Why, she wasn't sure. Walking through an avenue of poplars on a spring day. Wearing fresh clothes. Feeling her youth coiled in her, propelling her into the future: more days like this, Gérard, of sun shining through new leaves. It was at the back of her mind as she ordered a latté at the coffee stand – a little three-wheeler van specially kitted out with hot water and a coffee maker. The owner was from Spain or Italy and he liked to talk as he snapped on the espresso machine, frothed the milk and poured it into the paper cup.

– There you goes, lady, nice day, eh?

– Yes, beautiful.

He dropped the cup into a cardboard holder and squeezed on the lid.

– Is spring eh? Here are your latté.

– Looks great! *Perfecto*. Thank you!

Was that Spanish? It was close. Gérard would laugh. Sophie paid the coffee man, fumbling loose change from her purse. She caught a glimpse of herself in the window of an electronics shop. Smart in a grey two-piece suit with stylishly high heels. Her brown hair was twisted into a bun. She looked every bit like a PA walking to the office, superimposed on a row of TV sets that had the news playing silently. That woman from the White House, her mouth opening and closing like a trap. Then tanks rolling from left of screen and a man walking backwards waving a Palestinian flag.

Sophie had rented a room down from the main business area, below the city square where the trams came in. A neighbourhood of small shops and large tenements built before the war. There had been trams then, too, but they'd been taken away and the lines dismantled. Now they were coming back like in her grandparents' time. That was weird. *Regeneration.* She needed to call her parents this weekend. It'd been a week or so. She sipped the scalding coffee through the small hole in the plastic rim of the cup, noticing a smudge of lipstick as she pulled it away.

The entrance to the apartment block was light and tall, morning sun entering through a fanlight above the door and streaming into the stairwell. She preferred the stairs to the lift, balancing the half-empty coffee cup, feeling the pressure tighten her calves. Her ankles were her strong point, neat and slender in black court shoes. Expensively understated. That was the way she thought of them, of herself. Her first client was at 11.00 am so she still had over an hour. She might have time to read her novel or watch a little daytime TV. When she nudged open the door the flat smelled of lavender and just very faintly of the freesias that stood in a vase on the lounge table. There was a small kitchen, a bedroom with a double bed and built-in wardrobes where she kept her outfits, a lounge with a soft beige carpet, a sound system, and a glass-topped coffee table with magazines. A telephone was mounted on the wall.

Sophie pushed the door to with her foot and heard the catch click. She put the coffee cup down on the table, slipped the bag from her shoulder and then took off the thin jacket and slung it over a chair. She ran the back of her hand over the silk lining. It was sleek, sensuous. This morning, walking to work, anything had seemed possible. Sophie pulled the shade of the table lamp a little crooked. It was important to make the place feel lived in. It couldn't be too tidy or clinical. She looked in the mirror, wet her finger and dabbed a bit of sleepy dust from the corner of her eye. Grey eyes with the lashes lightly touched with mascara. She sat on one of the upright chairs to finish her coffee.

Last night she'd dreamed that she and Gérard had arranged to meet someone in one of those bars on the waterfront, where the Baltic ships used to come in, loaded with fur and timber. They'd travelled on a bus for miles past desolate dockland buildings. Some of them had been damaged by the recent storms. A huge tree with a flat trunk and flaking bark was being dismembered by workmen in hard hats with chainsaws and pulleys. The bus had stopped, shaking as the engine ticked over. They got off to find the pub closed down with thick dust on the engraved windows. *The Shakespeare.* It had been fitted out in solid oak by a team of shipwrights. Now a pair of workmen were sanding down the panelling, room by room. She remembered that she knew one of the bar girls from school. Where was she? Then it wasn't Gérard tugging her sleeve to leave, but a client she'd once helped. One of those who'd visited her a few times, then disappeared. She'd got out of bed remembering her work number on his cell phone, feeling bothered by it. She woke Gérard with a cup of tea, but he hadn't wanted to talk about her dreams. Anything before eight o'clock was way too early for him. Sophie had dreamed about that pub before. It existed in the geography of her mind. How many of her memories were really dreams?

Sophie went into the bathroom, slipping down her skirt, feeling the sheer lining against her thighs and knees. The toilet seat was cold. A wooden one would be better. She flushed the loo, then made sure the hand basin was spotless and the toilet bowl was clean and the waste bin empty. That was important. She kept some make-up on the shelves and there were clean towels in the airing cupboard. Many of her clients liked to take a shower before going back to their lives. That was important, too. It was a way of keeping things in their place, of leaving things behind. A Czech girl collected the washing every Friday, bringing freshly laundered sheets and towels. You had to remember not to add *Slovakia* when you spoke to her about home. Marta was tall, tanned and cheerful with a bright smile and Celtic tattoos on each calf, their blue flames twisting up from her ankles.

Sophie had seen working girls under the railway bridges behind the station, their short leather skirts and thigh boots and laddered fishnet stocking. Short jackets worn wide open to show their cleavage. All the usual clichés. Some of them were from Eastern Europe. Their minders would be watching from cars. Pimps, actually, if she was honest. And the other men, the punters, cruising by. Looking for hand-jobs, blow-jobs. It was hard to imagine that kind of life, what drove them to it. Except the obvious: a drug habit, kids, debt. Maybe all three. Sophie took a file and checked her nails. It was surprising how such a small thing – a hangnail scratching across a client's back – could upset everything. Not all of them could see the funny side. They wanted to feel special, after all, to escape from their lives or loneliness into the space she made for them. She believed them when they said they loved their wives. It was amazing how many of them told her that.

Sophie drew her chair to the window and watched the street beyond the net curtains. The flow of traffic and people was soothing, the city alive in all its dimensions. Sometimes she imagined it as a flow of electricity through millions of filaments. A huge brain teeming with information. Or water coursing through plumbing, sewers, culverts, pipework. Then radio waves that were woven together into an invisible cat's cradle of conversation and emotion. Or it might be journeys. Think of that: a city composed entirely from the journeys of its occupants. Short journeys within the city and journeys to it, like hers, like Gérard's or those girls under the railway arches, some of them still teenagers. Then it became a city of stories, not of cement and steel and glass and roads and rail, but a place that was *told*, a place that was pronounced, that existed only through utterance from the mouths of its citizens.

She'd tried to explain that to Gérard and he'd understood at once, how a place exists in the mind and imagination and speech of its people. *In France this is our culture. C'est vrai.* He made it sound simple. Gérard made it sound obvious. That was the nice thing about him. Matter-of-fact, to the point. It was his mystery, too, what made him cool and inaccessible. A bus paused just below the window and she saw a pigeon land on its roof and take off again. There were bird droppings on the window ledge she couldn't get to.

Two years after the fire Sophie had gone to secondary school and that was that. Her best friend Charlotte had been sent to a private school on the other side of town. She wore a tartan skirt and a green blazer and a smart Tam o' Shanter. Whereas Sophie was allowed to wear her own clothes to the local comprehensive. They didn't see each other much after that. Sophie made new friends. She made friends easily. She was a good sharer, so that hadn't been hard, really. It was funny how everything in her life had happened either before or after the fire at the mill. The night her father saw the fox.

After that, his business expanded. He took on three workers, including her uncle Pete, opened an office and employed a secretary. Mrs Rainer. *Anita*. Short grey hair, pink lipstick and gold bracelets, a picture of her grandchildren framed on the desk. Sophie's mother did an Open University degree, staying up late with the television. She had one of those old Amstrad word-processors with a green screen and tractor-fed printer where you had to tear off the paper. *Like a bog roll*, her dad said, predictably. After the degree she got a job as an office manager at the local council.

They were going up in the world. Everything was possible with a lot of application and a bit of luck. Her dad said that, too. He had three sisters who he never saw for whatever reasons. Her grandfather had been a farm worker and a drunk who beat Sophie's grandmother. When he died, her dad had gone out to celebrate. *The old bastard'll leave us all alone now.* Her mum's parents came to visit in a little Vauxhall with her mum's sister, Auntie Vera, who had scoliosis and still lived at home. They were altogether more civilised. Not that she'd ever met the other half of the family.

Then they moved from the terraced house overlooking the mill to a semi on the edge of town overlooking fields and farms. Sophie wanted a pony. For two years she wanted it more than anything else in the world. Something to look after, to feed and groom and ride around like royalty. A princess. Her father was tempted. Then her mother got pregnant. It was a massive surprise and, all of a sudden, she had a baby brother to think about. She was twelve years older than Daniel and the idea of the pony went away somehow. Not that they could afford one.

Dad bought her a telescope instead and they set it up so they could stargaze from the Velux in the attic room. One winter they watched a comet burning across the sky, a primeval omen of phosphorescent fire and ice. It raised the hair on the back of your neck to watch it. It was even on the news. It had a complicated name but her dad called it Fire Fox because of the way it slinked into the night sky as the light was falling. Because it reminded him of that night, the fox's eyes flickering from the larch woods. They watched it for weeks and then felt they'd lost something when it dropped out of view. Maybe that had been her childhood receding, burning up out there where there was no real time. Just incalculable distance and space.

These days Sophie got the odd text message from Dan. He'd Skyped with her from Thailand at the weekend, from an internet café, halfway to Australia for his gap year. Sophie felt sorry for him, really. It wasn't easy for his generation, the job market being what it was and student fees coming in. She'd graduated in Business Studies, then worked for a housing association before deciding that she wanted to work for herself. She still gave her father advice about market trends. They thought she was a consultant, which she was.

It was ten-forty. Sophie got changed for work. A short cotton nightie with a lace neckline, a damson nightgown with brocade, Moroccan slippers. She let her hair down and combed it, slipping off her bracelets and wristwatch, laying her earrings beside the bed. Pearl droplets in silver pendants. Gérard had bought her those. He'd moved in with her two months ago, an engineer from Lyons, working on a new pipeline at the oil terminal. He was tall, smart and funny. He liked good coffee and wine and nice food. He was an excellent cook and often had dinner ready by the time she made it home after a day's work, his Larousse *Gastronomique* open on the worktop, sipping a glass of wine, listening to Bartok, Hank Mobley or Dexter Gordon as he worked. Classical or jazz: that all depended on his mood, on the day he'd had.

Gérard knew what she did, was discreet, and didn't care. He was clean-shaven, smooth-skinned like a child, and tidy. He often worked late on his laptop as she slept. Being French made that small difference, opened that little distance between them. *Gallic.* She loved that word. She'd bought a Linguaphone course and was brushing up on her schoolgirl French. He laughed at her sometimes, mimicking her pronunciation. When they made love it was intimate and uncomplicated; he knew how to take pleasure and how to give it. She knew that half his pleasure was knowing she wanted him, wanted more. But that always stopped short of putting on a performance. He'd never told her he loved her and they never talked about the future. Not yet. Though in the summer she'd take a break and they'd spend a few weeks in Brittany with his parents, picking cider apples and drinking Calvados at the local bar.

Gérard was … well, too good to be true. Maybe one day he'd call her a name and that would be that. But not yet. There was something easy about the way they lived and worked around each other. Something that had clean surfaces, that wasn't sticky with feelings and possession. Even when they argued there was a coolness, a discretion that let it all go before it bit below the surface of things to corrode them. Right now she felt young; she felt capable of anything and she was happy that he'd be waiting for her when she got home with a cassoulet or braised poussin; a frank kiss on the mouth; a glass of Côtes du Rhône or Margaux to hand.

Sophie was at the window again as the blue Ford pulled into the parking space and the boy got out. She'd no idea how old he really was. Maybe twenty? Maybe more. His mother wound down the window and lit a cigarette, blowing smoke into the street. Then she handed him an envelope, waving him away as he hesitated. The boy had a vaguely lopsided walk, like a hare. He disappeared and a few second later the apartment bell rang. Sophie clicked on the intercom.

– Yes?

– M'th Mattinson?

275

– Yes. Is that Stephen? You're on time!

She pressed the button to unlock the door.

– Come on up.

That was twenty minutes ago. She'd helped him undress and taken him to bed. He'd fumbled the condom and she'd had to help him with that, too, stroking it on to make him ready. His harelip and cleft palate had been repaired as a baby but had left him disfigured, his speech muffled by his tongue as it tried to form consonants. After making love she kissed him – only him – as if she was grateful and he'd smiled and snuggled into the pillow. It's funny, but she *was* grateful. He'd sleep for twenty minutes as his mother smoked and read a paperback in the car in the street below. Then she'd wake him and he'd hand her the envelope and leave, smiling shyly from the doorway. His mother would have the engine running by the time he reached the car.

Right now there was peace. Tranquillity, in which he could dream; where she needed and wanted nothing. A space, a moment of satisfaction because things had gone well, unforced and natural. The space let her drift back to her dream: she and Gérard walking through rooms of varnished oak panelling which workmen were sanding down to the grain. Her dad would approve of that. That dream somehow turning into the night the mill burned down, when she'd watched with a blanket around her as her parents held her and rats had poured out from the flames. Rampaged into the night for the neighbourhood cats to hunt and kill. Before that, the fox in the snow, turning to look at her father, its eyes flaring. *Like it was daring me.* She still thought about that night as a watershed. The way their lives had moved, past and future sharply bifurcating.

Sophie's mobile phone beeped in the next room. She usually switched it off. It wasn't like her to forget. She slipped from the bed and into her nightgown, lifting the phone from her jacket pocket. It was Dan. *Phuket awesome. People (girls) ace. CU in a few months!* She smiled and typed a quick reply with her thumbs. *Missing you. SophieX.* When she got back to the bedroom the boy was awake and getting dressed. He handed her the envelope and Sophie straightened his collar and kissed him on the cheek.

– Thank you Stephen. You were wonderful!

– You w … w … were. Th … thanks …

He stammered a little and flushed. His hair was beautiful: ringlets of copper that had lain on the pillow like a hoard of spilled coins. When he left, she clicked the door closed and pressed her head to it, hearing the lopsided cadence of his footsteps.

Sophie wandered into the lounge, flexed her calves on tiptoe, picked up her novel and yawned. She was free until 2 o'clock when she had her next client. That would be another story. She'd have to strip the bed and tidy up a bit first. Today she'd finish around four-thirty. Afterwards, she'd walk back through the city as herself again. Through the poplars with pale new leaves. Over the tramlines in the city square to her bus. Home to Gérard in her other apartment, the one they shared now. Home to his seductive unforced surprise. *Sophie! Ça va, darling?* The kiss on her cheek as he balanced a glass of wine and a kitchen knife; chords from the sound system breaking into notes that fall like dust glittering from a comet.

ACKNOWLEDGEMENTS

'The Shoemakers of Nakasero' appeared in *Moving Worlds*; 'Terroir' and 'The Glover' (winner of the 2014 Short Fiction International Short Story prize) appeared in *Short Fiction*; 'Leverets' and 'Solomon' appeared in *Short Fiction in Theory and Practice.*

My thanks to Chris Stroud and Meg Vandermerwe of the Centre for Multilinguism and Diversity, University of the Western Cape, South Africa, for their hospitality during my 6-week Fellowship in April/May 2014 which enabled me to carry out substantial work on the manuscript of this book.

I am indebted to Marie Vidalenq of *Château Les Farcies du Pech* in Pécharmant, France, for her time and patience in explaining the working of that vineyard – and for the opportunity to taste some excellent wines. Any errors in the workings of the fictional vineyard in *Terroir* are entirely my own responsibility.

My special thanks to Penny Thomas of Seren Books for guiding the stories in this collection to completion and for her attentive reading of the text.

ABOUT THE AUTHOR

Graham Mort is a poet and short story writer who has also written for BBC radio. He is Professor of Creative Writing and Transcultural Literature at Lancaster University and has worked across sub-Saharan Africa and in Kurdistan on literature development projects. Graham's new and selected poems, *Visibility*, were published by Seren in 2007, followed by a new book of poems, *Cusp*, in 2011. His first book of short stories, *Touch*, was published by Seren in 2010 and contained the Bridport Prize-winning short story, 'The Prince'. *Touch* went on to win the Edge Hill prize for the best UK collection of short fiction in 2011. The stories in this new collection, *Terroir*, were written over a five-year period, including during a writing fellowship at the University of the Western Cape, South Africa, in 2014. A number of them have been published in literary journals, whilst 'The Glover' won the Short Fiction International Short Story Prize in 2014. In the same year, some stories from *Touch* were translated into Vietnamese by the writer Nguyen Phan Que Mai and appeared in the magazine *Tuoi Tre*. Graham is currently working on a new book of poems.